Daisy in the Doghouse

Joe Barrett

Black Rose Writing | Texas

ISBN: 978-1-68433-310-3
PUBLISHED BY BLACK ROSE WRITING
www.blackrosewriting.com

Printed in the United States of America
Suggested Retail Price (SRP) $18.95

Daisy in the Doghouse is printed in Book Antiqua

For Michelle, Joe and Sophie

Daisy in the Doghouse

Chapter One

It isn't a coincidence. It couldn't be.

I'm a person who understands the odds. I usually don't understand the actual odds, but I have a sense about them. In this scenario, worst case, the odds should be fifty-fifty. Maybe higher in my favor, assuming that anyone who knows anything would replace the toilet paper correctly. You know, hanging over, not under.

Someone is messing with me. It has to be deliberate. The numbers don't add up.

Three bathrooms in the house. Two adults, including myself, two children and a grandmother who typically stays thirty-six hours each week. The children probably don't factor in, but we can put them in the fifty-fifty category given the remote possibility that either would actually lift a finger in this house in a way that doesn't cause damage or a mess.

In my process of elimination, I decide to approach my son Sam first. Not necessarily because he is easiest to eliminate, but because he is the first child I see when I come out of the bathroom.

"Hey, bud."

"Hi."

"Whatcha doing?"

"Minecraft."

The ten-year-old equivalent of shooting heroin.

"Pause it for a minute."

"You don't have to pause Minecraft."

"Whatever. Hey, do you ever replace the rolls of toilet paper in the bathroom?"

"You want me to replace the toilet paper rolls in the bathroom?"

"Sam, that's not what I said, but yes, when you use the last of the toilet paper, you should replace the roll." A rare teaching moment. "But what I asked is, have you been replacing the rolls of toilet paper in our bathrooms?"

"Before they're finished?"

"No. Well, yeah, I would want to know if you've been replacing the toilet paper before it's finished because that would be wasteful."

"I wouldn't do that."

"I know, son. And I'm proud of you. But... well, let me put it this way. Have any of the rolls of toilet paper in this house been put into the holder by you?"

"In which bathroom?"

"Any of them."

"What time frame?"

"Ever."

"No."

"Awesome. Glad we were able to narrow it down to that level of detail before you answered," I say and walk away.

The grandmother should know better. She's old. She's lived a long life, and she isn't noticeably senile. She should weigh the odds in my favor. But I'm going to put her in the fifty-fifty category anyway in the event that her mind is slipping or that she's just too old to care. Plus, she hasn't been around much lately, me being between jobs and all.

The wife. She pretty much does everything around the house. Not because she's so industrious, but because the rest of us would be fine living in squalor. Without the wife, the children and I would probably die of dysentery, malnutrition or some other effect of plain laziness.

But there is one big chink in her apron. She almost never finishes the job. The children and I will step over little piles of rubbish she's left for a week after she's swept our wood floors. The kids and I have even discussed the fact that these little piles of sweepings are far more disgusting than dirt and grime evenly distributed over our wood floors.

And, in the space of a week, I cannot count the number of seltzer cans and cardboard coffee cups—minus only one single sip—that are arranged throughout the kitchen, den, living room and bedrooms of our home. It's like M. Night Shyamalan's movie *The Sign*, except worse, because the children and I are clumsy slobs who shuffle around the house like zombies and knock these "floaters" onto the floors and rugs with a frequency that would make you think we were trying to. But we're not. And despite how slovenly we are, not one of us can leave a fresh spill of flavored seltzer or coffee on the floor – so we are forced out of our comfort zones and into clean-up mode.

We all agree that getting out of our comfort zones isn't a good thing.

I also cannot count the number of times that I've finished a shower and opened the glass door to find no towels on the rack. Seriously? And I don't go to the bathroom without checking to see if there is a roll of toilet paper on the holder because I have learned—far prior to the arrival of my children—that toilet paper was very rarely ever replaced by my spouse.

All of which makes my current quandary even more strange. Possibly even diabolical.

My twelve-year-old daughter is sitting on the floor in her room, iPhone six inches from her face, hands like little talons on the screen board.

"Hey, String Cheese."

"Hi, Dad."

"I have a question for you."

She stops what she is doing and looks up at me with an evil glint in her eye as if I'm going to ask about her involvement in the sudden disappearance of neighborhood pets. But there's also a slight smirk, which lets me know that whatever she might be hiding, she thinks it's funny. Worse, she has the look of knowing that I'll think it's funny, too – in the event that I ever find out what it is she's hiding – which is why she never really gets in trouble for most of her mischief.

"It's probably not what you're thinking," I say, feigning knowledge of whatever she might be hiding, "but we will have another discussion when your mom gets home." I'll probably forget, but need to keep her on her toes. "What I want to ask is…"

"Sam has candy hidden in his bookshelf. I can show you where it is."

I'm mildly alarmed at this level of misdirection, indicating that there is, in fact, something of substance that she would very much like to avoid talking to me about.

"Don't be silly, Daisy. I totally know that Sam hides candy in his bookshelf. There is literally an entire colony of ants living in that bookshelf."

"It's right by his bed."

"I know where his bookshelf is."

"Does mom know about it?" she asks innocently, showing her hand.

I'm not sure if her mother actually does know about it. Probably something that I should have mentioned to her. Something Daisy would definitely use against me if her chips were down.

"Listen, this isn't about Sam's candy or your… whatever you're hiding, which we will discuss presently." Her misdirection has worked contrary to her original plans. I hate to digress from my own issue, but I feel like there's imminent trouble with the wife if I don't try to color this blank space a little more. "Actually, maybe we should talk about your thing first. Why don't you just tell me now and avoid a brutal interrogation."

I've always talked to children as if they were adults.

She nods her chin towards her chest and looks up at me with her wide green eyes.

"What if I told you that there is a dead body buried in the backyard?" she asks.

"I'd be very surprised and disappointed. Is there a dead body buried in our back yard?"

"No. So that's good news. Now, what if I told you that there's a dead squirrel down in the basement? A squirrel that probably died of natural causes, but was still so cute that someone like Sam might want to keep it as a pet? Like a stuffed animal, only real and dead."

"I wouldn't believe you because there's no such thing as squirrels."

My daughter and I have this thing where we don't believe in squirrels. We've decided that they're make-believe animals, like unicorns or coyotes, despite the fact that we live in Northern New Jersey.

"Well, whatever you think I'm hiding, it's not worse than those things. If there was anything that we needed to talk about, I mean."

"Daisy, first off, I just want to know if you've been replacing the toilet paper."

"The what? This is about toilet paper?!"

She seems thrown off her game and a little embarrassed.

"Yes, toilet paper."

"I've been using it!" she yells, indignant.

There was a developmental period in Daisy's life when she stopped using toilet paper. This was only a couple of years ago. Her mother and I had to have a difficult conversation with her about hygiene. It was her mother who did most of the talking while I tried to control dry heaves and to remember how much I love my daughter.

"I didn't say you weren't... but you have, right? I mean, you remember what we talked about." She drops her thick eyebrows, flares her nostrils and stares at me. My wife and I call it The Look. "Of course, I know you've been using toilet paper. You're twelve years old. What I was asking is whether you've been replacing the rolls of toilet paper on the holder when they run out."

Daisy's head shifts back towards her shoulders and The Look evaporates into a chin-in-the-neck, crescent eyebrow giggle that precedes a fit of hysterical laughing.

Of course, she has not been replacing the toilet paper when it's finished. On a daily basis, Daisy drops her jacket on the floor next to the coat rack. The trashcan in her room looks like a game of Jenga. She so lacks any instinct of household consideration that I have seen her remain seat-belted in the car on hundred-plus degree summer days throughout the duration of grocery unloading.

"Okay, stupid question. But we're going to talk when your mom gets home. About something other than toilet paper."

Though, what, in fact, I have no idea.

"Maybe it's the beaches," Daisy says in a slight Spanish accent as I walk out of her room.

"The beaches! Yes! And don't call them that."

The *beaches* is an endearing, but politically incorrect name that I have given to our cleaning people, who are sweet ladies of Latino descent. My kids had overheard this casual reference once when I was talking to their mother. It has, unfortunately, stuck. It probably doesn't help that I still continue to refer to the cleaning people as the beaches, but I figure the damage was already done.

Of course. It must be the beaches.

New beaches cycle through our house monthly in some form of immigration dodge. One of them must be so unfamiliar with the concept of toilet paper that she just puts the new rolls on with the paper hanging under whenever she cleans the bathrooms.

I feel a twinge of shallowness at the physical relief that my marriage and family life is saved.

But still, something about this conversation with my daughter doesn't feel right.

When my wife gets home, we always try to act like a normal family. Sam runs to the kitchen table and is concentrating on his homework before the door opens. Daisy stays in her room playing her iPhone, because anything different would only arouse suspicion. I mill around the kitchen acting like a house-dad might.

Catelyn is a philosophy professor at a state college nearby, so she has the kind of hours convenient for raising kids and a husband. I have been the CEO of a few small-to-mid-sized companies, the most recent of which I sold six months ago so I could take a year off to pursue my dream of writing a book. Pursue my dream sounds so gay – not the cool, homosexual gay that has become so hip these days, more like the Nineteen Seventies, eighth-grade slur gay.

I never really dreamed of writing a book. I do, however, feel like I have something to say about what happens in the rigged world of high finance and its impact on the common population. A book seems like the most convenient venue to make a statement.

It has been three months and, sadly, all I have done is perfected the art of procrastination.

My wife says "Hey" and drops her bags on the kitchen table, asks Sam how school was and kisses the top of his head. She asks me how my day was and gives me a tight-lipped kiss because sometimes I try to make out with her at inappropriate times, like in front of the kids. She yells "Hi" up to Daisy, who comes downstairs and gives her mother a trademark sideways hug. I grab a bottle of cabernet from the dining room and open it at the counter.

"Can we have a conversation about something?" I ask, pulling the cork with our cool next-generation wine opener that requires no screwing or tugging.

"What happened?" she asks, eyes widened in mild panic.

Catelyn kind of lives on the edge of an abyss, a part of her expecting any news to be of a terminal illness or personal bankruptcy variety.

"Nothing. Everything's fine. Relax."

She hates it when I tell her to relax and flashes me a contemptuous look.

"Have you been changing out the toilet paper rolls?" I ask.

"What? Why? Is Daisy not using toilet paper again?"

"No, she's fine."

"I'm right here," Daisy says in an annoyed tone.

Daisy's sitting off the kitchen at the tiny art table that we purchased when she was two and where she still does her homework every night, crouched like a giant little girl in a miniature world.

"I know, honey. We love you. What's wrong with the toilet paper?" Catelyn asks.

"I think it's the beaches," I reply.

"Dad!" Sam says, offended more by the fact that I'm punning on a bad word than by the casually implied racism-slash-misogyny.

"It's a term of endearment, boy!"

"Are the beaches… are the cleaning people stealing our toilet paper?" Catelyn asks. "You know, they could steal stuff that's a lot more valuable if they wanted to cross that line."

"No. Besides, stealing is something that you can address head-on. This is worse. Have you noticed, in the past few weeks, that every new roll of toilet paper in the house is hanging under, not over? I was working the odds, not in like a scientific way or anything, but there's no way that this could be happenstance."

"Happenstance?" Catelyn raises her eyebrows, looks at me as if I'm losing perspective on the situation.

"It's not a coincidence. The frequency… look, it happens too many times not to be deliberate. If you're not doing it—like, you know, to make some kind of point—then it's got to be the beaches."

Daisy has stopped doing her homework and is sitting on her tiny bench looking over at us like one half of the creepy twin duo in *The Shining*.

"What?!" I ask, turning to her, and she immediately goes back to doing her homework.

"You know, this toilet paper orientation thing is a pretty big issue for some weird reason," Catelyn says. "It's on the Internet. People get super worked up about it. Kind of sad, really."

"Don't be offensive. And how can it be a big thing? How can it be a thing at all? There's a right way and a wrong way to put toilet paper in the holder. There are absolutely no merits to the roll hanging under! You spin the thing and can't find the end-sheet. How can people even pretend to prefer that?" I say and go get my laptop to Google some research on the subject.

Catelyn takes a long sip of wine and sigh-moans in a way that I find sexy despite the contentious atmosphere in our kitchen.

"What if people don't like the way toilet paper looks when it hangs over," she says, "like when it unrolls and just hangs there six inches out from the wall?"

"So it looks better when it unrolls and hangs under down the wall?"

"It's not as sloppy that way, maybe. And I guess the wall might keep it from unraveling if the unravel end of the toilet paper is facing the wall."

"That's ridiculous. Wait, are you doing this? It's you, isn't it!"

"Easy, Francis," she says. My name is Jack. "It's not me. And it's not the beaches, either. They usually leave a nice folded triangle or flower type of thing on the toilet paper after they finish cleaning the bathroom. How do you not know that? It's a really choice gesture, makes you feel like you're in a nice hotel."

"That's right. Of course. It can't be the beaches. What am I thinking?"

I'm scrolling through my Google search results on toilet paper orientation when my mind suddenly turns to ice.

I look over at the tiny art table, and Daisy has disappeared.

My hand is shaking as I click on one search result that has appeared. In the Doghouse: Experimentations in Social Disruption at Home. A blog by Daisy Peanut Sullivan.

Chapter Two

"Daisy! Open the door. Now." She's locked herself in the kid's bathroom, or as I call it, "The Port Authority" because it is that disgusting. "Daisy Peanut Sullivan! You open that door."

Yes, that's her full name. Catelyn and I had been a little buzzed the night we came up with it.

"Can we name our baby Daisy if it's a girl?" I remember Catelyn whispering as she put her mouth against my ear.

Following a brief panic pending my confirmation that she was not, in fact, pregnant – which would have ruined the drinking part of our evening – I told her that I'd be fine with the name Daisy, as long as the middle name could be Peanut. It had just kind of rolled off my tongue, and I swear I could picture that little girl who came along a few years later.

"Daisy Peanut Sullivan," Catelyn had said out loud. "Okay, but I'm going to get mad if you continue to act like my getting pregnant would be an apocalyptic event."

"Daisy Peanut Sullivan," I said, redirecting the conversation. "It's perfect. I'm good with it."

"I can't wait to meet her," Catelyn had whispered, her mouth against my ear again.

"Daisy, you come out of there!" I say again through the door. My mind still feels like it's been cryogenically sealed. I rattle the bathroom door.

We'd bent the jam on the door to Daisy's room when we moved into the house, and it doesn't shut completely. The lack of privacy hasn't seemed to bother Daisy. Both of my kids have grown up to be very comfortable nudists around the house—coming from where I have no idea because Catelyn and I weren't ever into hippie stuff. But it means that their infrequent locked door situations require use of the bathroom.

This is good, in my opinion, because The Port Authority is gross enough to discourage any long periods of habitation.

"Look, Daisy. We're not mad at you. We just want to talk about this."

"I don't care if you're mad at me. Talk to me through the door."

She does care if we're mad at her. In most regards, Daisy is very delicate. She's polite and well mannered. She's an excellent student and does a great job of flying under the radar when it comes to the social politics of tweens. However, she also has a tendency to obsess. We saw this with the Disney Princesses and mermaids when she was little. Cute turned into super annoying turned into does she need to talk to a therapist? After that, Harry Potter led to a brief and frightening dabble in the occult wherein she printed dozens of Wiccan spells from the Internet, made twig and twine figurines like in *The Blair Witch Project*.

Somehow Catelyn and I missed the fact that she had gone off the edge, thinking that all of it was a harmless extension of the Harry Potter books, and it was actually Sam who ended up leaking the depth of Daisy's occult practices when he complained about her inability to resurrect his dead goldfish, Fireball.

I'd often wondered how her random obsessive personality trait would manifest itself as a tween.

"Daisy, you've got to come out eventually. It's disgusting in there," Catelyn says in a quieter voice. "How about we just skip the drama and get it over with. We've obviously read your blog."

"What did you think?" she asks.

I realize she is not aware of the many, many lines that she has crossed by deliberately messing with her own family and documenting it for public consumption. We need to cool down because anger isn't going to work here and I'm suddenly feeling as if our behavior is going to be judged by...

"Hey, Pumpkin? Just curious here. Do you know how many followers you have?" I'm thinking, how many could it possibly be?

"As of today, I've got thirty-four thousand, six hundred and two followers. But it goes up every day," she says. "Is that good?"

Meaning, is that a lot of followers? Not meaning, is it good that far more people than I have ever met personally have been enjoying the details of my sociopath daughter screwing with the weird private moments of my family?

"Uh, Daisy, sweetheart? Did it ever occur to you to use a pen name?" I'm thinking, if she's smart enough to set up a blog and carry out social experiments, there's no way that she simply didn't think to use a pen name.

"What's a pen name?"

"A nom de plume! A freaking fake name!"

"Why would I use a fake name?"

"So people wouldn't know that you're writing about us!"

"But that would seriously dampen my celebrity as a blogger."

"Dampen my celebrity" must be a term used by bloggers because there's no way that Daisy's mind could have come up with it on her own.

"Daisy, honey, I'm trying to keep it together here, but work with me a minute. All of these online friends that you have, you've never met them in person, right? They don't stop by the house or go out for pizza with you. So, what does it matter if you're using an online name? What does it matter if your celebrity, and more importantly our celebrity by association, is under fake names?"

I kind of feel like I'm arguing this point in order to sidestep the more important issue of our family being outed in a serial comic strip with over thirty-thousand subscribers.

"Huh, I guess you're right," she concedes, and I'm wondering what kind of leverage I can get out of winning this point when she adds, "but anyone who knows us would probably recognize you in the videos."

"You posted videos? Did you see videos on that blog?!" Catelyn screams at me, and I'm feeling like, maybe, I'm the one who's done something wrong here.

"I only skimmed the blog with you before we came up here to crucify our daughter."

I shouldn't have said that last part because this is where Daisy starts to cry. And when she cries, it's pretty much an uncontrollable flood of fear, shame and embarrassment of a depth that really shouldn't exist in a twelve-year-old.

"Honey, look…" I say, trying to recover.

"I know what crucify means," she screams through her sobs, and I'm thinking what a great idea it was to raise our kids Catholic.

"We're not going to crucify you," Catelyn says through the door. "We're just not sure how to react to this."

"Are you really mad?"

"I'm not sure if we're mad," Catelyn says and looks at me the way she looks when she's teaching a philosophy class, which is crazy annoying right now.

"I'm definitely mad," I say in a normal voice.

Daisy asks why, kind of innocently, but with a twinge of panic. As if there might be a depth to this situation that she didn't imagine, like she could be going to a reform school or something.

"Because we didn't agree to be the subjects of bizarre social experiments that you publish to thirty-thousand weirdos on the Internet."

"Sam did," Daisy responds.

At the bottom of the stairs, I see my son smack his forehead, Homer Simpson style.

"Dude!" I shout.

"I knew it! I knew she was going to drag me down with her!" Sam slumps his shoulders and trudges up the stairs, now thoroughly involved. "I'm actually glad it's out there. The pressure was killing me," he says.

Daisy opens the door when Sam gets to the top of the stairs, her face scarred with tear stains, but maybe a little hopeful. Which is weird. She tells Sam that she's sorry and he tells her "whatever" and we all go down to the kitchen to read Daisy's blog.

Chapter Three

"We're doing this as a family?" Daisy whines. "Why don't you guys just read it and we can talk after."

"We're going to walk through the entire thing on mom's laptop at the kitchen table," I say. "Who wants hot chocolate?"

"Are you trying to torture me with awkwardness?"

"Daisy, you not only messed with us. You also set up a blog to show the world how your family acted when messed with," Catelyn replies. "Awkwardness is your karmic reward."

"It was only you and dad, really. Originally the blog was going to be called 'My Idiot Brother' and I was just going to mess with Sam and write about that. But I needed Sam to help me set up the WordPress site, and he wouldn't help when he figured out what it was about."

Daisy gives Sam a mild version of The Look, and he responds with his own trademark "Are you freaking kidding me?" expression.

"I think *My Idiot Brother* was actually a Paul Rudd movie that came out a few years ago," I say. Catelyn rolls her eyes and gives me a this-is-not-the-time look, and I quickly get back on topic. "Daisy, why would you want to screw with any of us and write about it?"

"I needed something original to blog about. What, am I going to be the 'I love cute puppies' girl? There are like a thousand of those blogs out there already. I had to look at my surroundings and figure out what was uniquely me. And what is uniquely me is that you people are weird and I really enjoy making fun of it."

"Daisy…" I start to say, giving her what I think is an appropriately stern look even though I'm still not on solid ground with this situation.

"You do it too, Dad! You're like a freaking fountain of sarcasm."

She's right, of course. I sometimes feel like my entire consciousness is only one long string of snarky remarks.

"Okay," I say. "I'll own that. And I'll try to…"

"No, you don't understand," Daisy says. "What's so wrong with that? It's funny and doesn't hurt anyone. I mean, it's not like we're racists or homophobes or any other kind of real haters…"

"Dad makes racist remarks."

"Thanks, Sam."

"But he doesn't mean anything by them, really. He just tries to find funny stuff in whatever's going on around us. That's all I was trying to do. What's so wrong about it?"

"Okay, how about we just read through this thing from the top. We can reserve judgment until we actually know what we're talking about," I say and log into daisyinthedoghouse.blog.com

***

The homepage has a picture of Daisy's smiling face superimposed in the arched doorway of a cartoon doghouse. The last post is from yesterday.

"Come on, Daisy! What if the beaches read this?" I ask.

"Dad!" shouts an indignant Sam.

Daisy rolls her eyes. "The beaches don't even speak English, Dad."

"Don't call them that. And maybe one of the thirty-thousand people reading it could make a translation," I tell her.

"And you think they'd be all kinds of offended because you thought they were the ones putting toilet paper on the holders wrong?" Daisy rolls her eyes again and adds a puff of air blown through puckered lips, the kind of gesture you'd make if you were losing patience with a special needs kid.

"I think they'd be all kinds of offended that I call them the beaches. That's the sort of stuff that's supposed to stay in our family."

"You don't say it in a mean way. It's more like you're making fun of racism than being a racist. My readers know the difference."

"So, what, you've got enough of an intimate relationship with all thirty-four…"

"Thirty-four thousand six hundred and two, as of yesterday."

"And you're close enough to all of these people to know that they won't take something like that out of context?"

"They're following a blog by a twelve-year-old girl who screws with her parents and writes about it. I think they've got enough of an edge not to get too offended by the fact that you call our cleaning people the beaches," Daisy says.

"Okay, I'm not through with this discussion yet, but let's move on," I say.

Catelyn continues to read the blog out loud as we follow the screen with our eyes.

"You're embellishing the level of my frustration," I say to Daisy and the table at large.

"I've got to keep it interesting," Daisy replies carelessly, and we read on.

"Jesus, Daisy. You were the one who put dog poop in the living room? That's unsanitary!" I'm appalled.

"See!" yells Sam. "You all thought that was me!"

He's right. We did think he was behind the dog poop in the living room.

"Sam, I'm sorry," I say as kindly as possible. "It was not fair of us to assume you had something to do with the dog poop in the living room. But you are the filthiest member of our family." Sam shrug-nods in acknowledgement. "With no knowledge of your sister's premeditated, and in this case, disgusting experiment, we had to assume the dog poop in the living room had something to do with you."

"That's a fair point," Sam says maturely.

"What, Daisy? Did you just go outside and scoop up some random dog poop? And you put it on our rug? Do you know how disgusting that is?" Catelyn asks incredulously.

"It's from Elder across the street," Daisy says, referring to our neighbor's black lab. "I took it from their front yard. It was already dry, so it's not that disgusting. And it was so interesting to watch you guys trying to figure out how we got dog poop in our living room when we don't even have a dog. Can we get a dog? Please?"

"You went too far on that one, Daisy," I say, "and no, we cannot get a dog. I'm amazed that you think you can ask for a dog right now."

We continue to read.

"Ugh," gasps Catelyn. "Of course! You were the one that painted my toenails black."

"Only three of them, Mom. And about that… you had no reaction at all? Weren't you weirded out, or at least curious, when you woke up and three of your toenails were painted black? Even though it took dad a couple of weeks to approach us directly about the toilet paper, he didn't try to hide the fact that he was annoyed and then confused."

"How was I annoyed and confused?" I ask.

"You never used to yell curse words in the bathroom. I write about it a few posts down from where we are now."

"What made you think of the toilet paper, anyway?" I ask.

"I read about it on the Internet, how this small population was all amped up about which way toilet paper rolls are hung, and I thought, sounds like Dad."

"That's offensive."

"What's offensive about it? Wasn't I right?"

"What's offensive," Catelyn says, "is creating a context that makes me or your Dad appear neurotic so that you can watch our reactions and write about it for strangers."

"What about no reaction, Mom?"

"Can I go now?" asks Sam.

"No," I say.

"What about it?" Catelyn asks Daisy.

"My followers just thought it was odd, that's all. Read the comments for yourself. I mean, you obviously noticed that three of your toenails had been painted black. Didn't it creep you out that someone had gotten that close to you while you slept, and left an obvious sign? I mean, you're a doctor of freaking philosophy! I'd imagine there are loads of different ways to look at something like that."

"I felt violated," Catelyn says quietly.

"Maybe that's taking it a bit too far, Mom. It was only nail polish."

"Why didn't you tell me about it, Cat?" I ask.

"What if you were the one who did it? I'd just started the semester and was totally overwhelmed. I didn't want to deal with it. What if you were having some kind of mid-life crisis and needed to play out some strange erotic fantasy thing..."

"That's it, I'm out!" Sam walks out of the kitchen without asking permission. I figure we'll give him this one.

"...and it wasn't like I was going to avoid it forever," Catelyn continues, "but I didn't really have the bandwidth to get into something so complicated until the end of the semester."

"So, you were convinced it was me?"

"I wasn't convinced of anything. I certainly hoped it was you – and not, like, Henry sneaking in while we slept." Henry is our octogenarian neighbor, who has a key to our house in case we lock ourselves out. We have a key to his house, too. "But I started putting the chain locks on the doors at night. Just in case."

"I didn't catch that!" Daisy shouts. "I was looking for signs, and I totally missed that one!"

"I'm the first one up, and I unhook the chains every morning," Catelyn sighs.

"Interesting. So, it really got to you. Made you lock the doors in a sneaky way at night, made you avoid talking to Dad. What else?" Daisy asks, with an agenda that is obviously not related to her mother's well-being.

"Back off, Daisy. So, I'm getting the formula here. You think up these pranks…"

"Social experiments."

"Whatever," Catelyn says. "You think up this stuff, then you observe our reactions, but that's not really what the blog's about. It's obvious that you're only using our reactions, whatever they are, as a catalyst to talk about everything you think is wrong with the world." Catelyn is angry.

"What's a catalyst?" Daisy asks.

"It's an impetus – a starter, like the tip of a match," I say. Daisy nods.

"So, you didn't know that I reacted to the nail polish, and you use that as an example to start a rant about how people categorize and block things out of their lives. Now that you know how I actually reacted, you'll use that to rant about how people do stupid things to mitigate irrational fears and are too embarrassed to talk about it. Like putting the chain locks on our doors so that our eighty-something neighbor won't be able to sneak in and paint my toenails black when I'm asleep, and then taking the chains off in the morning before anyone else is up. Look, I know it was ridiculous on so many levels to think that Henry would use our key to creep into our house when we were all asleep, but it made me feel better to put the chains on – like I was doing something, not just waiting for it to happen again. But if I didn't even want to share this with you guys, how could you think it's okay to share it with a bunch of people we don't know?"

"We probably know some of them. I mean, it's more than thirty-thousand people," I say before thinking better of it.

"It's not like it's such a big deal," Daisy says. "I mean, you're not doing anything bad, and I'm not making up lies..."

"You embellish," I say.

"Just a little bit. But I don't make you guys look evil or stupid or anything. I don't think people are just sitting around waiting to see how the experiments turn out. I mean, what's really the big deal about turning around toilet paper rolls or dog poop or painting a few toes? I think they like to listen to my opinions on what's weird about the way we live. The experiments just give me a starting point to write about stuff that people my age deal with every day of their lives."

"I get it, Daisy, I do. But couldn't you have been a little more creative in finding an outlet for your words about life in the twenty-first century?" I ask gently.

"More creative than doing subtle and pointless experiments on my parents?"

"You know what I mean. More creative than... well, yeah, what you said. Because I didn't agree to be your straight man. You've got to understand I have an image to protect as an executive..."

"I thought you were an author now," Daisy says.

"You have to actually write something to be an author!" Sam shouts from his computer in the living room.

Apparently, he's remained passively involved in this conversation.

"Thanks, bud!" I shout back to him. "Yeah, well I'm not technically an executive right now..."

"So, what's the problem? And if you ever did, actually, write a book or article or whatever you're thinking about, then my following would only help with your publicity. Oh! And if your book were any good, your following would totally make my numbers spike!"

Daisy looks at me wide-eyed like we're suddenly in this together.

"I think we're targeting different demographics," I say, although my main problem is actually figuring out a demographic that I want to target. "And anyway, making me look like an idiot isn't going to help establish my authority when it comes to running an honest company in a society that's trapped in a rigged financial system."

"Maybe it would. Maybe it would help you stand out, give you a personality. Did you ever go to the business section on Amazon? There are almost two million books on business available as we speak," Daisy says.

"What are you doing in the business section on Amazon?"

"You said you were writing a business book – well, going to write a business book – and I wanted to size up the competition."

"My book…"

"It's not a book until you actually start writing something!" Sam yells again from the living room.

"My topic is a little narrower. It's about developing an organizational structure that can survive in today's lopsided financial environment, about helping small businesses grow into bigger businesses without damaging the culture or focus that made them successful in the first place."

I realize I should probably write that down.

"Small business and entrepreneurship, seventy-three thousand, six hundred and sixty-eight books." Daisy says. "Business culture, thirty-one thousand books. Management and leadership, two-hundred eighty-four thousand books."

Daisy inherited her mother's photographic memory, and it's a little freaky sometimes.

"My point," she says, "is that there seem to be more people writing books about running a company than there are people actually running companies, so anything that can make you stand out would probably only help."

I feel whatever might have been left of my motivation to write a book flush away forever.

"This isn't about me, Daisy."

"You just brought up how this is about you," she says calmly.

"Why do I feel like this is a negotiation instead of you just trying to get out of trouble."

"Because I want to keep writing my blog."

"Seriously?" I ask.

It hadn't occurred to me that she would want to continue with the blog.

"Seriously," she says. "I've got thirty-four thousand, six hundred and two people that are interested in what I have to say. I can't just stop talking to them. And the number's growing every day. It's an important part of my life."

"It's only been a few weeks, Daisy," I say and look at Catelyn.

I'm totally confused, and it looks like she is too. I don't think either of us is violently opposed to Daisy continuing to write her blog. There's even a part of me that's proud of what she's done. I'm just having trouble seeing the bigger picture right now.

"It's been six and a half weeks. Come on, Dad, Mom… You read it yourselves. I'm not doing anything wrong. I'm not doing any mean-girl stuff like calling people out at school for wearing stupid clothes. I just feel like there's a lot of stuff that doesn't make sense to me. Stuff people think is important that really isn't. And stuff that people ignore when it's right in their faces. And, like, when people do things because they think they're supposed to do them, even when it doesn't make any sense. I mean, if you look at it, I really don't spend too much time talking about you guys or the experiments. They just get me started. What I really talk about is how I see the world around me."

For the first time since coming out of The Port Authority, Daisy starts to cry. I am so screwed.

"If I can't blog about this stuff, it's going to stay all bottled up inside of me, and sometimes I feel like I could scream because it bothers me so much. It feels so good to get it out. Please don't take the blog away from me. Please!"

Daisy knows that I'm mush when she cries and she's working it. But there's also a lot of sincerity in her pleas. And I can't ignore the fact that what she's writing about in her world is eerily similar to what I want to write about in my world, in the context of business.

I look at Catelyn. She rolls her eyes, lifts her face towards the ceiling and then slumps her chin against her chest.

"You wouldn't be able to keep the same format. You've been outed as a social experimenter," I say quietly.

"That was going to get old, anyway." Daisy snuffles and wipes her eyes. "As long as I feel like I can keep being honest and talk freely about what bothers me, then I'm sure we can think of other ways to get me started."

"We?" I ask.

Daisy looks at Catelyn and then at me.

"It's still my blog," she says, firmly establishing our boundaries.

"I'm having nothing to do with any of this!" shouts Sam from the other room.

My cell phone rings. I look at the number, roll my eyes and walk into the living room for some privacy.

Chapter Four

"Amigo!"

"Jamie."

"Dude, please. I've asked you, like, a million times. Call me James, not Jamie."

Not to sound harsh, but Catelyn's little brother is a perpetual sophomore. Always aching for a seat at the big people's table. The only thing worse than someone who works at Goldman Sachs is someone who desperately wants to work at Goldman Sachs. Jamie's ten years younger than Catelyn and trying to build a career in wealth management—yuck—at one of the big banks that received government bail-out money during the 2008 financial crisis—vomit.

Regrettably, ever since I exchanged my company for personal wealth, Jamie will not leave me alone.

"Jamie, I know I've said this a million times before, but right now it's actually true. This is not a good time to talk."

"Two minutes. Believe me, you'll want to hear this. Just let me elevator-pitch you."

"Okay, this is a teachable moment," I sigh into my phone. "Firstly, only losers use the buzz term 'elevator pitch' as a verb, or, frankly, at all. Secondly, you 'elevator pitch' a product or service idea. You don't 'elevator pitch' a financial instrument offered by a major bank. My advice to you is to stop trying to say what you think everyone else is saying and instead just say what you mean. It might help your career."

Yuck again. People who use business buzz words might be losers, but people who use business buzz words incorrectly are wannabe losers, the worst kind of loser.

"Awesome! Good advice, bro," Jamie replies enthusiastically. It is impossible to insult this guy. "So, hear me out. Debt."

"Debt."

"Yeah, we're buying debt."

"You're buying debt," statement, not a question.

"No, I mean, you know, the bank is buying debt. We're setting up three new funds to purchase debt."

"That's not exactly a novel idea, Jamie. Have the taxpayers already signed on to underwrite your investments again?"

"Come on, it's not like that. The bottom dropped out of the debt market with the correction in 2008. After that, all kinds of debt instruments were artificially undervalued…" he goes on. And on. Finally, he finishes his pitch with a line about cherry-picking.

Jamie doesn't understand what his bank's new funds are actually set up to do. He's just been given a script to push at high net worth individuals, like myself. Banks call him a relationship guy. To me, he's more like that loud character who stands outside the strip club in tourist areas like New Orleans or Amsterdam and tries to hustle visitors from the packed street. I have no doubt that these funds have figured out a way to capitalize on market intricacies in order to make the rich even richer. But to me, it's a rigged game. It sucks.

"Jamie, do you realize that every time your bank buys low and sells high, it means that someone else bought high and sold low?"

"What do you mean?"

"I mean we live in a vacuum. Whenever you win, someone else loses. And typically, the people who lose don't even understand the rules. Doesn't that bother you?"

"I'm still not following you," Jamie replies.

This, in a nutshell, is my problem with writing a book. How do you talk about building honesty and integrity within a capitalist environment when even the lowest rungs of the ladder are completely oblivious to what I consider right and wrong?

"So, are you in or what?" Jamie asks.

"No, Jamie, I'm not in. And I've got to go. I'm dealing with some family issues right now."

"Okay, that works. Sleep on it, and I'll call you tomorrow."

He will, too. I hang up and walk back into the kitchen.

Chapter Five

"So, we're a blogging family now." Catelyn raises her eyebrows. "How very Digital Age of us."

"Technically, Daisy is the only one with a blog," I sigh.

Daisy has gone up to her room and is probably posting an update. I can't believe she writes all of her blog entries on an iPhone, a small one, her first phone, a birthday present three months ago. She was one of the last of her friends to get a phone because we wanted to slow down her foray into texting, Facebook, Twitter and all of the other social media outlets available these days. A strategy that obviously didn't pan out the way we had planned.

"She's up there writing right now," Catelyn says, looking defeated. "What do you think she's saying?"

"Don't worry about it, Cat. We read the stuff she was posting. I mean, from like before we found out about the blog. It was pretty hardcore honest, but it wasn't offensive, or wouldn't be if we weren't the ones peripherally involved."

"She knew we were eventually going to find out about it," Catelyn says, but I can see that she doesn't really think Daisy is subversive, or even that she's done anything really wrong. Like me, she just seems to be overwhelmed and confused about how to handle the situation. It's like Daisy was hiding a pet elephant in the basement, and then we find out about it, and then, somehow, we agree to accept it into our family. But it's still a freaking elephant, and we're uneasy about how it's going to be living with this big freaking elephant in our home.

"Look, we've got to spin this positive. It actually could be a good thing, help us to communicate. Bring us closer as a family," I say.

"I'm pregnant," Catelyn says and looks directly into my eyes.

I have no idea what my expression is right now. I might just have peed a little.

"I'm not pregnant, you idiot," she says without a smile.

"Not cool, Cat."

I still can't feel my legs.

"But I feel like that's the kind of bomb that she just dropped on us," she says, "like we've agreed to become a reality TV show."

"It's not like that. It's the producers who make those shows such a train wreck. No one's producing Daisy's blog." Then I rethink that statement since she actually was creating scenarios as a launching point for her rants. "Or at least we're involved in the production now that this thing is out in the open." I get why Catelyn is shell shocked, at least I think I do. "You know what's screwing with me? I think that I'm upset about a decision that Daisy made six-and-a-half weeks ago. When she actually decided to do all of this stuff behind our backs. If I could get over that, I don't think I'd be so upset at the conversation that we had tonight. It's just a lot to handle all at once."

"Okay, that's fair," she says. "Maybe that's what's bothering me too. So, do we let this whole thing settle, you know, like sleep on it, and talk about moving forward tomorrow?"

It's funny. When it comes to family issues, Catelyn is usually so decisive. I'm always the one that's clueless. But this time it seems like she's really asking what I think we should do.

"It's only seven-thirty, so we've got some time before bed. How about we finish that wine, try to put the six-weeks-ago trauma away somewhere, and just talk kind of shallow about how this could be a good thing. We don't need to untangle it all, but maybe just talking about some positive aspects would put a better tilt on it before we let this stuff settle overnight."

Catelyn nods, gets up, grabs the bottle from the counter and says, "You first."

I start with the obvious, surface stuff, how this is much more about us as a family than about people reading the blog because there are so many blogs out there that Daisy's is probably just one of dozens that each reader follows, and there's obviously a huge dilution effect. Catelyn nods and gives me a tight smile, as if she's waiting for something else, as if she's waiting for me to get to a real point.

"You have something that you want to talk about, and you're avoiding it," she says.

"Why do you say that?" I'm feeling transparent, maybe a little selfish.

"Because I call tell when something's itching you, so why don't you stop thinking about what you should be saying and just talk."

"We've got a lot going on. I feel weird turning it into a conversation that's about me when we've got so much stuff to work through."

"Now I'm curious. Come on, we're not going to get any further on processing this blog stuff tonight anyway. And we're both pretty shook up and vulnerable right now, so just talk to me."

"Okay," I say. "This is unfiltered, remember that. Kind of like free association."

"Go for it, Rocky."

"That was a weird thing to say, but okay. It's just that a part of me had kind of a breakthrough when we were reading Daisy's blog. Or maybe it was when I was talking to your brother, afterwards."

"My brother's an idiot. But anyway, how so?"

"Well, you know how I've been stuck trying to write something about... how I feel like the whole country is trapped in this rigged bureaucracy of banking and corporate finance. Why I feel so bad about my selling out to private equity, becoming part of a system that I think is so wrong. That kind of thing."

"I thought you were trying to write about creating an honest organizational structure and company culture in a dishonest environment," she says, repeating the words I typically use to describe what I'm trying to write about.

"Yeah, but I don't know. I mean, I'm proud of what we did with Tree Fort, but at the end of the day we sold out. So, who am I to talk about honesty and integrity? And anyway, who's going to listen? It feels like I'm just spinning my wheels, you know? And then I read Daisy's blog, and it's genuine, and it's innocent and, most of all, it's meaningful."

"Our daughter messes with us and writes about it, Jack."

"I know, but she's just trying to find an outlet to write about what she thinks is wrong with the world. The only difference is that her audience seems to give a damn. It's everything that I've been missing."

"Oh, my god!" A light finally went on in Catelyn's head, and she understands where this is heading. "No way, Jack..."

"Wait. Now, just… just wait a second. It's not what you're thinking." I feel beads of sweat forming on my forehead as my wife glares at me from across the table.

"You're not thinking of finding a way to hijack your twelve-year-old daughter's blog?"

"No, I'm not. Not really. And you're making it sound so much worse than it actually is."

"You cannot be serious. How many levels of irresponsible parenting are we looking to explore here?"

"Just hear me out."

"Daisy is twelve. This is an important developmental stage in her life. This is not the time to experiment on her psyche. You can do real damage, you moron."

"Just hear me out. And this innocent twelve-year-old is also the same anarchist who constructed a bunch of experiments to mess with her parents so she could write about it for strangers," I remind Catelyn. "I'm not thinking about hijacking her blog. She likes to write about what's wrong with the world. She needs a new set of catalysts to jumpstart her rants because we've outed her. I need an outlet for all of my thoughts or I'm going to lose my mind. What I realize is that my biggest problem has been figuring out how to find an audience that cares about what I've got to say."

"Then start your own blog," Catelyn says.

"Am I a millennial? I'm not going to start a blog. But listen, if I were able to break down and distill some of the stuff I've got to say… if I were able to translate these thoughts into something that a twelve-year-old could follow and understand – and we're talking about what's wrong with the world here, which is right up Daisy's alley – then maybe a twelve-year-old girl could use these thoughts as a catalyst for her own online rants."

"Daisy has no context for what you're talking about," Catelyn says. "She's never been in business. Hell, I'm an adult with a Ph.D. and it's tough for me to track your rants without dropping you into the category of conspiracy theorist."

Catelyn has clearly spent more hours than she would have liked listening to me rant about how the rigged system of corporate finance is ruining society. I guess I spend a lot of time on my soapbox.

"Then I'll need to rethink what I'm trying to say, what I want to say, and I'll need to contextualize it and break it down into something that Daisy can understand, something that she'll want to write about. Otherwise, the experiment will fail."

"Since when is it okay for our family to want to perform experiments on each other? I mean, this started out as a normal day…"

"Did you take the chain locks off the doors this morning before we all came downstairs?" I ask. Catelyn drops her chin to her chest and sticks her hands into her hair. "We're past normal here," I say. "I think this blog stuff is going to be a part of our lives, at least for a little while. What's the harm in a little active participation? At least it will give me a target, some structure to my rants, as opposed to me just spewing random thoughts on the evils of modern society."

"If you screw up my daughter, I'll kill you in your sleep. I'm not joking, Jack."

"I'm not going to screw her up, at least not any more so than what we're dealing with now."

"Daisy's not going to let you steer her blog anyway. She won't even let me pick out a shirt for her. She has a problem with authority."

"She's one of the most obedient, best-behaved kids I've ever met."

"She has a problem with authority when it comes to the stuff she thinks is her domain. Like fashion or art. And I imagine her blog falls into the same category. I don't know why I'm even worried," Catelyn shrugs.

"She's twelve. I've run companies. I can manipulate her… for her own good, obviously."

"Good luck with that," she says and gets up from the table.

"Believe me, you're going to be happy about this. It's going to be fun," I say and follow her upstairs.

Chapter Six

Daisy's sitting on the floor at the end of her bed, fingers stabbing at the small screen of her iPhone. I creak open the door that doesn't shut properly. She doesn't look up.

"Dai-sy," I say, in kind of a slow singsong because how else do you say a name like Daisy.

"Dai-sy Dad-dy," she replies in a monotone singsong. Daisy Daddy is what she's been calling me since she was a baby. She hasn't raised her eyes from the screen, her fingers pecking at the screenpad.

"Daisy, put the phone down."

"One sec," she says politely.

I wait about twenty seconds. "Daisy!"

"One sec."

"Daisy, now!"

She taps a few more times on the screen and then raises her head and gives me a look that says this better be quick.

"Bad Daisy!" I say, making her smile the way she always does when I speak to her like she's a puppy. She whimpers as she looks back down at her iPhone. I question my parental authority.

"Put it away. We need to talk."

"Awwww…" she whines, but puts the phone on the floor beside her.

"It's about your blog," I say, standing in front of her because at my age sitting on the floor isn't an option.

"I can keep it, right?" she asks eagerly.

"I think we can find a way for you to continue writing your blog, but you're going to have to compromise a little bit." I now have her full attention, since she is clearly not interested in any kind compromise. "Just listen to me. I think we can help each other."

She gives me The Look. I'm handling this poorly.

"I don't have anything that's really mine, except for my blog," she whines. Totally not true.

"It's still going to be yours, Daisy. Keep an open mind for a minute, okay? What I'm talking about here is a lot more deceptive and inappropriate than your old format of messing with mom and me as a launching pad for your rants."

I need her to think that she will be doing something wrong, that she will be conspiring with me on the kind of shenanigans that should never be allowed for a kid her age. It's the only way to turn her. Luckily, I have a long history of poor parental decision-making to back me up here.

"Remember who you're talking to. This is Daddy. I'm the one who tried to teach you how to drive our car when you were six years old. I'm the one that showed you how to build a fire when you were four. You know I have really bad judgment when it comes to parenting. And what I want to talk to you about is so far out on the edge that even I'm questioning whether it's a good idea."

"You've intrigued me," she says, eyes half-closed as a wry smile sets on her lips. "Go on."

"Maybe I shouldn't," I say and start to turn my back.

"Daddy, seriously!"

"Okay. Sit up here on the bed with me," I say, settling down on the mattress, leaning back against the headboard. She gets up and sits on the bed, leaving her iPhone on the floor, an indication that she's actually interested in what we're going to talk about. I wish I'd prepared more, but I'm just going to have to wing it. "Here's the deal. You know how when you played your pranks on us…"

"Social experiments, not pranks," she says, "and if you don't take my process seriously, then I don't think we're going to be able to work together."

I appreciate her candor.

"Sorry. It's your process that makes me want to have this conversation – a very adult and probably inappropriate conversation – in the first place." Daisy nods, satisfied, and I continue. "Your experiments were about setting up mom and me to react to weird stuff so that you could criticize our behavior and use it as a launch point to write about what you think is wrong with the world, right?"

"What gives you that idea?" Daisy asks confrontationally, as if anything I say about her blog is going to be wrong.

"That's what you told us an hour ago at the kitchen table."

"Oh," Daisy says thoughtfully. "Okay then. Go on."

"Well, I'm old."

"You're not old, Daddy," she says in a saccharine tone.

"Oh, shut up," I say. "What I mean is, I've started a few companies and run a few others. I've lived in different states and different countries. I've seen things, some really strange and bad things. And I have some ideas about why these bad things happen."

"You mean in business?" Daisy asks.

"Yeah, well I've seen a lot of really bad things in business, but I'm actually just talking about how people treat each other. Whether it's business or school or family, situations come up, and people react to them – like with your experiments on mom and me. I've seen people react to situations in ways that I think are bad for the world. It doesn't matter if it happens at work or at school or at home, you know? People shouldn't hurt other people and then lie about it. Or try to convince themselves that they're right when their actions are wrong. People should speak up when they see bad things happening, don't you think? When people make the world a worse place, it's important to expose it, so it doesn't stay hidden, right? Isn't that kind of what you were getting at in your blog? Using examples to show what you think is wrong with the world?"

"Well, I wasn't really writing about bad stuff like you're describing. You're kind of, way out there, Dad. But I guess I was trying to call it out when people act strange," Daisy says.

"Why?"

"Because it's super frustrating when people act weird and nobody talks about it."

"Right, exactly. Now let's take it to another level, a more grown-up level. Think about how frustrating it is when people do bad things, and nobody talks about it. Think about how, if people let that kind of thing go on unexposed and undiscussed, it can make the world a worse place."

"Okay," Daisy says.

"So, if you knew about bad things that people do over and over again, would you want to write about it in your blog? If you could look at different scenarios where bad things happen as if they were experiments, do you think you could use them as a launching point to talk about how you see the world?"

"I guess so. But I don't know about really bad things that people do over and over to make the world a worse place."

"What if I told you some stuff?" I ask.

Chapter Seven

The next morning is Tuesday. Catelyn doesn't have classes on Tuesday, and I'm obviously not engaged in writing a book so we can talk while the kids are at school.

"I need your help with this, Cat. You've got to get behind me."

"Daisy agreed to work with you?" she asks as if she doesn't believe me.

"She didn't say no," I respond. "Please, Cat. Give me a hand. You're a critical part of the process."

"The process to subversively insert your own insurrectionist ideas into your twelve-year-old daughter's blog," she says, deadpan. "Yeah, that sounds awesome. How can I help?"

"I've been thinking a lot about this. I want to expose the subversive corporate financial system. It's really hurting people. It's all around us, everyone knows it's there, but people don't even know how to talk about it. There's no way to take it down, but maybe there's a way to give it a black eye."

"And you think you can do this by working with Daisy on her blog? That's a stretch, Jack."

"If you rail against the system, you sound like a conspiracy theorist. But a twelve-year-old girl with a blog following? That might be a different story."

Catelyn agrees to let me pick up Daisy from her singing lesson that afternoon and take her to Ruth's Chris Steak House.

Daisy is a born carnivore. She is also a soft touch. When we go out to eat as a family, her go-to order is the filet mignon, medium-rare, which typically costs as much as the sandwich, salad, and chicken fingers respectively ordered by me, Catelyn and Sam combined. I love this about her for reasons that I can't explain, despite the fact that it has caused me some serious stress in times when money was tight.

I took Daisy to Ruth's Chris for our first Daddy-Daughter birthday dinner when she was seven. It was just the two of us because the restaurant is expensive and Catelyn doesn't eat meat, Sam only eats chicken. It has since become her favorite restaurant, and we have Daddy-Daughter birthday dinners about once a quarter. Sam and I have father-son dinners at Buffalo Wild Wings, where we play trivia and use the questions as conversation starters. Sam costs me a lot less money than Daisy. I need to remember to thank him someday.

"Daisy," I say after she's ordered a Sprite and I've ordered a glass of Cabernet.

"Daisy-Daddy," she replies, looking me in the eye.

"How's school?"

"Really?" she rolls her eyes, brings them back to mine, "School's fine. Is that what we're going to talk about?"

"I thought we'd just ease into things," I say, surprised that she seems more anxious to dive in than I am.

"I need something to write about for my blog," she says abruptly. "I already wrote about how you guys outed me about the social experiments and the whole blow up that came next. That dialog is done. I need something else to write about, or I'm going to lose my followers."

I'm amazed that she couldn't get a few more miles out of being outed by her parents for her previous format. It hasn't even been twenty-four hours.

"I don't have time to ease into things," Daisy says. "We need a plan, something I can start on tonight."

"I have a plan, Daisy," I say. "Relax." I take a gulp of my wine. I don't have a plan. I thought the whole scheme would take a little more coaxing. That was the point of this dinner. Daisy gives me the same look that Catelyn gives me when I tell her to relax. I'm thinking maybe it's not a good idea for men to tell women or girls to relax, like ever.

"What's the plan, then?" she demands.

She isn't fooling around. Thankfully, the waitress comes and takes our order. As usual, I have to reiterate to the waitress that my daughter really does want the filet cooked medium-rare – red, not pink, in the center – since sometimes restaurants cook her steak medium because she's young and they think she doesn't know any better. When this happens, we have to send the steak back. And this happens more often than you'd think. Daisy would order the steak rare if we let her. She would probably dig into the flank of a living cow if allowed.

I need a plan.

"Dad," she says impatiently as the waitress walks away.

I reach for my wine and take a sip, the last sip. I wave at the waitress and raise my glass, indicating another. All the while Daisy's fiery eyes burn into me like Poe's raven. She knows I'm stalling. I set down the empty glass. A plan. A starting point is all I need.

And... I've got it.

"Daisy, I want you to write about me. Something that I did, something that I feel bad about. I got myself into a situation, and I reacted in a certain way. It's different, but in the same ballpark as reacting to one of your pranks..."

"Social experiments! Geeze."

"Sorry, it's kind of like one of your social experiments, where you put mom and me into certain situations and we reacted a certain way. Well, this is a grown-up situation, and I reacted in a certain way, and I'm not happy about it. But I'm even more unhappy about the fact that I didn't feel like I had much choice, you know?"

"Did you do something illegal?" she asks eagerly. Like she wants the answer to be yes. Like maybe she's losing some perspective here.

"No, I didn't do anything illegal, you psycho."

She deflates a little bit, then perks up. "But it was bad, right? Or was it just weird? There's a difference."

"It's complicated. But in general, I feel like the situation is more bad than weird. And it's real. And it's all connected to something that I think is really bad. Something that most people can't put words around. Something that affects the lives of grown-ups."

"Mom, too?" she asks.

Maybe the eagerness in our complicity is being diluted by some apprehension.

"Mom, too, yeah. But to a much lesser degree because she's an academic. It's really more about the world of money and business jobs. Government too, I'm sure, but I don't have any direct experience with that side of it, thank God."

"Dad, what are we talking about here?"

She's either nervous or impatient, I can't tell.

"It's nothing that you need to be nervous about, Daisy. It's nothing that's going to hurt you or Sam or mom. Did you ever play with kids who try to make up the rules of a game as it goes along in a way that helps themselves more than it helps the other players?"

"Cheaters?"

"Kind of like cheating, but more like people who bend the rules around and then try to convince other people – maybe even themselves – that what they're doing is allowed. Like they're not doing anything wrong."

"Like playing Monopoly with Freddy, down at the beach." Freddy is her younger cousin, my sister's only child. He's a notorious liar and a self-obsessed tool. I wonder if most corporate lawyers and investment bankers are only-children. "He always does that. Sam and I hate it," Daisy says, nodding. "He smells weird, too. He always smells like chicken. Why do you make us play with him, anyway?"

"Because he's your cousin and it's important to mom that we maintain good family relations, but that's not the point. And you're right. He does always smell like a roast chicken dinner. I wonder why that is? But anyway, the point is that you're not scared of Freddy, right? You and Sam know what he's up to. In fact, I bet it drives you crazy that you can't just call him out when he tries to bend the rules."

"We do call him out, but it doesn't stop him from doing it."

"Right. Exactly! The frustrating part is that he doesn't seem to know the difference between right and wrong, correct?" Daisy raises her eyebrows and nods as if she had underestimated my parental insights. "Well, what I'm talking about in the grown-up world is a lot like what Freddy does. There are people who think that rules exist only so that those rules can be bent and twisted for their own personal gain. And there are a lot of those people out there. And they dedicate their lives to abusing the rules instead of just playing the game. And they make the world a bad place for people who are trying to play fair."

"So what, Dad? You acted like Freddy?"

"No, I didn't act like Freddy. But I sold my company to a bunch of people who act a lot like Freddy. And I feel bad about it. And I feel bad that people who act like Freddy have become so powerful by abusing a big, complicated system of rules and money that only they understand. Freddy types twist up the jobs that grownups have to do to support their families. They play games with the stock markets where people are trying to save for retirement or for their kids' education. They make life miserable for regular people and take what isn't theirs by abusing the rules, and real people get hurt. If I can explain what's really going on, in a way that you can understand, I thought that maybe you'd want to call out some of these people on your blog."

"Okay, go on." She raises her eyebrows and gives me a diabolical smile. "That could work."

So, I totally unload on Daisy. I give her a complete history of the rise of a lopsided financial bureaucracy and how it has led to the current economic crisis for all of the regular people who are not part of what I consider to be a thoroughly rigged system. I talk about selling my companies to people like Freddy, about my choices – good and bad – and about how few endgames there are left to people who try to create something meaningful in business.

It is eloquent. Daisy is enraptured.

Unfortunately, throughout this whole process, I vilify Freddy beyond any possible sort of redemption. That part was stupid.

"We need to bring Freddy down," Daisy says in all seriousness.

I should have thought this through prior to giving her my sermon.

"Freddy is eight years old. I was using his personality-type as an example. Freddy didn't actually do anything wrong. He had nothing to do with this."

"Yet," she says.

"Okay, yet. I'll give you that. But he's just a type of person who this unfair financial system would cater to, someone who is likely to abuse a set of rules for his own gain."

"Then we need to take him down. Before he starts."

"Let's forget about your cousin Freddy for a minute, okay? What about all the grown-up Freddies who are actually abusing the system and making people's lives so painful, hurting other people if it means they'll make more money or gain more power?" I've got to redirect this conversation away from the actual Freddy.

"We need to take down all the Freddies!" Daisy says.

That's a little better.

"These people, these Freddies," I say, feeling I'm really on a roll now, "they delude themselves. They protect themselves from any kind of ridicule by hiding behind a broken system that they perpetuate..."

"Perpetuate?"

"The system they help sustain, help cultivate, like adding fertilizer to a garden. They want the system of rules to grow bigger and more complicated so they can justify to themselves that what they're doing isn't illegal, so it isn't really bad." I've been sipping my second Cabernet and I realize I'm talking louder than I should be. I amp it down a bit. "They use all kinds of tricks to convince themselves that what they're doing isn't wrong. But listen, let's take a step back. Don't you think it's also partially the fault of the people who get abused? Don't you think that the people who get taken advantage of should be doing something about it?"

"How do you mean?"

"Well, we see these people who abuse the system every day. They're at the grocery store, they're watching the soccer games you play, they're at church on Sunday..."

"How would you know? You never go to church," Daisy snarks, as if not going to church is a bad thing.

"I have an issue with the Catholic Church. You can make your own decisions about it when you're older. Anyway, these people that abuse the system are all around us. Every day they mix with the people they hurt, as if nothing's wrong. So, tell me, if someone on our block broke into the houses of old people and stole their retirement money, then built a big McMansion with the stolen money right on the corner, don't you think the neighborhood would at least say something about it?"

"McMansion?"

"A big freaking house that looks like every other big freaking house that rich people build, like the Mahoney's house down the block," I say.

"Oh. Okay."

Catelyn and I often talk about the monstrosity that the Mahoneys' built on our block, leaving them about six inches of yard on either side of their huge freaking house. They built their additions in 2009, no less, only a year after the bank bailout.

"So, if these people stole from their neighbors, even if they got away with it from a legal perspective, don't you think everyone on our block would at least make them feel bad for what they did?"

"Sure," she says. "Mischief Night would be epic."

"Well, Mr. Mahoney is a corporate banker, and I haven't seen anything ever happen to his house on Mischief Night. And he's a perfect example of people who generate a lot of wealth by working a system that makes it okay to take money away from people who don't know the rules."

"So why doesn't anyone make Mr. Mahoney feel bad about it?"

"Because there are, like, thousands of little steps in between the people who abuse the system and the people who get abused. Everything's so far removed that these Freddy-types don't get blamed. I think the people who abuse the system need to be exposed so that we can all finally treat them the way that they deserve to be treated."

"So, who is it we're calling out here?" Daisy asks.

"Let's start with me. I'll answer any questions you have about why I sold Tree Fort to the private equity company. And the money for our house, for your school, for your music lessons, even for this dinner, right now, all of it is coming from me helping to sell the company into this rigged system."

"Okay, I get your part, and we can talk about it," Daisy says, sounding a lot like a journalist. "But who do we call out next?"

"That's easy. The people who deserve to be called out are the people who benefit most from the rigged financial system. The more they benefit, the more they deserve to be called out. But any corporate banking, any legal position, any accounting job..." A couple more sips of wine and I'll be ready to jump on our white table cloth and start yelling "Power to the People!" I better ratchet things down—don't want to get eighty-sixed from Ruth's Chris—but I'm still pretty worked up. "Any McMansion, any eighty-thousand-dollar automobile, any forty-thousand-dollar prep school is probably a good place to start. These are all big red flags as far as I'm concerned."

"Can we get the check? I'm ready to go home." Daisy says with a look of violent determination all over her twelve-year-old face.

She's in.

I'm suddenly a little worried about how this is all going to play out.

"First, you need to promise me," I say, "that you're not going to write anything about the actual Freddy. Nothing about your cousin."

My sister would knife me in the head if she knew how I steered Daisy's understanding of unfair people via the analogy of her son. Or that we were talking about how he always smells like roast chicken, for that matter.

"Deal," Daisy says and waves down the waitress with a pantomime of signing the check, something that I've never seen a twelve-year-old do.

When we get home, Daisy kisses her mother, answers "Good" to Catelyn's ask about how was the dinner, and then goes to her room.

"Where'd we land?" Catelyn asks me.

"I don't know, really," I say. "It was fine, I think. We talked a lot. I talked a lot. I don't really remember everything I said."

"And..."

"And, that's it. I'm not sure where she's going to take it. We'll just have to read her blog."

Chapter Eight

At eight o'clock the same evening I get a call from Steve, one of my old partners at Tree Fort. That was quick.

"Seriously, Jack?"

"You read Daisy's blog," I say. Statement, not a question.

"We've been reading it for weeks. My daughter follows her. I was wondering when you guys would find out about it."

"Thanks for the heads-up."

"Not my place," Steve says. "At least it wasn't my place when your daughter was just messing with you and Catelyn. How could you let her write about Tree Fort?"

"She needed something new to write about. She didn't actually name the company."

"Come on, man. This is serious. My kid thinks I'm a jerk. Did you read what Daisy wrote?"

"I did, yeah."

"It makes us all sound like greedy sell-outs."

"We all are greedy sell-outs," I say.

"Whatever, dude. My kid doesn't have to know that."

"Hold it. I've got another call…" I look at the number and switch lines. It's Pete, another Tree Fort partner. "Hey, Pete."

"Whoa, dude. Interesting little blogger you've got there."

"I've got Steve on the other line, want me to conference you in?"

I join the two lines, but before anyone can speak, I get another call. This time it's Louis, a third Tree Fort partner. I add him to what has nearly become a full ex-shareholder meeting. Colin and Tony, the other two partners, call too but are out of luck because my phone can only conference four people at a time, including myself. I give the others a chance to vent, all of it pretty much amounting to the fact that I had no right to let Daisy blog about the sale of our company. Blah, blah, blah.

"Look, Jack. We all know how you feel about selling the company," Louis says, "but you like the guys at Western..." Western Capital is the Chicago-based private equity firm that purchased our company. "How do you think they're going to react to this?" Louis has always led the group when it comes to paranoia, especially during and after the private equity transaction. As if, somehow, for any reason, Western could decide to just take the money back.

"It's a twelve-year-old girl's blog. One of thousands out there on the Internet. What makes you think they'll even see it?" I ask. "And what's the difference if they do? It's not like Daisy wrote anything about the transaction details or included any sensitive information. As far as the reader is concerned, we're just another example of shareholders letting their employees down by selling out to the big money people. That's the new American Dream, isn't it? Build up a company so that you can sell it to private equity, regardless of what happens after the fact? Anyway, I didn't write the blog, my daughter did. And I'm okay with her voicing opinions on the situation. In fact, I'm happy that she called us out. If any of your kids want to write a blog about what's wrong with the world, I'm fully in support of it."

"You took the money, too, Jack," Pete says. If only Pete and I had owned the company, I don't think we would have sold it.

"You guys are talking about this as if we robbed a bank," Steve breaks in. "Look, selling was a good thing. We were up to our eyes in debt. We didn't have money to expand or even hire the type of people we needed to run a company doing fifty-plus million in annual sales. We lacked both capital and infrastructure, not to mention management. How long were we going to be able to keep growing?"

"Did you get recruited by the Western guys?" I ask Steve. "Because you sound just like them. And the problems we had weren't really any different than what we dealt with at five million or ten million or twenty-five million of revenue."

"The stakes were a lot higher," Steve says.

"No, they weren't," I reply. "The numbers just got bigger. The worst that could have ever happened is that we'd have had to declare bankruptcy and we'd lose everything. We had it all on the line from the start. We weren't any further from personal bankruptcy at fifty million in sales than we were at five million. We were fighting to survive as soon as we decided to grow the company. We didn't have more to lose. We just lost our nerve."

"Maybe we didn't have more to lose," Steve says, "but we never had as much to gain as we did when we sold. There's no way that we could pass up the opportunity."

"So, we traded everything we built, including all of our people, for the money we now have in the bank," I say.

"It's done, Jack," Pete says. "There's no use beating yourself up about it. We all had mixed feelings about selling the company."

"Pete, I get it. I take full responsibility for my part in our decision to sell. Hell, I was the CEO. We weighed all the options, we voted on it, and none of us tried to swing things the other way – me included. I totally own what we did. But I freaking hate it."

"So okay, Jack," Steve says. "See a shrink. Work through your problems. But don't hang our dirty laundry out in public."

"I think we're all forgetting the fact that it's not my blog," I say.

"Then control your kid."

"Relax, Steve. Daisy didn't actually name any of you guys. Like I said, she didn't even name the company."

"She's your daughter," Louis says. "Anyone who knows who she is knows who you are and so they also know who we are."

"That's a lot of degrees of separation. Anyway, I wouldn't worry about it. It's all going to be backwash soon."

"How do you mean?" Pete asks.

"You read Daisy's blog. She finished up her last entry with a request that her followers ask their parents what they do for a living, what kind of future world they're contributing to. What kind of world their kids will inherit…"

"How does that make our stuff backwash?" Steve asks. He's always been kind of a dim bulb.

"I'm guessing there are going to be a whole new wave of people called out on Daisy's blog tomorrow," I say.

Chapter Nine

"I know what a bank is," Daisy says, her mouth full of fries. "I have a bank account. But explain to me exactly, what is a banker?"

It's Wednesday night, and we're at Buffalo Wild Wings, Sam's favorite restaurant. Daisy has intruded on my father-son dinner with Sam. I thought he'd be steamed since I took her out for a solo dinner at Ruth's Chris the prior evening, not to mention the fact that she's taken over the conversation, but he appears rapt. Sam soaks up new information like a sponge.

"There are lots of different types of bankers. I need more information to answer your question accurately. Exactly what kind of banker are you asking about?" I ask.

"I'll let you know," Daisy says and pecks the screenpad of her iPhone. "How about a lawyer? I mean, I know what a lawyer is. But what does a lawyer really do?"

"Same answer. There are a lot of different types of lawyers. All of them have invested themselves in learning about law. But there are laws that govern people, and there are laws that govern companies. There are lots of different laws for lots of different circumstances."

"Yeah, but what do they actually do?" Sam asks, and I give them a rudimentary explanation of contract law.

"So, you wouldn't need lawyers at all if people just kept their word," Sam sums up.

"Yeah," I respond.

"Good to know," Sam says.

I have no idea why that's good for him to know.

"Okay, is there anything wrong with being a nurse?" Daisy asks.

"No. I mean, I'm sure there are good nurses and bad nurses, but there's nothing inherently wrong with the profession. Nurses help people. That's generally a good thing."

"Doctors?" she asks.

"Same."

"Teachers?" she asks.

"Anyone who teaches, all the way from preschool teachers to high school teachers, should be showered with praise and money by everyone in society."

"Seriously? Why?" asks Daisy.

"Because, and I'm not trying to offend you guys here, but children are awful. Teenagers are worse than awful. And teachers get paid, like nothing. Teachers teach because they want to make the world a better place. And more often than not, it's a losing battle. Teachers fight for the next generation to survive. Teaching is the most important profession in society and, at the same time, it's probably the most neglected profession when it comes to earning enough money to make a living. Teachers are the closest thing we have to heroes outside of wartime."

"What about during wartime?" Sam asks.

"They're still heroes. That wartime thing is just a saying."

"So why don't you teach?" Sam asks.

"Because I don't like teenagers or children," I say. "You two being the exception, most of the time."

"So, what about college?" Sam asks.

"What about college?"

"You said teachers are heroes, from preschool to high school. What about college teachers, like mom?"

"First of all, mom is a huge, medal-of-honor type hero – if only for dealing with the three of us. We need to recognize that because we're difficult to live with, especially me. Second, teachers at college are called professors. And most of them are heroes, too. The only exception might be professors who teach MBA programs. And I actually don't know, because I don't have an MBA."

"What's an MBA?" Daisy asks.

"It's the Hitler Youth of today's society."

"The Hitler what?"

"An MBA is a Masters of Business Administration. It's a degree people get after they've finished college that teaches them how to manipulate the systems of law, politics, and economics in order to make money for themselves in business."

"There's actually a college degree for that?" Sam asks.

"Effectively, yes."

"So, what about accounts?" Daisy asks.

"What about accounts?"

"What are they? What do they do?"

"Accounts don't do anything. Do you mean accountants?" I ask. Daisy looks at her iPhone, scrolls and nods. "Would you please eat some of your boneless wings and not just the fries?" I ask. I have no idea what the difference is between her boneless wings and Sam's chicken fingers, but aside from pizza, my kids refuse to ever order the same thing. "Accountants are people who get certified to assure that a business isn't lying about their numbers – meaning companies aren't trying to say they made less money so that they can pay less taxes, or trying to say they earned more money than they actually did if someone is trying to acquire them."

We discuss accountants and lawyers through the end of our dinner.

"So," Daisy says, "what about veterinarians? Same as nurses and doctors, right?"

"Right," I say and get up from the table. Sam spills an entire cardboard sleeve of catsup and fries onto the front of his hoodie as he rises from the table. He watches the sleeve tumble to the floor and then makes his way to the door as if nothing happened. Sometimes I really think that he is mentally challenged.

"What about HR?" Daisy asks.

"What about HR?"

"First, what does it mean. Second, is it good or bad?"

"First, HR means Human Resources," I say, holding her hand as we walk to the parking lot. "And second, it's almost always bad."

Chapter Ten

"Okay, what's an investment banker?" Daisy asks, picking pieces of pepperoni off a steaming hot slice of pizza.

It's Thursday night. Same as Wednesday, Catelyn has late classes. She and I haven't spoken much since this all started on Monday night – when this all started for her and me, at least. We actually haven't had much time together, I remind myself, since she teaches graduate classes through the middle of the week and doesn't get home until after eight pm most days.

Used to be, her mother would come to our house for one or two nights during the week to take care of the kids, but since I've decided to make a career of not writing a book at home, this routine has somehow ended. So now I'm Mr. Mom for the middle part of the week. And in lieu of cooking them dinner, I decided to take the kids out for pizza. Good daddy.

"Dad?"

"What?"

"What's an investment banker?"

"An investment banker is someone who has studied all of the crooked rules of business and law and accounting to a point where he can help to sell a company to someone else, or to the public market, for the highest possible price."

"That sounds bad."

"Yeah. You can put investment bankers into the bad column," I tell her. "The parasites of the business world."

I explain again what a parasite is, as well as the rudiments of investment banking.

"Parasites," Daisy says. "Got it. They're bad."

"Daisy, eat some actual pizza, not just the pepperoni," I say.

"What about policemen? Or policewomen?" she asks.

"All good."

"Dad, how do you know the worst of the worst when it comes to different types of jobs?" Sam asks.

"Bad can pretty much be measured in proportion to the amount money that parasites make in business. And I'm talking about people who work within what I keep calling the rigged economic system as opposed to actually building or creating something. In other words, people who earn money by coordinating and connecting stuff according to the rules of the system, as opposed to actually producing anything. As a general rule, anytime you've got people who don't really produce anything, you can assume that the more money they earn, the worse they are."

"Got it. Thanks," says Daisy.

She smiles at me and then, oddly, smiles at Sam. I like the fact that they seem to be on the same team with this stuff. It makes me feel like a good parent. Maybe a little twisted, but generally on the good side of the fence.

When we get back to the house, the kids split, Daisy to her room and Sam to the family computer in the den. I take out my laptop and sit at the kitchen table, scrolling through junk mail, checking our accounts, looking for something to help me avoid opening up my WORD document and getting started on my book.

After a few minutes, I bail, sit down on the couch and turn on the television. Five hundred channels and nothing's on. I get up, walk to the cabinet where we keep our booze and pour myself a Jameson's, neat. I circle around the kitchen island and grab a can of black cherry flavored seltzer out of the fridge as I head back to the couch.

This is the life, I think. I'm on the chaise part of the couch, my feet outstretched. My right knee is draped over Tippy, the name we've given to a stuffed giraffe shaped like a beach ball. It eases the pressure on my back. When I'm running a company, I never seem to have the headspace necessary to just veg out. I'm not stressed about money. I'm not getting ready for a trip. I'm just here, enjoying the moment.

I am super freaking bored.

Sam walks into the room, lays on top of me. This is pretty much standard procedure in our house. Both kids just lay out on me as if I were a Barcalounge. It's how we used to fall asleep on Sundays when they were babies, watching whatever Disney or Pixar feature was in fashion. And they just kept the habit, even though they're now ten and twelve years old.

"What's up, bud?"

"Nothing," Sam replies and grabs the remote. "Have you started your book, yet?"

I swear to God this kid puts more innocent pressure on me to get my life together than anyone else in the world.

"Not yet."

"Do you even know what you're going to write about?"

"I want to write about the stuff that I've been talking to you and Daisy about. I just can't figure out how to communicate any of it without sounding like a crazy person. Do you know what a conspiracy theorist is?"

"A crazy person?" Sam asks.

"Yeah. Someone who goes around talking about how there's some hidden plot or plan by some organization… like big business or the government. I'm having trouble not sounding like that, you know? And no one listens to people like that. Not to mention the fact that there is no conspiracy, even though I talk about how big business is a corrupt system. It is corrupt, but there's no evil genius pulling the strings. It's just a bunch of greedy people. A bunch of greedy people who build on rules and structures that were built by other greedy people, who built their rules on top of earlier rules created by earlier greedy people. There are layers and layers of this nonsense. And it all makes things so complicated that the people who get hurt by the broken system can't even figure out who's fault it is. That's what drives me crazy."

"I can see how you would sound like a crazy person. Trying to explain this stuff," Sam says thoughtfully.

"Thanks, bud."

"So, let me get this straight," Sam says. For a ten-year-old, he's pretty big on stepping back and trying to grasp the big picture. "You just want the people who take advantage of the system for selfish reasons to get their comeuppance?"

Who says "comeuppance" these days?

"I just want to make it part of the conversation, you know. Like, if you choose to be a part of things that end up hurting other people and you do it for personal gain, then at least it should be out in the open. If you want to be selfish and greedy at the expense of others, fine. But you shouldn't be able to fool yourself or fool other people into thinking you're a good person."

"I understand," Sam says. He gets up and walks back into the den.

"What are you doing, bud?"

"Just playing Scatch," he replies.

Scatch is some kind of a programming game that I don't understand. I think it's a community-approach to coding basic stuff. I close my eyes. The next thing I know Catelyn is standing over me asking if I'd read Daisy's Blog.

"I fell asleep," I say, coming out of a fog and recognizing in Catelyn's tone the implication that she had, in fact, read Daisy's blog.

"It's a rant about how investment bankers are the devil."

"That's ridiculous," I say, still groggy. "Investment bankers aren't the devil. They're more like the miserable little cretins that work for the devil. Saying that they're the devil gives them way too much credit. Investment bankers would probably get off on the idea that anyone thinks they're the devil."

"I'm serious, Jack. Daisy's rant is a response to one of her followers, whose father and mother are both investment bankers. You're messing with people's families, here."

"Well, maybe some families need to be messed with. Jesus, both parents are investment bankers? I can't even imagine how horrible that must be. And if she's following Daisy's blog to the point that she feels comfortable enough to dialog about it…"

"It's a boy," Catelyn interrupts.

"What, your imaginary baby?" I ask, remembering her pregnancy head-fake three nights ago, which still has me a little shaken. "Did you have an imaginary sonogram?"

"The follower, Jack. It's a boy, not a girl."

"What's the difference? I mean… you know what I mean. But what's the difference if the follower is a boy or a girl?"

"I'm just clarifying," Catelyn says.

"Whatever. Anyway, I'm glad the kid is getting a different perspective on what his evil, parasitic parents do for a living. I'd love to hear how they explain themselves."

"This is out of control, Jack. Daisy's twelve. It's irresponsible of us. No, actually, it's irresponsible of you to fill her head with stuff that can damage people's lives."

"Let's agree to disagree on that point."

"Stop being so nonchalant about this. She listed out what investment bankers made last year and compared it to what grade school teachers make."

"Interesting. I wonder where she got that information. I guess everything really is on the Internet these days."

This piece of news has Sam written all over it. I guess it's nice that they're working on something together.

"I'm going to go talk to her. This has got to stop."

"Cat, wait a minute," I say and get up from the couch. "I totally understand where you're coming from here, but we need to talk before you try to put the kybosh on Daisy's blog. Seriously."

Catelyn stops and turns around. Then we walk to the kitchen table and sit down.

"I'm her mother, Jack. I don't need to try. I can put the kybosh on anything that I want."

She's angry. Catelyn is an exceptionally gorgeous woman but, oddly enough, she is not beautiful when she's angry. Angry-Catelyn looks like a cross between a Japanese anime character and a potato. I mentioned this once, during an argument years ago, and she didn't find it amusing.

"Stop looking at me like that," she says. "We both know I'm mad."

"Catelyn, I'm not much of a parent," I say, and her big eyes roll towards the top of her angry potato face, "but some things are really important to me. This is one of those things. It's like when Daisy was right on the age cusp, going into kindergarten, and we had to decide about whether she was going to be the youngest person in her class or the oldest. I knew in my bones that we didn't want Daisy to be the youngest kid in her class – her mind and her body having to play catch up with the other kids in school, in sports, in social situations. We discussed it, and we agreed to pull her back rather than push her forward. And we both still agree that it was the right thing to do."

"Get to the point, Jack."

"Well, this time I think it's important that we push her forward. Or at least we shouldn't hold her back."

"You've already been pushing her forward, Jack. She's not basing the past few blog entries on her own twelve-year-old opinions. She's championing your ideas."

"No, not exactly true. I admit to shifting the direction of her blog towards what's important to me, yes. But we had to do that anyway, once we caught on to her messing with us. Daisy is going to blog. She's passionate about it, at least for now. And if she's going to blog, then why not let her blog about something productive? It's not like it's dangerous. I mean, she's calling out business people, for God's sake. It's not like she's going after the mob or street gangs or anything. And we both know Daisy. If we don't steer her blogging into something that we think is productive — and that she thinks is edgy — then she's going to find something edgy on her own. Look, I know I'm biased here because I like what she's doing, but I really do think our best bet is to let this play out. When I try to think about it objectively, that's what I think."

Catelyn puts her face into her hands. "We need to watch this, Jack. We need to stay on top of it so that no one gets hurt. Not Daisy, not her followers. I'm totally going against my better judgment here. This whole thing is way too combustible for a twelve-year-old to handle. Would you pour me a glass of wine?"

Catelyn is putting her hammer away, at least for now. She gets up from the kitchen table and walks upstairs to kiss the children goodnight.

Chapter Eleven

I look at my cell phone. It's the same nine-five-four area code that I've ignored three times this morning. I decide to pick it up.

"Jack Sullivan," I say.

"Mr. Sullivan?"

"Yes, this is Jack Sullivan. What can I do for you?"

"Mr. Sullivan. Ah, my name is Morton Greenly."

Wow, I think. It's the investment banker from Daisy's blog. It's got to be. No one but an investment banker would stick to the name Morton as a go-by. Not Morty or Mort or whatever more normal middle name he must have. He goes with Morton, straight up. I bet he thinks it makes him sound wealthy or important.

"Ah, I'm an investment banker in Fort Lauderdale," he says. "Mr. Sullivan, there are some matters that we, ah, need to discuss."

"What can I do for you, Morton?"

"Ah, it's about your daughter's blog."

"How did you get my cell number?" I ask.

"Oh, right. Well, your daughter wrote about you on her blog, and her last name is Sullivan, so I just Googled 'Sullivan' and 'private equity' and got your press release. Congratulations on the Western deal, by the way."

"Thanks."

"So, anyway, I know your deal guy." Meaning he knows Danial, the investment banker we used for the transaction. "It's a small world, you know. So, I asked Danial for your contact information, and he forwarded me one of your e-mails. You put your cell phone number in your e-mail signature?"

"So clients could get hold of me if they needed anything. Back when I was running my company."

"Right, well, ah. That's how I got your cell phone."

"Got it. So how can I help you, Morton?"

"Ah, it's about your daughter's blog."

"You already said that. What about it?" There's a woman in the background haranguing Morton. I assume it's his wife. The other investment banker. She's telling him to give her the phone. She sounds like a shrew. "Do you two actually work at the same firm?" I ask incredulously.

"Hello?" The wife investment banker has obviously grabbed the receiver.

"Hello!" I shout jovially.

"Is this Mr. Sullivan?"

"I think your husband established that it is."

"Mr. Sullivan, this is Ginny Greenly."

"What a lovely name. So much nicer than Morton. What was your maiden name? Was it alliterative, too?"

I can't stand investment bankers. In the background, Morton asks what I'm saying and Ginny tells him that I said she has a nice name.

"Mr. Sullivan, this is about your daughter's blog."

"Your husband established that, also. What can I do for you, Ginny?"

"What you can do for me is take that slanderous blog post down immediately!"

"I can't do that, Ginny. It's not my blog."

"Did you see what your daughter wrote about investment bankers?"

"Did you see what my daughter wrote about me?" I respond, and it seems to put her off balance.

"Yes, well, that was unfortunate. Congratulations on the Western deal, by the way."

"Thanks."

"So, I'm very surprised that you, of all people, wouldn't be putting a stop to this blogging nonsense. My son read the blog post she wrote about investment bankers!"

"Your son responded to her blog and asked her what do investment bankers really do. Talk to your son. No one is making him read Daisy's blog."

"What we don't need is some little brat slandering our profession on the Internet. Morton and I work eighty-hour weeks to give Matthew the kind of life we never had."

"Who's Matthew?" I ask. I can't help messing with her. No one actually works eighty-hour weeks.

"Matthew is our son."

"Oh," I say.

"So, anyway," Ginny says, trying to recapture her prior momentum, "Matthew is too young to understand what we do, and your daughter's slander has made a mess of our household. I want that post taken down, now."

"No."

"Why not?" she asks.

"Because it's true."

"What?"

"What Daisy wrote about me is true. What Daisy wrote about investment bankers is also true. If you so violently disagree with what Daisy wrote, then just explain to your son how she got it wrong. Explain to Matthew how you and Morton are actually making the world a better place by being investment bankers. Or respond to Daisy's blog with the same explanation. I'd love to read it."

"Mr. Sullivan, I don't want to get our lawyers involved."

"Wait a second. So, you're talking about suing a twelve-year-old girl for telling the truth about your profession on her blog? You can't be serious. Did I mention she's twelve? I mean, I know you think you're serious, but listen to yourself for a minute."

"Matthew is talking about becoming a marine biologist!"

Like we need more of those. I never understood why every do-gooder kid wants to be a marine biologist. Don't they know how hard biology classes are at the university level? I think it's just something that sounds cool.

"Mr. Sullivan, what your daughter wrote, it was public slander!" Ginny yells. "We certainly have grounds to get a lawyer involved!"

"Google 'why do investment bankers suck.' I bet you get a million hits. Are you going to sue everyone that comes up in the search results for public slander? I mean, Daisy didn't even name you guys. She was talking about what you do for a living. You know, why you two spend eighty hours a week away from Matthew. I hope the nanny's nice."

That was just mean of me.

"She responded directly to our son! The whole post was a response to Matthew!"

"Then limit what sites Matthew is allowed to go to on the Internet. Or better yet, stick him into therapy. Long sessions, back to back, every afternoon after prep school. Maybe that will keep him off the Internet. Maybe that will even help him to avoid growing up and becoming a sleazy deal broker like you and Morton," I say.

I'm suddenly more than tired of this conversation. There's a tussle on the other end of the line. I wait.

"Hello? Mr. Sullivan?"

"Hi, Morton."

"Mr. Sullivan, my wife and I would sincerely appreciate it if you made your daughter take down that blog post."

"I'm sorry, Morton. Not going to happen."

"Well, that's very unfortunate."

"Okay," I say, and after a few seconds of silence we both hang up. Weird.

***

I pick up Sam and Daisy from school that afternoon at three-ten pm. No play practice, no cross-country practice. After they've both buckled in, I mention my interesting conversation with Matthew's parents.

"Who's Matthew?" Daisy asks.

"Matthew is the kid that has two investment bankers for parents."

"Oh. His user name is downinthedumps," Daisy says.

"That's an uplifting user name," I say. "It sounds like he was already having some problems before you explained to him what his parents do for a living."

"Tonight, I'm writing about corporate lawyers," Daisy says enthusiastically. "In response to user name allaloneesquire. His or her dad is a corporate attorney, which means business lawyer."

"Thanks for the explanation," I say. "How was your day, bud?"

"Fine," Sam says.

"Did anything happen?" I ask.

"No."

"Did you learn anything?"

"No. Not really."

"Awesome," I say.

"Daisy-Daddy?" Daisy sing-songs from the front seat.

"Daisy?" I respond in a flat tone.

"Can we maybe talk a little bit more about business lawyers?" I sigh. Man, don't get me started on corporate attorneys.

***

I'm asleep on the couch again when Catelyn comes in at six-thirty pm. The kids have done their homework, and the kitchen is reasonably clean, so I don't expect any issue regarding my nap. But I can see from her look that we're not going to talk about me falling asleep in the middle of the afternoon like some kind of hobo.

"Did you see it?" Catelyn asks.

"Cat, I just woke up. I've been asleep for a while, I think. I don't even know if the kids are still in the house."

"So, you didn't read her blog post about corporate lawyers." Statement, not a question.

"No, I did not. Was it good?"

"Lawyers, Jack? Seriously? I thought you were going to monitor this stuff. I thought we agreed to that last night." I don't recall agreeing to anything like that, but in the interest of self-preservation, I allow her to continue. "She calls corporate attorneys, and I'll quote because I remember this clearly, she calls them 'useless parasites who only exist because people don't do what they say they're going to do'."

"That seems pretty accurate," I say. "What's the problem?"

"This is in response to some kid whose father is a corporate lawyer."

"Right, user name, all-alone-esquire," I word it out for Catelyn. "Daisy told me about him. Sounds pretty sad, no? Just the user name, I mean."

"Jack, if Daisy continues to rip these jobs apart to the sons and daughters of these professionals, we're going to end up getting sued."

"For what?" I ask.

"For something. I don't know. We can't let a twelve-year-old girl mess up family dynamics, mess up relationships between sons and daughters and fathers and mothers. It's not right. It's too much power for a twelve-year-old. And she's blatantly attacking all the people of position in our society. How can you think nothing bad will come of this?"

"It's just a blog, Cat. Thirty-thousand people out of hundreds of millions. Yeah, she's stirring things up. But it's a small population. And maybe she's doing some good, too. Maybe these are conversations that sons and daughters and mothers and fathers should be having. These kids obviously are having a hard time regardless of Daisy's blog. Have you checked out the user names? It's like roll call at a methadone clinic."

I decide not to tell Catelyn about my conversation with Morton and Ginny Greenly. Under different circumstances, I think she would have enjoyed the story.

"You're way too cavalier about this, Jack."

"No, I'm not. I'm just being cavalier with you because of your reservations. Reservations that I think are unfounded. Get on board, Cat. Daisy is doing something that I think is awesome. In her own small way, she's undermining a broken system through the bureaucracy's own kids. These business parasites are bulletproof when you come at them head-on. How they behave in their family lives versus how they behave in their business lives is totally hypocritical, but they've been able to keep it thoroughly categorized. They don't feel any remorse about teaching their kids to be good people at the dinner table, when in their business lives they do things that are the complete opposite of being a good person. Daisy is reaching the one population that can actually make a difference to these money junkies. Their kids. It's freaking brilliant."

"Remember that she's your daughter, Jack. She's got to grow up and live in this world."

"That's exactly why I'm so happy about what we're doing."

"What we're doing?" Catelyn asks.

"What she's doing. What Daisy is doing," I say.

Chapter Twelve

On Thursday morning, I drive Daisy and Sam to school. From the front seat beside me, Daisy casually offers up the fact that she has launched another website.

"What do you need another site for, Daisy? Won't that dilute your celebrity as a blogger?"

"It's a different set-up, the kind I couldn't make work on 'Daisy in the Doghouse.' But it's going to be linked, so I don't think it'll hurt traffic any."

"So, are you going to tell me about it?" We have about five minutes before we get to their school.

"I was getting too many responses from kids asking about what their parents do for a living. I had to get more organized."

"Organized how?"

"Well, this other site is much more interactive. Kids walk through these steps where they can, you know, input their information – like where they're from, what's their parent's job, how much time they spend with their parents each week, what their home life is like, their happiness quotient, that kind of thing."

"Happiness quotient?" I ask.

"How happy they are, on a scale of one to ten."

"Oh."

"So on the back end," Daisy continues, "the program categorizes this information into groups of people with similar problems, or questions, or things that they want to discuss. And you end up with kind of a dashboard on the homepage so people can easily join whatever conversation works best for them. And everybody can score the posts that they find most interesting or helpful so we can rank the posts and put the top ones on the homepage dashboard. It's really cool."

I look in the rearview mirror at Sam, who stares back at me with an expression like "What?" We pull up to the stop sign across the street from the school where Daisy can give me a kiss goodbye without being embarrassed in front of her friends. Sam has never minded kissing me goodbye in front of his friends, but he sticks his head up from the backseat and kisses me at the stop sign anyway because that's what we do. I drive across the street, and we exchange love you's and have a good day's as they get out of the car.

Daisy pulls her ridiculously heavy backpack from the seat well, and I ask, "What do you call this new site?"

"Stuff That's Wrong with The World dot com. You can get there from the link on 'Daisy in the Doghouse.' Love you, bye!"

Sam turns around outside the school door and waves to me, like he always does. I wave back and pull out of the school driveway into morning traffic. I skip my usual coffee stop and head straight home to check out Daisy's new site.

***

Back at the house, I open my laptop and go to "Daisy in the Doghouse." She's changed the picture on her homepage. It's still her face superimposed on a cartoon doghouse, but she's gotten rid of the sweet smile and replaced it with a pouting expression. Otherwise, it's still the same WordPress format with Daisy's latest post about corporate lawyers above the fold.

But in the right-hand corner, big enough that it can't be missed, is a logo of a blue and green cartoon globe spinning slowly beneath a big, grey, drizzling cloud. "Stuff That's Wrong with the World" is in block letters below the globe, with a red cursive subscript beneath the title that says, in all lowercase, "let's talk about it."

I click on the hyperlink and am redirected. Whoa.

The cloud-raining-on-globe logo is on the top right of the new site. Below it is the Daisy's-head-in-a-doghouse logo linking back to her original site. The rest of the homepage looks like something that NASA might have built. The center of the page is filled with what appears to be an interactive map of the United States. Different size, color-coded dots cover the map, some blinking, some not, with heavy concentrations in the coastal cities and some areas of the Midwest. To the right is a list of the top posts, the header indicating that this list was refreshed a few seconds ago when I came onto the site.

I refresh the browser and the timestamp changes, as does the order of the top posts. Under the map are four color-coded columns, each containing rows of abbreviated posts with headers like "my father is a hypocrite…" or "mom loves money more than…" or "I can't even look at them anymore…" That kind of thing. Rather than scanning the posts, I click on the Start Here button that sits beneath the link back to Daisy's original blog.

I'm redirected to a page where Daisy gives a short explanation of why she created the blog. This part is followed by a "tell everyone about yourself, but only if you want to" area populated with text fields and drop-down lists. These fields take the user through a series of steps to acquire their age, gender, race, location, school, father's profession, mother's profession, etc. All of the steps are optional, so the user can skip anything that she or he doesn't want to share.

I fill out a profile, adopting the user name "bewildered," and move on to a page where I can post whatever is on my mind.

There are drop-down lists at the top of the page to help fit the posts into general categories that can't be extrapolated from the personal information that the user's provided. The design of the whole site is amazing. I click back to the homepage and browse the categories. I play around with the legend on the interactive map, looking at the user groups arranged across the country by age, by gender, by parent's profession, by degree of unhappiness.

I'm flabbergasted. It's brilliant.

My mind scans everything from front to back, and I really can't find anything illegal or even dangerous about the site. I bask in fatherly pride for a few seconds before bringing myself back to reality and the more practical parental issues at hand. Like finding out who actually built this site. Like figuring out how to handle this whole thing when Catelyn finds out.

***

Daisy has play practice until five o'clock. It's raining, so Sam's cross-country practice is canceled and I pick him up at three-ten. We could use a little alone time, Sam and I. He throws his backpack into the back and climbs onto the front seat of the car. I look at him, expressionless.

"Hi," he says.

"Hi," I say back.

"What?" he asks.

"Let's cut the charade, shall we? You will please let me know exactly how involved you are with Daisy's blog." It's a command, not a request.

"What do you mean?"

"I mean Daisy's new site looks like it was built by God. Spill it."

Sam slouches into the seat.

"I helped her with it," he says.

"You helped her with it?"

"Yeah, well, me and the guys from Scatch," he says. "A bunch of them follow Daisy's blog. And when she got into the business stuff, we started to have a conversation about different possibilities."

"When she got into the business stuff? You mean on Monday?"

"Yeah."

"Sam, it's Friday. Are you saying that you and your friends from Scatch concepted, designed and launched "Stuff That's Wrong with the World" in like, three days?"

"Two days, actually. Maybe less. But it's really just preexisting components and programs that we stitched together. All of them have API's, and it's all freeware, so it wasn't like we did any original programming. And the guys in India and Australia were working opposite hours to ours, so that helped move things along."

I know nothing about the world that my kids live in.

"You coordinated all of this?"

"No, no, no, no. I just explained what we were trying to do. Appleboy loved the idea. He took it and ran – project-managed the whole thing. But everybody helped."

"Apple boy?"

"He's one of the senior moderators at Scatch. I think it's a he, at least. With a user name like Appleboy, right?"

"How old is this apple boy?"

I know I should be more worried about sexual predators and other bad actors participating in my ten-year-old son's global network of computer hackers, but if Sam explained it right, the capacity to build this type of "complaints clearinghouse" for sons and daughters of the corrupt minority, it could be important in our efforts to rally a lot of good people behind our cause.

It is a cause now, I think.

"No idea. I don't know anything about him aside from the fact that he's a really awesome project manager," Sam says. "But the site's good, right? There's a lot of bells and whistles that I don't think it needs. Like the map and the filters. I mean, they're cool, but they don't really serve any practical purpose. But the way that different people can talk about different parent problems in their own sections? It really gets rid of the noise. And the rating system, that's totally awesome. Not only does each section have top-rated posts, but the whole site has top-rated posts across different sections. It really keeps the discussions focused and moving."

"The site is impressive, yes," I say, still trying to drive while Sam keeps his eyes locked on mine from the passenger seat, an annoying habit he has. "But, Sam, where do you think this is all going?"

"I don't know," he replies casually. "You wanted a discussion about all of the stuff that's wrong with people who take advantage of an unfair system. We set it up so that their kids could have that discussion, with their parents and with each other. I say we just let it play out. Can we get frozen yogurt?"

***

Sam and I walk into our house with frozen yogurts. I tell him to do his homework, and he says that he will, but then makes a beeline for the family computer in the den. I'm about to call after him when my phone rings. I look at the caller ID and can see that it's Bill Ingram, the attorney who represented me when I sold my first company, before Tree Fort. I haven't spoken to Bill in probably eight years. I should clean out the contacts on my phone.

"Hello, Bill."

"Jack, do you want to explain to me why my daughter now looks at me as if I'm something that she scraped off the bottom of her shoe?"

"Well, I'd guess that she's either gained some deeper insight into your personality or that she's been following Daisy's blog. The family's all good, then?"

"You've read her post on corporate attorneys, I assume."

"I have, yes."

"She called corporate attorneys pond scum. And she went into an elaborate defense of that statement."

"I read the post, Bill."

"What are you going to do about it?"

"Why does everybody think that I'm going to do something about it?" I say into the receiver. "She's right, Bill. You know that your job doesn't make the world a better place. It just makes you rich. Tell your daughter that you got into a slime-ball profession so that you can buy her nice things. Maybe that will make her feel better."

"Who do you think you are, criticizing all the lawyers and accountants and money people?"

"First of all, it's not me publicly calling everyone involved in our lopsided economy to the carpet. It's Daisy. Second, I'm just as complicit as you and the rest of them. I'm a sell-out, and you're a parasite. At least that's how it looks through the eyes of a twelve-year-old girl, given a little bit of understanding about what people like us do. Maybe that's how it looks to your daughter, too. And maybe we should stop blaming the kids and take a long look at what they're saying is wrong with the way we live our lives."

"Put a stop to it or I will," Bill says ominously.

"If you try to concoct some weird lawsuit against me, Bill, I'm pretty sure that it will be posted in its entirety on Daisy's blog. And that's the type of thing that gets picked up in the syndicated news and on talk shows. It would shine a huge spotlight on what a litigious little cretin you really are. How do you think your daughter would react to that?"

"Are you threatening me?" he asks.

"Are you threatening me?" I respond.

There's an uncomfortable silence. At least I assume it's uncomfortable, for Bill.

"Put a stop to it," he says.

"No," I reply. Print me a freaking T-shirt. He hangs up.

***

Sam stays at home when I go to pick up Daisy from play practice. Since school started this year, we've begun to let each of them stay at home alone. Typically, it's when Catelyn and I run errands, go out for a quick dinner or drink. I think my parents used to let me stay home alone when I was six years old. Different times.

I pull up to the school and Daisy seems to be surrounded by more kids, more older kids, than usual. She throws her backpack into the back and jumps into the front seat.

"Hi, Dad."

"Hey, Peanut. So who are all those kids you were hanging around with when I drove up."

"They're seventh and eighth graders. They follow my blog."

"Since when?"

"I don't know. Some of them have been following me for a while. Some of them started this week. They have issues with what their parents do for a living."

All of them?" I ask.

"Well, two of them, really. The others just like the fact that I'm sticking it to The Man."

I've stopped wondering where she gets these expressions. I don't think she understands what they mean in a literal sense.

"Did they join your new site?" I ask. I'm trying to keep it casual.

"You saw it! What do you think? It's awesome, right?"

"It's very impressive. By the way, I outed Sam. I know he's involved. He helped you set up the site by leveraging his network of underground computer hackers from all over the world."

"He must be relieved. Sam hates keeping things from you guys."

"That's apparently not a problem for you."

Daisy batts her eyelashes at me, gives me an impish smile.

"Look, honey," I say. "You know I love you and in a lot of ways I'm actually proud of what you're doing…"

"You asked me to do it," she says.

"I didn't ask you to do it," I reply. "I merely offered — as a suggestion — that you turn your blogging efforts towards people who capitalize on an unfair financial system for personal gain. Instead of messing with your mother and me."

"So, you invited me to do it. Big dif."

"Daisy, I'm not talking about your motivations. It just seems like you've got a pretty enthusiastic following here. Tell me, has your follower base gotten any bigger in the past week or are you still around thirty-thousand?"

"It's gotten bigger," she says quickly.

"Okay, how much bigger? Sixty thousand? Did it double?"

Daisy purses her lips and blows her bangs off of her forehead.

"What, a hundred thousand?"

"As of this afternoon, it's four-hundred and sixty-five thousand and change."

Just Monday, Daisy had felt it necessary to quote her numbers down to the single digit of users. I can see where Catelyn might get concerned with the type of sway she's building.

"Wow. Okay. Impressive. Uh…"

"The idea of getting kids to ask their parents about their jobs, about whether they were making the world a better place or only helping themselves at the expense of other people, that's what did it," Daisy says. "I never thought that so many kids would have such a big problem with what their parents' do for a living. Who knew?"

"Did you? Did you and Sam have a problem with what I did for a living, I mean?"

"God, no!" she says. "We never even thought about it. At least I didn't, and I think Sam would have said something if it bothered him. But we weren't rich, right? I mean, it was only after you sold Tree Fort that you and mom stopped arguing about money."

"You knew about that?"

"Neighbors all the way down the street knew about that. You and mom used to get really wound up."

"Sorry about that."

"No problem. We didn't really care that much. But after you sold Tree Fort, the arguing stopped and then you got really bummed out. Me and Sam were confused about that."

"Is that about the time you started blogging?"

Daisy thinks, then says, "Yeah. I guess it is."

I'm starting to feel the weight of being a parent. How my moods and actions can affect my kids in their developmental stages. You never really think of yourself as such a big influence in another person's life.

"Did the way I acted have anything to do with why you started blogging?" I ask.

"No, not at all," Daisy says as if I had asked her whether Mercury in retrograde had been the reason that she started blogging. I wonder if she can hear my bubble of narcissism pop. "When you guys finally got me my own iPhone, I started reading blogs. And I thought most of them were pointless. Then I got the idea of performing social experiments on you and mom and started my own blog. And just look at how far we've come!"

"Thanks for the level-set. That brings me back to the original point of this conversation. You're getting a lot of attention here, Daisy. You have a lot of followers that are all jazzed up about what you're doing. You've got seventh and eighth graders huddled up around you after play practice, which is something I've never seen before. I'm worried that it's going to mess with your head."

"Mess with my head? How?"

"Well, when people – especially kids – get too much attention, too fast, then it can sometimes distort their perception of reality. It can make them think that they're unrealistically important. Like kids who become TV stars at a young age. Do you know anything about the normal life trajectory of a little kid who becomes famous on TV?"

"I saw a Bravo special on Gary Coleman. Wow, that was messed up. Especially when they jumped the shark by bringing that little redheaded cousin onto his show. That put Gary into a tailspin."

"Yeah, well I'm sure Gary started out as a nice, reasonable little boy..."

"He was a midget," Daisy says.

"Little person, I think, is the politically correct term. And what's your point?"

"Okay, he was a little person. Gary Coleman was going to have to deal with a lot of stuff when he grew out of the cuteness and into an older version of a little person. I don't think he's a good example. The midget thing skews it."

"Wait, look at Peter Dinklage! He was on the cover of Vanity Fair a couple years ago. Little people can grow into big little people and still do awesome stuff without the whole small size thing getting into their head and making them spiral. Little people — or anyone who has to live with something that makes them different — are just a lot stronger than the rest of us," I say, then thoughtfully add, "Except for Gary Coleman. You obviously know what happened to him."

"Okay, I think we're getting kind of far away from whatever point you were trying to make."

Right, we were talking about the potential inflation factor of Daisy's head.

"Look, honey, it's just really important that you don't let all of this attention go to your head. It's important that you don't start thinking of yourself as a celebrity."

"I've always thought of myself as a celebrity," she says mildly.

I pause for thought.

"That's true," I say. And it is. Ever since she was a child, Daisy has always maintained a kind of regal attitude. As if she were gracing everyone in her vicinity with her presence. Not in a bad way, but it was there. I suppose if anyone is going to gain rapid celebrity, it's probably best if they've always considered themselves a celebrity. "Okay, I just don't want this blog to make you into someone different."

"Why would I ever want to be anyone different?" she asks.

Silently I credit Catelyn for her parenting.

Chapter Thirteen

By the time Catelyn comes home at a little after six pm, I've cleaned up the kitchen and made sure the rest of the house looks as nice as I can imagine it should look. Catelyn looks worn out, more so than from a normal day at the college. I've got an impending doom feeling in my gut.

"Hey," she says wearily.

"Hey."

"You've obviously seen the new site."

"Yeah, I have," I say.

"You spoke to Sam, I imagine."

"Of course. The brains behind the mouth." I roll my eyes. I'm trying not to offer any opinion on the situation until I get a better read from her. "Kids these days, right?"

I immediately regret saying that.

"Our kids, Jack. I really don't know how to be a parent in this situation."

I'm about to ask her what situation, just to get a little more insight into whatever she's feeling, but I think better of it. Instead, I pour each of us a glass of wine and sit down at the kitchen table.

"What's up, Cat? I mean I know everything that's going on around us, but what's up with you, right now?"

"I got stopped, three times today, by students at the college. About Daisy's blog. They know about it, Jack." She takes a gulp of her wine. "And they love it."

"Really?"

"They think it's the best thing since Occupy Wall Street."

"That's a pretty low bar," I say, immediately regretting the fact that I've shown my hand. Occupy Wall Street was a serious movement that fell apart because it had no plan, no what's next. Not that we have a plan. It's actually a pretty solid analogy, I guess.

"I'm serious," she says. "They're comparing it to a national movement like Occupy Wall Street. How many followers does she have now?"

"Ah… how would I know?"

"How many followers does she have, Jack?"

"Almost half a million," I say, like a kid caught in a lie.

"And they're all kids?"

"Of that, I really have no idea. I don't think there's any way to check. You've got to assume a bunch of them are just Internet predators."

I look at her, but she has no sense of humor about this.

"Okay, we're in this," she says. "How do you suggest we handle it as parents?"

I'm about to make a snide comment about parenting being her field of expertise, but I hold back and instead give it to her from the heart, maybe with a little ranting thrown in, seeing as I know myself.

"Look, Cat. What Daisy's doing is a good thing. And me, filling her head with the stuff she writes about, that's a good thing too. She's reaching the only people who can make a difference when it comes to the whole backward world of manipulating the financial system for personal gain. She's talking to the only people who these self-deluding parasites might listen to – their kids. She's wedged herself right into the weak underbelly of their hypocrisy. We're making people—people who have deluded themselves for years—finally stand up and explain what they do, say exactly what they contribute to the world. And they have to explain it to their own children."

"You switched from 'she' to 'we' again, somewhere in there," Catelyn says.

"Okay, it's we. It's always been we. You know that. We talked about it. Daisy is the front person for my theories on what's bad about the corporate world, just like she's the front person for Sam's technological site building miracles. He and I are both on board with this, Cat. And you're the only sane person—the only objective person—in this family. We need you."

"Other than you, I'm the only person older than twelve in this family. Do you think you and a couple of tweens can peer pressure me? I'm thinking about Daisy, here. She's a baby. Our baby. She is not equipped to manage this type of situation. It's too public. There's too much energy behind it."

"She's equipped to handle it if we're with her. All of us. Regardless of the consequences. Let's get behind her and see where this goes. People are living the wrong way, whether they know it outright or whether they're able to delude themselves into thinking otherwise. And we're coming in at an angle here that none of those parasites could have possibly expected. We need to see where it goes. We need to get behind this, as a family. Look, Cat. You know this is important to me. And you know I love our kids more than anything in the world. I recognize that it's potentially dangerous for Daisy to be in this situation and I recognize my part in putting her there. But this is bigger than proper parenting. And we're in this situation, so we need to be together in it."

"Okay," Catelyn says.

"Okay, what?" I ask, honestly not sure what she means.

"Okay, I'll get behind this. I won't fight it. I'll support it. I'll help however I can. This can be a family mission, Daisy's site."

"Sites," I say.

"Sites, then. Look, I know you think it's necessary. And I know I've never been in your world, so I don't have the kind of hate you do for this whole unfair economy thing. But I've always trusted you to take care of the family, from a financial perspective at least. And this seems like one of those macro issues where we just need to commit, where I just need to commit and trust your judgment. So I will. We'll be in this as a family."

"Okay. I'm not sure what to say here. So, you're on our team? And we can be a team?" I'm more than a little concerned about accepting this level of responsibility.

"Yeah," Catelyn says. "We're a team. What's next?"

I honestly don't know.

"How about we let the wheels spin a bit," I say, "since they're already in motion?"

Catelyn nods. She's a very good wife for me.

Chapter Fourteen

For the next couple of days, it's the same routine. And it has become a routine, but the type of routine that spins in smaller and smaller cycles, like a rope spinning around a metal axis and the rotations get shorter and shorter as the spin progresses. It's becoming more focused. It's going somewhere. Though exactly where it's going, I have no idea.

Daisy asks me about different professions, and I answer her to the best of my knowledge and opinion. The follower base continues to grow – five hundred thousand, one million, one million five. It seems like all of the kids in the country either are hating their parents for making the world a worse place or cheering their parents for making the world a better place. The latter category being mostly civil servants and teachers.

I have a gnawing feeling that we are making all of this too black-and-white. Kids holding their parents to the fire for choices that they made decades ago, choices that they never thought to consider wrong in the first place. It's unfortunate. That's all I can think.

Unfortunate is the word that always pops into my head. Unfortunate. But it is also unfortunate that these people chose to invest themselves in a way of life that contributes to hurting people for their own gain, no matter how far they have removed themselves from reality, the reality being that we don't each exist in a vacuum.

Still, it's an exciting—although simultaneously sad—time. Remarkably, even though Daisy's blogs connect with huge amounts of people, the only personal connections that we've had to deal with still come from me, from our last name and people who deduced my identity. I ignore a dozen phone calls daily from people in my past lives. The conversations would all end up being the same. But other than these people from my past lives, we're in the cloud. Life seems almost normal.

"Jack." I hear my name called in a voice that isn't Catelyn's.

"What? Hey, Daisy." I'm sleeping on the couch again. It's Sunday afternoon. "What did you call me?"

"Jack," Daisy says, suppressing a giggle. "I was hoping that you and mom would let me call you by your first names now that I'm a big-time blogger."

She walks over to the couch and lies on top of me. Twelve-years-old, her feet almost touching mine when she stretches out. And although rail thin, she is still the type of heavy that will do some damage to my back and my hips when she eventually gets up. Still, I wouldn't trade it, figuring the bank of times my daughter will lie on top of me to watch TV will eventually run dry. Like when she turns eighteen or something.

"I prefer Daisy-Daddy," I say, "but you can call mom by her first name. She'll like that."

Catelyn's at church, selling cash cards to the parishioners of the diocese to which my kids' school belongs. She really is our only link to the community at large, I think.

Then I remember Daisy.

Sam comes into the room like a sleepwalker, despite the fact that it's one-thirty in the afternoon. He puts his arm around my neck and wedges onto the left side of my body. Shoving Daisy over, just like the two of them used to do when they were toddlers. Daisy gives him the space to lie on one half of me. She never used to do that. It was always a surreptitious elbow and knee battle when they were younger. I suddenly feel like I'm being played.

"Okay, what do you guys want?"

"Us?" Daisy asks sweetly.

And the jig is up. The melodrama on Daisy's voice is a dead giveaway. She always sounds like she's reading from the script of a Nineteenth Century play when she's putting on an act. Sam looks at her in disgust.

"What..." She says, but she's not asking.

"Okay, here's the deal," says Sam, manning up for both of them. "We need money."

"What?" I ask. "How much? And why? And more importantly, how much?"

"We need three hundred dollars."

And I'm like, okay, whatever. Do these kids not know how much it costs every time I take them to the Outback Steak House? Which is, like, often. Sure, whatever, three hundred dollars. No problem. But why?

"Why?" I ask guardedly.

"Field trip," Daisy replies as if that is going to be enough.

"A field trip for school?"

"Not exactly, no," she says. "More like a field trip for our family project."

When we're talking about what she's going to write, it's her blog. When we're talking about money, it's our family project. I lift my right hip and vault both of them off of me and the couch.

"What do you need three hundred dollars for?" I ask.

"We hired an organizer to set up a meet for the Northwest Chapter of our group. It's at Strumpner Field, right by school," Sam says.

"The Northwest Chapter of our group? Is having an in-person meet?" I'm thinking about a field day for sexual predators from the Internet. "And you need to pay three hundred dollars for what?"

"We just need to put up a thousand dollars in advance for the organizer, like a deposit." Sam says, "Everything else is taken care of by our sponsors and the food trucks."

"So where does the other seven hundred dollars come from?" I ask.

"We're Northwest Jersey. Our sponsors are putting up seventy percent of the total deposits for each of the events in our state. So Southeast Jersey and Mid-Jersey and Southwest Jersey each have to put up three hundred dollars for their events, too," Sam says. "We get the deposits back as long as the event clears at least fifteen thousand dollars. But the sponsors don't get the deposit back."

They're estimating fifteen thousand dollars' income for each public gathering? I actually have no idea if this is a high or low number.

"Who are these sponsors?"

"Oh, you know. Scatch, Twitter, Facebook, Instagram, those types of companies. All of them have programs to help groups like us."

"How did you get in touch with these sponsors?"

"My friends from Scatch," Sam says, "and their friends. Everyone knows someone in the web development community."

"The hacker community," I say. "How did you get permission to use Strumpner Field?"

"The organizer," Sam says.

"How did you get permission to have food trucks?"

"The organizer," Sam says, "which is the same answer that you'll get for probably most of the questions that you're about to ask us."

"Who is this organizer?"

"Event Planning International, Inc." Sam says. "It's a group contact. A mom who divorced a partner at some corporate accounting firm. And it turns out she hates the guy. I think the name of her company is a little ambitious for North Jersey."

"Please give me her number," I say calmly.

I send the kids upstairs and call the organizer.

***

"Event Planning International," the receptionist answers, "How can we make your special day unforgettable?"

"My name is Jack Sullivan. I need to talk to whoever's in charge there."

"Well, Mr. Sullivan, do you have an event planner that you're working with?"

"No. Actually, I don't know. I'm Daisy Sullivan's father, and I need to talk to whoever is organizing her event at Strumpner Filed this Saturday."

"Oh, Mr. Sullivan. I had no idea! I'll put you through to Nancy right away."

There's a hold click and a connection click.

"Mr. Sullivan!" the person I assume is Nancy shouts. "I have been dying to talk to you!"

"And here we are, Nancy." I say, "and I'm going to skip pleasantries to get immediately to the financials. Nancy, let's just walk through the economics of this deal you've got going on with my daughter so I can catch up. Now, as I understand it, Daisy's group is going to give you a deposit of three hundred dollars."

"Which she gets back if they hit the minimum spend," Nancy says.

"Sure, that makes sense. But I understand the minimum spend is fifteen thousand dollars, among food trucks and other promoters. Is that right?"

"Yes."

"So, as an organizer of this type of thing, I'm assuming you get thirty percent of the gross, right?"

"Anywhere from twenty-five to thirty percent, typically, yes."

"And you're expecting at least fifteen thousand from this event, given that's your minimum so as Daisy doesn't lose her deposit, right?"

"Well, that's the minimum, yes. You see, we don't know how many people will show up for something like this. It's quite extraordinary, you know."

"I know. But I'm wondering about why Daisy's group doesn't share in its profits if it actually were to generate profits for everyone involved?"

"Well, Mr. Sullivan, this isn't an ordinary event…"

"I'm sure you know Mort Greensburg," —I totally make up this name— "who's on the council for Rudolph, New Jersey. Well, he assures me that the town always gets fifteen percent of the gross revenue when they sponsor events like this. Now, in my daughter's case, I assume you'd have to pay for use of the field…" Silence on the other end of the line, and I'm actually sure the town would let any event use the field for free if it potentially brought people in. "…but I can't imagine you think you're going to keep all that profit, after any expenses, for yourself?"

"Mr. Sullivan, this isn't a town event. You have to understand that there is some risk on my part."

"And that risk, I assume, is covered by the three hundred dollar deposit. Nancy, what is your last name?"

"Birmingham. But I'm in the middle of a divorce, and I'll be taking my maiden name, Henley."

"Okay, Ms. Henley, I understand that your kid is a follower of my daughter's blog, yes?"

"Oh, absolutely! My daughter really had her eyes opened to the type of person my soon-to-be ex-husband is thanks to your daughter's blog!"

"So, Ms. Henley, how do you think your daughter is going to feel when we tell her that you tried to screw Daisy's group out of standard profit sharing for this type of event? You're looking to take a deposit and give the group no upside. That's not fair. And fair is what Daisy's group is all about."

"Well, it is an unusual sort of event. There's more risk than a town event."

"For who?" I ask sternly, like I'm talking to a bad child. "The food trucks? I'm pretty sure they've got nothing on the line for this thing, Ms. Henley. In fact, I'm pretty sure the deposit is just there to make sure you don't waste your time if this event ends up zeroing out. And if it blows up, you make thirty percent. You're sleazy, Ms. Henley. And the funny thing is, you were all over your daughter joining Daisy's blog because it makes your soon-to-be ex-husband look like a creep. But you're just as much of a creep as he is. I'm sure Daisy and your daughter will be very interested to learn this. I'm sure they'll be very interested to talk about your company on her blog."

"Is she even incorporated?"

"I am," I lie. I realize that we definitely should incorporate this group as a limited liability non-profit company so at least there's limited liability in case of God knows what.

"Okay, then. I wasn't aware of that. I thought it was just a bunch of kids. We can organize the event with no deposit and Daisy's group can have twenty percent of the total revenue," Nancy says quickly, trying to undo the damage that her greediness may potentially cause to her reputation within the group, or with her daughter.

"Whatever," I say. "We'll think it over, and my son will get back to you. He's ten, by the way."

I add this last bit to make her feel like the slimy little cheat she is. And she's a small business, not the typical corporate mogul that I rail about. Why can't people just be fair, I ask myself? Why do people think that a little extra money is worth sacrificing their integrity for, I ask myself. There are good people and bad people in every profession, I tell myself. My fight is with the bad professions, I tell myself. I'm talking to myself a lot these days. It would make me feel better if things were more black and white.

I go to a do-it-yourself website to incorporate Stuff That's Wrong with the World. Surprise. The name is available. I apply for the federal and state tax exemptions. And in a few minutes, we have Stuff That's Wrong with the World, Inc. A non-profit, 501 (c) company.

It sounds ominous.

Chapter Fifteen

Sam calls Nancy Birmingham-Henley the next day, gives her our tax ID and sends her a basic contract outlining the profit-sharing terms for the meeting scheduled for the next Saturday. I drew up the contract yesterday, back-of-the-napkin type of stuff because I'm not an attorney, but I do know what's fair.

On principle, Sam tells her, a verbal commitment is fine for our company. But given the fact that Nancy has already acted unethically, we're going to have to go with a paper contract this time. I listen to the conversation and give him a thumbs-up.

I'm not normally involved in any kind of event planning, but six days seems like a pretty tight timeline. That said, the speed with which the kids launched and grew the user base of the new site was astonishing enough to help me keep an open mind.

Interspersed with her rants about the banking system and professional services, Daisy has been putting up more posts that celebrate careers like school teachers, nurses, police and firefighters. This is positive, even though every post has a nasty edge digging into exactly how the altruism of these careers highlights the selfishness of corporate slime who are making the world a worse place for everyone who is not a professional money-maker.

At least it puts a more positive spin on her research conversations with me and Catelyn. And we like encouraging kids to feel good about what their parents do for a living – when it's justifiable. Especially parents who are generally overworked, underpaid and underappreciated – like teachers and other civil servants.

It's like we're giving these kids a reason to be proud of their smaller houses and older cars. Giving solid, hardworking parents the kind of grass-roots recognition that they have always deserved and have probably never gotten. Maybe even causing the bankers and corporate service professionals some embarrassment about filling up every square inch of their suburban properties with McMansions and luxury automobiles.

We're getting into a good groove here, I think to myself, trying to ignore the foreboding pit in my stomach that I always get when things are going too well. Still, I have this feeling, like it's only a matter of time before the other shoe drops. And time moves very fast these days.

***

At eight pm on Tuesday night, I read Daisy's latest post and feel a chill run up my spine. It's basically an exposé regarding the very specific impact of the 2008 financial crisis on the North Jersey Teachers Pension Fund. She lists the schools in each district, and she lists the involved banks and fund management companies that received government bailout money. She lists the compensation for executives at these firms in 2009 as well as 2010 and compares them with the residual state of the pension fund in the same years.

I'm immediately thinking of the interactive map one click away, where anyone can sort and search to figure out where the people that work for these firms might live. At least, if their kids have input enough information. We're making this personal.

"Daisy, honey?" I call up the stairs. "Can you come down for a minute?" I pause for thought. "Sam, can you come down, too?"

"One sec," Daisy shouts down, her standard reply to a request for her presence. Sam comes down right away.

"Hey," I say.

"Hey," he says back. We head to the kitchen table and wait for Daisy.

"You read what Daisy posted tonight?" I ask.

"Yes," Sam says.

"She didn't source all of that information on her own. Neither did you. Where did it come from?"

"One of the users."

"How do you guys know it's accurate?" I ask.

"Oh, it's accurate," Sam replies.

"Daisy!" I shout towards the stairs.

"One sec!" she shouts back.

"Now!"

Daisy hisses an exasperated okay and trudges down the stairs.

"You got pretty specific in your blog post tonight," I say as she sits down next to her brother.

"Yeah, I've got, like, weeks' worth of material on how the little guy got screwed by The Man. I'm going to do the fireman's pension fund tomorrow, then the police and then nurses. It's great, right?" she says enthusiastically. "And we've got moderators who are starting their own blog contributions on, like, a regional basis, and they're doing the same thing. We're really pulling back the curtain on these corporate swine."

Daisy's obviously still picking up terminology from her contributing users.

"How do you know that what you're saying is accurate?"

"I quote my source on every piece of information I offer. Well, I quote someone's source, whoever actually sent me the information. I think it's some sort of professor of something. That's how he or she sounds, anyway."

Great, I think, we've got academia involved. No conspiracy theorists on that side of the fence.

"And the sources are all public records," Daisy continues, "so it's not just according to some looney out there."

"How did you know to do it that way?"

"The person who sent the information told me to do it that way," she says innocently.

"Daisy, I want to look at any data that's sent to you before you post an entry about it."

"Daddy, that's not how this works! You said…" she whines as if I'm going back on an agreement.

"I don't need to read your entry before you post it. I just want to see the data you're getting. It's really important that you don't post anything that can't be very easily backed up by a legitimate public source."

"You sound just like the professor-type person who sent me the data," she says.

That makes me feel a little better. Maybe there are some good people out there. People with brains and research capacities who can contribute to the fight. But there are a lot of nut-jobs, too, I remind myself. We're deep in the heart of the Internet here.

"Just show me the source data before you post anything about it," I say.

"Fine," she replies, gets up and scooches me from in front of my laptop. She goes to her site, logs in, enters an admin code, does a quick search and then shifts the screen back towards me.

"Whoa," I say after perusing the attachments from a user response. "Someone's been staying up late." There are literally dozens of pages outlining specific wrongdoings perpetrated by the corporate bureaucracy on the innocent populace and their money. The attachments outline the specific winners and losers involved in each situation, with an eloquence and brevity that blows my mind. Every piece of hard data is nailed to a source in public record. It's amazing.

On impulse, I highlight and copy a few paragraphs. Then I open a new tab, paste the content into the Google search field and hit search. I click on the first result, and it takes me to a .pdf of a paper written by an economics professor at one of the New Jersey state colleges. Hello, Dr. Gregory Greenburg. The paper was published four years ago. And a lot of good it did, apparently.

Dr. Greenburg has dumbed down his incriminations for Daisy's blog. No, I correct myself, he hasn't dumbed them down. He's just made them more concise and understandable – turned his work into something that a twelve-year-old is able to digest and comprehend. Maybe he gets it, too. How the message needs to be simple enough for a kid to understand.

I Google his name, do an image search. He's probably in his mid-sixties, or at least he was when the picture was taken. Weather worn, a big ragged beard that makes him look crazy in a beatnik sort of way.

You had something to say too, huh, Doc? I ask him silently. And we both needed a twelve-year-old girl who had the ear of greed's sons and daughters before anyone would pay attention. Though I shouldn't really put myself on a par with Dr. Greenburg since he actually wrote something.

"Daddy?" Daisy sounds as if she's asking for a summary judgment and then to be excused.

"Yeah, honey. You can use this stuff for your posts. But if you get any source material from other users, can you please show it to me before you post any facts from it?"

"Deal," she says and skips back upstairs.

"Can I go, too?" Sam asks.

"Yeah, you can take off, too. Go do whatever it is you do."

"Hey, Dad?" Sam asks, getting up from the kitchen table.

"Yeah, bud?"

"Do you think what we're doing is right?"

"Yeah, of course. I mean, I definitely think it's more right than it is wrong. Why do you ask?"

"You know my friend Blake. The rich one? Who took all the boys in class to a Yankees game for his birthday last year?"

"Yeah, I know which one you're talking about." Blake's your prototypical entitled rich kid. I never liked Sam hanging around with him.

"Well, he told me he hates his dad."

"Oh," I say. I want to tell Sam if you're going to make an omelet, you've got to break some eggs. But that's too callous. This is the problem with using kids as a wedge into their parent's conscience. It's effective, but what does it do to the kids?

"He asked me if I hated you," Sam says. "I told him, no, I love you. And he asked how I could love a sell-out."

"What did you say?"

"I said that maybe you've done some stuff that didn't make the world a better place. But I said that it bothered you so much it made you nuts, and now you're trying to make things better. I told him that everyone deserves a chance to try to make things better."

"Good answer," I say.

"Blake always looked up to his dad," Sam says. "He always bragged about all the things they have and all the trips they take. And now he's so into Daisy's blog, I don't know. It's like he's too into it. All he does is bash his parents. Maybe it's so the other kids won't hold it against him, all the money his parents have and how they got it. But I also think maybe he's all mixed up and needs something he can hold on to. So he holds on to this whole movement we've got going, and it's the same movement that makes his parents look so selfish and greedy. Which has got to be really confusing for a kid. I'm not sure how he's going to find his way back."

I wonder if that's my responsibility, helping these kids find a way back to normal. If I, or Dr. Greenburg, or any other soapbox heroes, so passionate about raising the awareness of a problem… If we succeed, are we also responsible for cleaning up the mess we make? I've got to think that we are, though I don't know where to start on that part of the project. And I have a feeling it's going to get a whole lot worse before we have a chance to start thinking about how to make things better.

"Tell Blake to talk to his dad," I say. "Either Blake will change his mind, or maybe his dad will decide to figure out how to live a better life. That's about all you can do at this point."

Sam nods and heads to the den, to the computer.

Chapter Sixteen

The next morning, when I drive the kids to school, I see John Mahoney pulling toilet paper out of the trees around his McMansion with one hand while simultaneously hosing egg yolk from his front windows. Catching my eye as I cruise by, he slowly raises his middle finger at the car. I shrug my shoulders in response and then look over at the children. Daisy's fumbling with the radio, so she missed the brief scene. Sam is…

"He gave you the finger!" Sam shouts. "Oh, man. He just gave you the finger! Did you see that?"

"What?" asks Daisy, looking up and scanning the houses.

"Nothing," I say.

"Mr. Mahoney just gave dad the finger!" Sam shouts again. "Did you see that?"

"I missed it," Daisy says, deflated.

"It was nothing," I say.

"It wasn't nothing, Dad. He just stuck his middle finger up at you! Should we turn around?"

"Turn around and do what?"

"I don't know, shouldn't you fight him or something?" Sam asks, "What do you do when someone gives you the finger?"

"You ignore it. It's a juvenile gesture. And anyway, Mr. Mahoney is upset about the fact that someone toilet papered and egged his house, so let's cut him some slack on this one. And, I shouldn't have to ask, but you guys didn't have anything to do with what happened to Mr. Mahoney's house, right?"

"No," they say in quasi-unison.

"So, who do you think did it?"

"Probably their kids," Sam says. And he's right. It probably was the Mahoney children defacing their own house. I wonder why he doesn't have them outside cleaning it up before school. Probably, family relations are a little strained at the Mahoney house right now.

"I can't believe he gave you the finger!" Sam repeats several times on the drive to school.

After dropping the kids off, I start thinking that some proactive measures might be in line here. Avoid the escalation of any random *Lord of the Flies* type behavior from the disgruntled neighborhood children. And not just in this neighborhood. I have no idea how many of these kinds of incidents are sparking up around the country this morning.

***

I pick the kids up later that afternoon and tell them that after their homework we're going to watch a movie. Daisy complains until I agree to let her post the next blog entry before my impromptu family movie night.

When Catelyn comes home at nine-thirty that evening, the kids are both lying on top of me on the couch in front of the television.

"Hey, guys!" Catelyn says. "What are you watching? And why is everyone still downstairs so late on a school night?"

"Mom! You don't have to pause it, Dad!" Daisy says and gets up to hug Catelyn. Sam has fallen asleep, so I remain pinned to the couch. I pause the movie.

"What's this all about?" Catelyn asks me.

"Gandhi," I say.

"You're making them watch *Gandhi*?"

"Well, Sam nodded off about a half hour ago, but I'm sure he'll want to pick it up tomorrow." Sam finishes everything that he starts. "Daisy's going to finish it now."

"Can't I go to bed?" she asks her mother.

"No," I answer for Catelyn. "Get over here and let's finish this."

"How much longer?" Daisy whines.

I click the play button on the remote. "Look, it's only fifteen more minutes. Come on."

"Listen to your father," Catelyn tells our daughter, a hint of question in her voice. Daisy slumps her shoulders and walks over, nudges Sam as she climbs back on top of me.

"Good Daisy!" I say. She lets her tongue fall out of her mouth and pants like a puppy. When the movie ends, I ask what she thought of it.

"It was long," she says. It really is a long movie. I shouldn't have waited until seven p.m. to start it.

"I know," I say. "Sorry about that. I didn't remember it being so long. But did you take away any meaning from the story?"

"I'm really tired," she says.

I tell her to go up, brush her teeth and get into bed. But I ask her to think about it. I tell her we'll discuss it in the morning, and she walks upstairs. I carry Sam up behind her, kiss them both goodnight and come back downstairs to Catelyn, who is halfway through a glass of wine.

"You made them watch *Gandhi*?" Catelyn asks for the second time.

"We've got to get ahead of some stuff," I say, "like, make sure that kids don't act out against their parents, or any other parents on the naughty list, in a way that's destructive or dangerous. You saw the Mahoney's house, right?"

"Yeah and three other McMansions, all victims of mild vandalism, on my drive to the college this morning. I thought you'd be happy about it. It's not any worse than Mischief Night."

"Oh, I am happy about it. Don't get me wrong. A little toilet paper and a few eggs – harmless. Productive, even. But we don't want it to spiral. Daisy's got to make a statement on the blog about non-violent, non-destructive resistance. Or exposure. Or whatever it is we're doing. We just want to make sure that we let everyone know we're against violence and destruction."

"So, *Gandhi*?"

"I wanted to get her into the right head space for our discussion about this stuff. Prime the pump a bit."

"Makes sense, I guess," Catelyn says and pours herself another glass of wine.

"So, how was your day?"

"Well, Daisy's blog – both sites, actually – have officially become the talk of the college. It's an academic vacuum, so there's nothing but positive feedback. She's becoming a hero. Or prophet. Or something. I don't know. I think a lot of students are going to this event on Saturday."

"I talked to her, and I don't really think all this attention is going to Daisy's head. Strange as that may seem."

"How could it not be going to her head?"

"I don't know. I told her I was worried that all of this sudden celebrity would change her. She told me that she'd always considered herself a celebrity, so why would she act any different when other people finally start to treat her that way. And there's a lot of truth in that. I mean, she's always had this air of royalty about her – like a good princess, you know – and it never seemed to be coming from how other people treated her. Aside from us, I mean. Who knows, maybe she's a natural. Maybe she's got the build for this type of thing?"

"I hope so, Jack. I mean, I'm on board and supportive of letting this play out. But I'm relying on you to make sure it doesn't mess Daisy up. God help you if it does."

"We're surfing a giant wave here, Cat. I'm trying very hard to be Zen and rational and stay ahead of any potential pitfalls. I know it's dangerous and I know we're talking about Daisy – and Sam, for that matter. So maybe you could ease up on the ominous threats a little. Help me stay on game."

"I'm fully behind you and this whole… project. I was just reminding you, if it goes the way of Chernobyl, you are a dead man," Catelyn says, but she says it with a smile.

"Thanks. That's all I was looking for. I appreciate the support."

***

I drive the kids to school again on Thursday morning. The Mahoney's McMansion has been trashed with toilet paper and eggs for the second night straight, but John isn't outside cleaning it up when we drive by.

"So, let's talk about Gandhi," I say.

"I fell asleep. Don't spoil it for me!" Sam shouts.

"Spoiler alert," Daisy says. "The British government hands over control of India, they louse it up, and Gandhi gets shot."

"Seriously, Daisy?" Sam whines.

"Daisy," I say sternly.

"What? It's based on historical events. I don't think anyone should expect a surprise ending."

"I'm going to watch the rest of it anyway," Sam says.

"Okay, but what happened in the movie… was any of it meaningful to you guys? Do you think any of it is applicable to our situation today? To what we're doing?"

"You want me to go on a hunger strike?" Daisy asks. Something in her voice makes me think she's actually considering it as a publicity stunt. We'll be at school in a few minutes. There's not enough time for me to wait for them to deduce my meaning.

"No. Look," I say, "Gandhi was a leader who hated violence and destruction, right? He actually brought down British rule in India without any fighting from his side. Instead of trying to kill the enemy, he exposed what the British Empire was doing – made it public to the world. I mean, we watched the movie less than twelve hours ago. Is any of this ringing a bell?"

"Sure. Get to your point." Daisy says in a tone light enough to retain a modicum of respect for her father.

"My point is, Gandhi was very vocal with his followers about the fact that he didn't want to achieve this victory by causing harm to other people, even the British." I cut to the chase. "I think we need to take a similar position with the blog and the site. And I think we need to do it as soon as possible."

"Why, because the Mahoney kids' toilet-papered their own house? Twice?" Sam asks.

"No, toilet-papering houses is harmless. But this type of thing can escalate quickly, especially when people are all wound up, and when there's no clear position on violence or destruction on behalf of the movement. How would you guys feel if tonight, instead of throwing eggs at the Mahoney's house, someone threw a rock through their window? What if it hurt one of the kids? How would that make you feel, knowing that our project is responsible?"

"I'm almost positive that the Mahoney kids are the ones vandalizing their own house," Sam says.

"That's not the point. This isn't just happening in our neighborhood. It's happening in a lot of places around the country. At least I imagine it is. And throwing rocks isn't too far a leap from throwing eggs, especially when Daisy continues to pump out very localized indictments based on Dr. Greenburg's data."

"It's not just me," Daisy says. "There are dozens of moderators pumping out localized blog posts based on Dr. Greenburg's data. We've got material for weeks, for hundreds of posts."

"I understand that, Daisy. That's why it's so important that the movement make a clear statement on its position towards violence and destruction, that statement being we don't approve of it. And this has to happen tonight, while things are still under control and no one has acted out in a bad way, at least that we know of. Do you read me?" I ask.

"Okay, I read you," she says and thinks for a second. "Can we come up with other ways to act out, though? Ways that aren't violent or destructive?"

It's a question that I wasn't expecting.

"Sure," I say. "I guess so. As long as we make it very clear that no one gets hurt and nothing gets destroyed."

I pull up to school. We forgot to kiss at the stop sign. Daisy, shy in front of her friends, lets me kiss the top of her head. Sam leans over from the back seat and plants a big one, right on my lips. I love this kid.

Chapter Seventeen

That evening I wait by my laptop, Daisy up in her room. She shouts down the stairs that she's done and I refresh the site.

Oh, no. Not good at all. I don't read the words, but am looking instead at the redesign of her logo. It's still Daisy's pouting face in a cartoon doghouse. But now that face is superimposed on top of a tiny, stick-thin body, sitting cross-legged in a white sheet. The head-to-body proportions are like Hello Kitty.

"Daisy! Please come down here right now!" I shout from the kitchen table.

I hear her get up and walk down the stairs. She knows my serious voice.

"What?" she asks, walking into the kitchen.

"Is this your face on a photo of Mahatma Gandhi's body?"

"Is it too much?" she asks innocently.

"It is disrespectful in ways that I can't even begin to describe. You superimposed your face onto one of the most iconic civil rights leaders who ever lived. It's totally offensive!"

"Oh," she says, "I didn't realize. Who would find it offensive?"

"We can start with the almost one-point-three billion people who live in India, I imagine."

"Really? Because in the movie it seemed like Gandhi had a sense of humor…"

"That's a picture taken of him during one of his hunger strikes, Daisy. It's like superimposing your face on Jesus's crucified body. So not cool."

"Fine, I'll have my people change it. Did you read the post?"

Who exactly are "my people"?

"No," I say. "I'm not going to read the post until you redesign the logo."

"Fine, give me a minute."

***

About thirty minutes later Daisy shouts "Done!" from her room.

Her "people" are quick. I refresh the site, and it's the old, pouting Daisy-face logo. And sitting, fully intact, beside the cartoon doghouse is a black-and-white silhouetted image of Gandhi, including his own head and face. I guess that works.

"Is it okay?!" Daisy shouts down the stairs.

"Much better!" I shout back.

"Did you read the post?!"

"I just refreshed the site!"

"Let me know when you've read it!"

"Okay, but I don't want to continue this conversation by shouting between two floors! Come down in five minutes!"

"Okay!"

Daisy's post is simple and eloquent. Like all of her writing, it's without pretense, straight from the heart. There are times I wish I were a twelve-year-old again instead of being trapped in a mind so twisted up by years of other people's language and motivations, years of me trying to be what I believed other people thought I should be.

She comes down into the kitchen, and I give her a kiss.

"It's good?" she asks.

"It's good," I say.

"Cool. I need to go write about the firefighter's pension plan."

She heads back upstairs.

Catelyn comes in a couple hours later. She'd read Daisy's post about our position on violence and destruction when she was at school. She gives me a look of approval like I'm holding up my end of the bargain. I smile and shake my head.

***

On Friday morning I drive the kids to school again. The Mahoney McMansion is trashed with toilet paper and eggs, but I can't tell if it's a fresh batch or residual from two nights before. I pass a few more toilet-papered McMansions that I hadn't noticed on the prior two days. I've been pretty engaged in conversation with the kids on these drives, so maybe I missed them.

I slow down about two blocks from the school, cruise by a small split level. I'm looking at a little red doghouse on the front lawn. Like what Snoopy had in the Peanuts cartoons. I can't tell if it's made of wood or plastic. Does anyone keep their dogs outside anymore? Maybe I'm delusional, I tell myself. Maybe the stress is getting to me.

I drop the kids off. As I drive home, I notice two more small red doghouses on two more front lawns. I pull up to our house more than a little freaked out. I call Catelyn, who's already at the college.

"Did you see any little red doghouses on your way to work?"

"Ha," she laughs. "Yeah, I saw some little red dog houses on the way to work. And there are dozens of them at the college, too. One in front of almost every building."

"These are obviously in support of Daisy and her message?" I say more than ask.

"You think?" Catelyn replies.

"Where would people get little red dog houses? I mean, it's been less than two weeks since this whole thing really started."

"Check the site. This feels like Sam to me. Okay, I've got to run," Catelyn says. We exchange love you's and hang up.

I go to the Daisy in the Doghouse blog site, scan the page. It's just Daisy, Gandhi and her posts, same as last night. I click through to the "Stuff That Is Wrong with the World" site. Bingo.

Sitting on a promotional shelf right above the fold is a bar ad featuring a picture of a little red doghouse and asking for support. I scroll down below the fold of the site, but the promotional shelf doesn't move with the scroll. It stays in front of the user. Nice touch.

I click on the bar ad. It takes me to a simple e-commerce site. One product in the gallery, a red doghouse in sizes small, medium and large. Next to the doghouse, in the slots where other products would be, there are a few "Coming Soon" banners. For t-shirts. For hats. For a Gandhi-style toga sheet. That will have to be removed from the site as soon as the kids get home from school.

I click on the doghouse. It's being drop-shipped by Amazon and is eligible for overnight and two-day delivery. I click on a "Coming Soon" hat. It's all available for pre-order.

At least the stuff is reasonably priced.

Too bad they couldn't have had the hats and t-shirts ready in time for the big get-together on Saturday. Which is tomorrow, reminding me that I haven't seen any kind of agenda for the event. I wonder if all the kids are just going to show up at the park and text with each other.

I call a copyright attorney I know and get him started on the process of protecting the site's trademark designs and logos. Standard housekeeping and probably unnecessary, but all of the profits from our sites will ultimately be donated, so we don't need anyone else trying to capitalize on our goodwill in order to sell their own stuff.

Daisy's got play practice until five and Sam's done with cross country at four-thirty. We follow the normal Friday routine. I pick Sam up, we buy three packs of Pokémon cards from the Main Street Smoke Shop—yes, our little rural town still has a smoke shop—and then we walk over to Smart World Coffee. I get a large black "Mud," he gets an apple juice, and we sit at one of the low-top tables in the seating area.

One time, about five years ago when I used to work from home on Fridays, we decided to sit at one of the high-top tables beside the floor-to-ceiling windows. Sam loved being up so high. It felt like a grownup moment. Until he reached for a Pokémon card and toppled off the seat, knocking the wind out of him.

Not being fluent in parenting a five-year-old, I thought that the fall had collapsed his lung and immediately began performing my own version of cardiopulmonary resuscitation on his gasping body. A female barista pulled me off of Sam, calmed him down and gave him some ice for his bruised elbow. She refilled my coffee with a disappointed look.

The regular three-thirty pm coffee shop crowd, mostly old people, thought the whole scene was hysterical. For a few weeks, we were coffee shop celebrities. Not the good kind. So now, five years later, we still sit at the low-tops.

After we sit, Sam selects one of the three packs of Pokémon cards, which I then open. I hold the deck in front of Sam and flip the top card as quickly as I can so that he only gets a glimpse of the picture on the front. Then he guesses the name of the Pokémon on the card. But I wouldn't really call it guessing because ninety-nine out of a hundred times he's correct. After he guesses, I hand him the card, which he then stacks in one of three piles: Pokémon that he doesn't have; different versions of Pokémon that he does have; and duplicates, or cards identical to what he already owns.

Now that he's ten, I have a feeling he performs this ritual more for me than for himself. But he still seems to enjoy it enough, and we've got thirty minutes to kill. The mindless card flipping makes for good conversation time.

"So," I say, flipping a card, "nice e-commerce site you've set up."

"Arbok," Sam says, naming the Pokémon. "I know, right?" "Appleboy connected me to some Magento people who follow Daisy's site, and they totally hooked us up. It's the freeware version, but it has everything you need to sell product."

"Where are you guys at?" I ask, flip.

"Ninetails. What do you mean?"

Sam puts the card into the appropriate pile, a duplicate.

"I mean, how many doghouses have you sold? How much money have you brought in?" I ask, flip.

"Sandslash... I don't know. Here, can I use your phone?" Sam asks, takes my phone and hacks at the screen. A moment later he says, "We're at three-hundred, seventy-four thousand dollars in sales so far. But the store's only been up for three days."

"You got that from my phone, real time?"

"Butterfree... We're hooked up to Google Analytics. It's also freeware. We're on the wi-fi here, so I just downloaded the app."

"You're only selling one product. And you're telling me that the site has made three-hundred, seventy-four thousand dollars in three days?"

"Poliwrath... Yeah, two-and-a-half days, actually," Sam says. "And we're not doing any search engine optimization or e-mail marketing, either. It's all organic. Crazy, right? And we haven't 'made' three-hundred, seventy-four thousand dollars. All-in we net about fifty percent after costs, so we've only made like one-hundred, eighty-seven thousand dollars."

"In two days?"

"Yeah," Sam says, and suddenly he doesn't appear to know if I think this is good or bad. "But all of the events are coming up tomorrow, so I think we'll do a lot better over the weekend."

"All of the events?" I say.

"Venonat... Yeah."

"About how many events would that be?"

"Arcanine… I think it's about four-hundred, twenty-three in total. In the United States."

"About four-hundred, twenty-three?" I stop flipping cards.

"As of this morning. Here, let me check," he says and hacks at my screenpad again. "It's up to four-hundred-fifty. But I don't know if the last twenty-seven will be able to pull it off. I mean, they only have twenty-four hours."

He rolls his eyes.

"You said in the United States. Are there events going on in other countries as well?" I ask, flip.

"Not that I know of."

"So why mention it?"

"Why not?" Sam asks.

I drop it, move back to our prior discussion and flip another card.

"Event Planning International, Nancy's company, isn't handling the organization of all these events, is it?" I ask.

"God, no!" he replies. "Every moderator is coordinating their own event with an independent event organizer in their area. Oh, that last one was Golbat, by the way."

"I asked Daisy how many moderators there were. She said dozens?"

"Yeah, about thirty-eight dozen," Sam says.

"Sam," I say, "you know how Event Planning International tried to rip you guys off?"

"Yeah," he says. "That was my bad."

"You're ten. It wasn't your bad," I say, flip. "But how are you making sure that the other moderators aren't going to get ripped off in the same way?"

"Onix… I explained the terms we used with Ms. Birmingham-Henley on Monday and posted all of the moderators the same contract. It's all good," he says.

I feel a twinge of discomfort.

"Do they all have their own nonprofit tax ID numbers?" I ask and flip another Pokémon card. Sam pumps his fist. The card is an EX that he doesn't have. I don't know what exactly EX means in the Pokéverse, but the graphic on the card is super impressive.

"This one's a Mewtwo. It's really rare," Sam says, settling down.

"Anyway, no. We're all using the Stuff That's Wrong with the World, Inc. tax ID that you set up."

"Same for web site sales, I gather? The doghouses?"

"Yeah. Are we done already?" Sam asks, referring to the packs of Pokémon cards.

"No, we've got one more pack left," I tell him.

I think about it. Twenty percent of fifteen thousand dollars, average for each event, multiplied by four-hundred-fifty events. That's over a million dollars. Not counting web sales. I've never run a nonprofit business before. I was not expecting to manage a million dollars in nonprofit revenue over the next two days. We don't even have a bank account.

"Sam, I don't want to bog you down in a lot of administrative details, but how are the vendors getting paid? I mean, the suppliers that sold you guys the doghouses in the first place?"

"Oh, we set it up through Amazon. They handle everything on the back end and take a percentage."

"Didn't you have to give them a deposit? I'm sure they didn't front you the money for your first order of doghouses from whatever vendor you're using." I flip a card.

"Gyarados… You don't get it, Dad," Sam says. "Amazon is the vendor. After everything is said and done, they just cut us a check for about fifty percent of sales. We set everything up through our existing Amazon account."

Uh, my Amazon account. Where my credit card is on file. No harm, I suppose, since sales seem to be going through the roof.

"And where do you put the check when Amazon sends it to you?" I ask.

"Snorlax… We haven't gotten one yet," Sam replies. "I guess I'd put it in my room."

We pick up Daisy and then go to the local branch of TD Bank and set up a business account for Stuff That's Wrong with the World, Inc.

When we get home, Sam posts the account details to all of the moderators with an ask that these details be forwarded to all of the event organization companies, who can set up wire transfers for the event proceeds. This way we can avoid receiving, like, four-hundred-fifty checks at our home address.

I give my tax lawyer a call to talk through any loose ends. He doesn't seem very happy to speak to me, and I remember he has two teenage sons who likely follow Daisy's blog. But he takes our information, gives me the advice I need, agrees to file a few more forms with the tax offices and says that he'll send me a bill. He sighs when I tell him to address the invoice to Stuff That's Wrong with the World, Inc.

***

Catelyn gets home at five-thirty. We decide to take the kids out to a brick-oven pizza place nearby rather than make them dinner at home. We wait for Daisy to finish her post, for Sam to finish whatever he's got going on with the online hacker community, and then pile them into the car.

"So, are you guys nervous about the meet tomorrow?" Catelyn asks from the front passenger seat.

"Why would we be nervous?" Daisy responds. "You're still letting us go, right?"

"We're all going," I say and watch in the rearview as Daisy gives Sam a look, as if this weren't a part of their plan. "Of course, we're all going. What did you guys think, that mom and I were just going to drop you off?"

"That's not an option?" Sam asks.

"No," Catelyn responds, "not an option. So, what's going to happen tomorrow?"

"I don't know," Daisy says. "There are going to be food trucks."

"You don't have any idea what's going to go on at the meet?" I ask. "Isn't it your meet?"

"A lot of people who follow the site wanted to get together in person. So I said, okay, let's get together in person. Maybe the organizer has some stuff planned."

"Are you going to say anything?" I ask.

"I'll probably say a lot of stuff," Daisy answers.

We arrive at the restaurant, and everyone gets out of the car, silently.

"I don't mean to harp on this," I finally say, after we've been seated and ordered drinks, "but there's absolutely no agenda for tomorrow? There might be more than a hundred people there. Aren't you going to have any speeches or anything?"

"We're just going to hang out. Geeze, Dad," Daisy says. "Think of it like a big play date at the park. We'll figure it out when we get there. Can I get a side of meatballs?"

"Sure. You want it on the side of what?" Catelyn asks.

"Can I get a side of sausage with meatballs on the side?"

Always the carnivore. Sam hasn't said anything since we sat down. We order and watch the games on TV until the food comes.

"Are your friends going to be there too, Sam?" Catelyn asks.

Between Sam's underground hacker friends and the myriad of Internet predators bound to attend, I'm thinking this event is probably on some kind of NSA watch list.

"Maybe," he says. "I don't really know where they live. I doubt anyone is going to fly in for it."

"And I know that hackers typically don't want to make that long walk up the basement stairs of their parent's house," I say. Sam rolls his eyes at me. "Anyway, I think you guys should put together some kind of rough agenda, at least."

"Look, it's just a bunch of people getting together. People who like our blog and believe in our message," Daisy says. "I don't know why you're making such a big deal about it."

She has vacuumed up three meatballs and one Italian sausage before Sam has finished his first slice of pizza.

"I'm done. Can we get the check?" she asks.

"The rest of us just started eating, you animal. Are you worried about any of this?" I ask, looking at Catelyn.

"She always eats fast. That's her thing," Catelyn responds, smiling, her mouth full of eggplant parm.

No one is taking me seriously.

*****

When we get home, Daisy goes into our room to watch television and hack on her iPhone. Sam goes to the computer in the den.

"Do you think we're being irresponsible parents with how much screen time we allow our kids?" I ask Catelyn. "I mean, Daisy's double-screening up in our bedroom."

"I think we might be irresponsible parents for a number of reasons beyond just screen time," Catelyn responds. She walks to the foot of the stairs and yells for Daisy to turn off the TV if she's going to be on her iPhone. Daisy shouts down okay, and we hear the television set click off.

"Really, Cat. Are you worried about tomorrow?"

"I'm worried about all of the stuff that's been happening for the past two weeks," she says. "But as long as we don't think it's dangerous, I'm okay letting it play out. Just like you asked me to. It's a little late to get cold feet, Jack."

Chapter Eighteen

There's a lot of open space in Northwest New Jersey, a lot of preserved farmlands and state parks. Randall's State Park sits at the edge of our town and abuts my kids' school. It's massive. Several thousand acres. Strumpner Field is the name given to a wide, flat span of ground which sits on the edge of the park in the valley between four surrounding hills.

There are baseball backstops in each corner of the valley, diamonds spreading towards the middle, outfields bordering six multipurpose playing fields. The fields are arranged two-long and three-deep at the bottom of what looks like a giant inverted dome. This is where our town has its fireworks show on the Fourth of July. Concerts and other events are also held at Strumpner Field.

But I have never seen anything even remotely like what I see at Strumpner Field on this Saturday morning.

Traffic is a mess all through the town, and I'm thinking, great, our meet just happens to be on the same day as some other major suburban event. We end up parking at my kids' school and walking about a quarter mile to Strumpner.

There must be a whole bunch of games today, maybe even some kind of state final, because there's a large, loose crowd walking in the same direction as we approach the park. I ignore the fact that more than a few people are wearing red doghouses affixed to their heads.

I'm honestly wondering what's going on, whether we'll even be able to have this meet. Despite the random doghouse wearers, there's only the slightest glimmer in my mind that these crowds could be in any way connected to us.

"Whoa!" says Sam, looking around at all the people. "Good turn-out."

"Don't be ridiculous, Sam," I say. "There's probably a big game."

"The organizer said that there weren't any games at Strumpner today," he says.

"Well, there must be something. Where is your meet supposed to happen?"

"The organizer just said Strumpner Field," he replies.

"What else could it be?" Daisy asks, hacking away at the screenpad on her iPhone. "Yeah, these are our people," she says, apparently informed by something on her phone. "Oh, can I get a Diet Coke?"

I hand two dollars to some kids sitting in front of a tub of ice and soda, then give Daisy the Diet Coke. There are news vans in the parking area at the top of the hill. I look at Catelyn, and she shrugs, but her eyes are wide.

***

"Can you open it?" Daisy asks, handing me back the ice-cold can. The tab is jammed tight against the wet metal. My fingernails have been bitten down to nearly nothing in nervous anticipation of, well... now.

Daisy and I continue to walk towards the news trucks. Catelyn has fallen back with Sam. She's giving him her phone so that we can keep in touch if he wanders off. I can't seem to budge the tab on Daisy's soda.

"Daddy, I'm really thirsty, and I need to go say hi to everyone," Daisy says.

In an act of nearly super-human stupidity, I bring the can to my face and try to wedge my lower teeth in between the tab and the metal top, just to get the tab started. As I'm doing this, I see the news people turn around and look at us, as if they've been informed by something on their phones. They start to jog our way. My bottom teeth are still trying to find some purchase between the tab and the metal as the news people get closer with their microphones and cameras.

At this absolutely perfect moment, my lower jaw cramps up. Very badly.

I don't know if jaw cramps are a common occurrence among other people, but for those unfamiliar with the phenomenon, it's when the muscle that lies between the throat and the tip of the chin wrenches itself into a vicious knot of unbearable pain. Typically, this happens when you try to do something stupid with your mouth, like use your bottom teeth as a can opener. It's happened to me under different scenarios as well, but only a few times, over the course of my life. Once it happened when I yawned too big. Anyway, it's gut-wrenchingly awful.

So I'm standing there, gripping the can of soda, my mouth wide open in what looks like a soundless howl, my head twisting side-to-side in an effort to release the cramp, my eyes clenched to slits. Picture a paraplegic adult having a stroke.

The news people step up to me and Daisy. It appears that all of the major news stations and affiliates are represented. Great, thinks a clear, comedic spot in my brain, a spot that has somehow separated itself from the god-awful pain that's contorting my face and body. It's nice that there's a part of me that can always find the humor in these situations.

"Daisy, is that you?! I'm Martha Chase, with CNN," a newswoman shouts and shoves a microphone towards Daisy's mouth.

"Hi, Martha! I'm Daisy!" Daisy shouts enthusiastically for the camera, not even a little bit nervous. She looks at me, beaming at my hideously contorted face. This jaw cramp isn't going anywhere fast.

"Is this your Dad?"

I can see through my squinted eyes that the news lady is focused exclusively on Daisy when she asks the question.

"Yeah, it is!" Daisy says.

The CNN lady looks at me for the first time. Her jovial face disappears, replaced by a look of shock and possibly disgust. My cramp is only getting worse.

"Hyawullluh," I groan from the back of my throat as she mindlessly raises the microphone towards my face. I sound like someone is torturing Chewbacca.

"Does... does he have special needs?" the visibly shaken reporter asks Daisy, quietly, but into the microphone.

"He sure does, Martha!" she replies brightly into the microphone, unaware, I think, of what the reporter was actually asking.

"Nuuhwal murh sjaw!" I say, trying to unclench my eyes and shrug off the cramp as if it's no big deal. I can tell by the look on the reporter's face that my attempt to smile only makes me look that much more grotesque. Her body does a quick, involuntary shake before she regains her composure and turns back to Daisy.

"Did you expect so many people to come to the... what are you calling this?" the reporter asks, smiling again for Camera One.

"We're just calling it a meetup! And I didn't know what to expect!" Daisy shouts. She thumbs something into her phone while still on the air.

My chin is jammed tightly against my chest, and I've closed my mouth into a deep frown, making me look more like a neckless simpleton than a bad impression of Stephen Hawking. Not that any impression of Stephen Hawking is good.

I see Daisy hit send on her phone. Despite the wrenching jaw cramp, I crane my neck to look beyond her, down into the valley that is Strumpner Field. Like a ripple, heads nod towards their phones in this sea of people. Then, like some variation on the stadium wave, they all turn and look at us on the hilltop.

It is really neat to watch.

"Hi, everybody!" Daisy shouts ecstatically, arms extended halfway above her head, corkscrewing the palms of both her hands at the crowd below. As if she were born for this moment. The crowd erupts into shouts and applause. I glance behind Daisy and see Catelyn, who seems to be in shock at the number of reporters surrounding us. She looks at me, and that's all it takes to break her trance.

"Jack! Stop making that face! You're ruining Daisy's moment!" she shouts.

As if I've contorted my face into something that would freak out Lon Chaney, Jr. as some kind of prank on my daughter's spotlight moment. As I point at my jaw, trying to inform Catelyn of my temporary disability, I feel the cramp finally starting to let go. I have a feeling that my brief scene with the CNN reporter is going to go viral, if it hasn't already.

"My jaw cramped up. Real bad," I say to Catelyn, who's looking at me as if I'd just punched a baby in the face.

"Pull yourself together, Jack," she says through a tight-toothed smile. "We're on TV."

***

The reporters follow Daisy down the hill. Daisy's head is continually bobbing down to look at her iPhone and up to scan the crowd. Catelyn shouts her name over the crowd.

"What, Mom?" she asks, a third of the way down the hill.

"Keep your phone on, so we can reach you!"

Daisy looks at her phone and then back at Catelyn as if her mother is insane. As if Daisy's going to turn off her phone at any time during this event. She turns her palm up and gestures towards the entire crowd, everyone jogging between the physical world around them and the digital world of their smartphones. She waves and continues to walk down the hill.

"Where's Sam?" I ask Catelyn.

"He got on my phone and found some of his friends. We can call him if we need him."

We look at the scene on the field below. The food trucks along the edge of the valley have people lined up at least fifty-deep. Followers of Daisy's site have put together make-shift booths and banners: The Police Benevolent Association, The New Jersey State Firefighters Association, The New Jersey Teachers Pension Association, and a bunch of other different schools and community organizations. Everyone in the crowd is looking at their phones and then scuttling among different ad-hoc assemblies of people.

"Hey," I say to a teenager as he walks by. He looks up from his phone and then there's a hint of recognition.

"No way! Stroke, dude!" he shouts. "Right on!"

It's been like a minute, and he's already seen a stream of me with the reporter.

"Hey, come here for a second, would you?"

"Me?" he asks.

Yes, you kid. I nod my head and make a come-here motion with my cupped palm. The kid checks his phone, as if for guidance, then ambles over.

"I'm really glad you're OK, man," he says. "That looked like a super bad seizure you were having. That's what it was, right? I mean, you're not retarded like everyone first thought?"

To be a teenager again. No filter.

"No, I'm not retarded, and that's not the politically correct term."

"Oh. Sorry, man. You have special needs."

"I don't have special needs."

"Your daughter said you have special needs. Anyway, it's an honor to meet you, sir," he says with random formality.

"Great, thanks. You, too. So, tell me, why is everyone looking at their phones?"

"What do you mean?" he asks.

I struggle to come up with a more literal way to say what I just said. Maybe if I say it slower.

"Is there something about this event on your phone?" I ask.

"Oh, yeah, of course," he replies. "There are like fifty Twitter feeds going. Different groups are talking about different stuff, you know what I mean?" I give him a funny look. "Well, if you want to join the conversation, you go to, like, hashtag North backstop to see what they're talking about, and then you head over."

I go to Twitter on my phone and spend less than a second trying to figure it out, decide instead to hand my phone to the kid and ask that he get me where I need to be.

"What's your user name?" he asks. I look at him blankly. "Your Twitter handle? You know, your user name?"

I don't have a Twitter account.

"Use mine," Catelyn says and gives her user name to the kid.

"You have a Twitter account?" I ask.

"Everyone has a Twitter account," she says.

The kid hands Catelyn back her phone and gives us a look that asks if there's anything else we need.

"You can go now," I say. "Thanks."

"Selfie?" He steps behind me and lifts his phone in the air. "Can you make the stroke face?"

"No, I can't."

"That's all right," he says with compassion, lifts two fingers in a sign of peace, captures the selfie and walks down the hill.

"Don't eat the brown acid," Catelyn says, finally warming up to me. I can tell she still holds some residual anger about how, on TV, I made it look like she married one of Jerry's Kids.

We look at my phone. Daisy has her own Twitter feed so we can follow her movement throughout the crowds and discussions. Hashtag Daisy hashtag Northwest sideline. Hashtag Daisy hashtag Korean barbeque. It looks like it's other people hashtagging Daisy at the different assemblages because when Daisy actually tweets something herself, it comes from @daisydoghouse. I really don't get Twitter. The comments move at a fast pace. There are a lot of people with hashtags, like Daisy, who get combined with location hashtags to let others know where they're at. I think.

I look at the hillsides below where Catelyn and I are standing. Around the sides of the inverted dome, not actually in the valley, there are small groups of what look like parents, standing in twos and threes, a dozen here and there. And on the far hill, there's a larger group of parents, maybe a couple hundred or so, standing together. What looks like a lot of intense conversations going on.

It hits me that this larger hillside group is the country club crowd. The dispossessed wealthy, the people that this whole movement is calling out. Wow, I think, how much must it suck to have your kids turn against you and then you have to stand around all day at a public event while they talk about what selfish people you are?

Catelyn and I walk down the hill and into the flat valley, striding through the bustling playing fields. A few people recognize me, make the stroke victim face in a friendly way, give me a thumbs-up or peace sign. We try to follow the Twitter feeds to put ourselves in the vicinity of Daisy.

I call Catelyn's phone to find Sam.

"Hello?" he answers.

"Hey, Sam."

"Hey, Dad."

"Where are you?"

"I'm in the back of a van," he says.

"You're what?!"

"Just kidding, do you really think I'd get in a van with someone? There must be a thousand Internet predators out here today," he says.

"Don't do that. This is an intense situation," I say, but I'm glad he's on his toes.

"Don't have a stroke or anything," he replies, laughing.

"Whatever. Where are you? What hashtags should I follow to know where you are?"

"I'll be around hashtag geek, hashtag nerd, hashtag hackernerd – all the cool kids. I'm meeting a lot of people from Scatch. It's amazing."

Ahead of me, I see a familiar face looking at a smartphone.

"Okay, cool. Have fun, Sam. Call every thirty minutes or so to let us know you're alive."

I walk forward and approach the man I recognized. He's weather-worn with a scraggly beard, the professor who sent Daisy her economic data. Catelyn follows.

"Dr. Greenburg?"

"Mr. Sullivan," he recognizes me as well. The image of him that I found on Google didn't capture the amount of personality in his face. He looks like a little kid in a bearded old man's body. "Unfortunate about that stroke thing when you were talking to the reporters. Good to see you still up and about," he says, shaking my hand, smiling.

"This is my wife, Catelyn." They exchange greetings, shake hands.

"We're fans of your work," Catelyn says.

"Right back at you," he says with a slight wink.

"Are you following this whole Twitter organizational scheme so easily adopted by the younger generations in play here?" I ask.

"I'd say I'm about thirty-percent up to speed. It's amazing, really. Coordinating the discussions through geocentric Twitter feeds. I can't imagine the amount of planning that went into this setup..."

"None, to my knowledge," I say, and he raises his eyebrows. "Yeah, they pretty much just fell into it when they got here, I think. I guess we old people put a little too much weight on the whole planning thing. Sometimes I guess it's better to just let things evolve as they evolve."

"Remarkable," Greenburg answers. "You know, when I wrote my papers, I feel like this is what I was trying to achieve. Not this exactly, but something like this. I thought that, if the winners and losers were clearly spelled out, people couldn't ignore what happened to them in the 2008 financial crisis. Like I was untangling the whole bureaucracy and putting it into a format that would make sense on a neighborhood level. I felt like I was a primary or secondary charge that would jump-start a social revolution, or at least an extreme period of discontent at the way society had been treated. I didn't know what shape that discontent would take. I just believed it would happen. And then I published the papers, and nothing happened. It was just one of a million academic papers complaining about the rich getting richer and the poor getting poorer." He looks sad.

"Yeah, you were trying to spell things out for grownups. It seems like you should have been talking to the kids."

"Clearly," he says, looking around at the crowd. "So, what happens now, do you think?"

"I was actually hoping you'd have some idea," I say.

"Well," he begins to pontificate a little, even a little more than me, "it looks like people have come to grips with some specific facts about what's wrong with the financial system. I mean, everyone knows there's something wrong with the financial system, but it looks like Daisy's blog has taken it to a personal level. Something that isn't way out there on the news channels, but right here in the neighborhood. And we've identified the good guys and the bad guys. The bad guys being anyone who contributes to and benefits from the unfair financial system, the good guys being anyone who has been hurt by the same system. And the kids are what connects these two camps. Kids, who in their new awareness, now have a conscience about these things. And now, with Daisy's sites, they also have both a voice and a platform for organization. I was only hoping to accomplish half this much with my papers. Whatever happens next, I guess we better let it evolve as it evolves."

Now he smiles the smile of someone who feels like he has finally made a difference, even if it is only in the background.

"It was nice meeting you, Doctor," Catelyn says and shakes his hand again. "I hope we see more of you."

"Very nice meeting the both of you as well. Oh, and I liked the whole Gandhi thing," he says as he walks towards the food trucks. "We don't want things to take a violent turn. Best to stay ahead of it."

We watch him walk away. Catelyn smiles at me like maybe we should invite Dr. Greenburg over for dinner sometime.

I notice a kind of humming noise coming from the direction of the East backstop. I look at Catelyn. She hears it too. Weird. Now it's like it's coming from all of the backstops, superseding the buzz of conversation all over the field. It sounds like...

"Is that...?" Catelyn asks, tilting her head as if to improve her hearing. But it's become very clear by this point.

"Blur, blur, blur... We're not gonna take it, anymore..." the crowd seems to murmur as one.

"Look at your phone," Catelyn says. I do, holding it at an angle so that she can see the screen as well. All of the Twitter feeds are showing the lyrics to "We're Not Gonna Take It" by the 1984 transgender-progressive hair-metal superband, Twisted Sister. Seriously?

The tweet feeds are just repeating the lyrics to the chorus, priming the pump as the crowd gets into it. But it's not the hard-metal version of the song. It's a beat or two slower, more of a hymn like it's being sung on a Coca Cola holiday commercial. Within seconds the whole crowd is singing – kids, police, firefighters, teachers – everyone on the field. It looks like the only ones not singing are me, Catelyn and the dispossessed parents on the far hill. No, wait, now Catelyn is singing, too. She's taken my phone so, not having the lyrics in front of me, I just hum along and look at the crowd.

> Oh, we're not gonna take it
> No, we ain't gonna take it
> Oh we're not gonna take it anymore
>
> We've got the right to choose it
> There ain't no way we'll lose it
> This is our life, this is our song
>
> We'll fight the powers that be just
> Don't pick our destiny 'cause
> You don't know us, you don't belong
>
> Oh, we're not gonna take it
> No, we ain't gonna take it
> Oh we're not gonna take it anymore

At this point in the song, without breaking the slow melody, everyone singing lifts an arm and turns to point. Most people, including the adult service workers, point at the largest crowd of dispossessed parents on the far hill. Some kids are pointing at the smaller groups of parents on the surrounding hills.

Wow. Powerful. Kind of mean, but still. Wow.

> Oh, we're not gonna take it

No, we ain't gonna take it
Oh we're not gonna take it anymore

Oh, you're so condescending
Your gall is never ending
We don't want nothin', not a thing from you

Your life is trite and jaded
Boring and confiscated
If that's your best, your best won't do

Oh, Oh,
We're right – yeah!
We're free – yeah!
We'll fight – yeah!
You'll see – yeah!
Oh, we're not gonna take it
No, we ain't gonna take it
Oh we're not gonna take it anymore

I'm amazed at how appropriate the lyrics are and wonder if they've been adapted for this meet by the kids. Probably not, as that would take too much advance planning. Once the song's over, the Twitter feeds reappear, and the crowd picks up its prior buzz of discussion, like it never even happened.

My generation would have been hooting and cheering to congratulate itself after that kind of a display. Catelyn is shaking her head. She takes my hand, and we walk towards the food trucks. The rest of the afternoon is just people using the Twitter feeds to bounce around discussions, no more songs or other displays of solidarity.

Chapter Nineteen

"So, what did you think?" I ask after we've all gotten into the car, winded from the walk. "How did it go?"

"Good," says Daisy, hacking at the screenpad of her iPhone.

"It was awesome," Sam says. "I met like thirty kids from Scatch. A few of them were the ones that stitched together some components of Stu-widdu site. Can I have a playdate with Sneakypete?"

"What's Stu-widdu?" I ask.

"Stuff That's Wrong with the World," Sam replies. "It's an acronym, like SCUBA, so you say it like a word. Can Sneakypete come over this week?"

"We know what an acronym is," Catelyn says. "Who's this Sneakypete?"

"Wouldn't the acronym for Stuff That's Wrong with the World sound out more like 'Stu-Wittuw' or something?" I ask.

"Yeah, but Stu-widdu sounds better," Sam replies.

He's right. It's like a character from Star Wars. No, Stu-widdu... I AM your father.

"Who's this Sneakypete?" Catelyn asks again.

"He's a moderator from Scatch, super cool. He said he can get me the Pokémon mods for Minecraft. The new ones."

"How old is Sneakypete?" Catelyn asks.

"I don't know. Like nineteen or twenty, probably?"

"You're ten, and you want to have a playdate with a twenty-year-old? That doesn't seem odd to you?" Catelyn asks.

"I don't think he'd call it a playdate. He just said he'd come over and help get the mods for me. He has his own car, so you don't have to pick him up or anything."

"Let's talk about it," I say, not wanting to rain on his parade at the current moment.

"Daisy, who came up with the whole Twisted Sister thing?" Catelyn asks.

"What's Twisted Sister?" Daisy asks.

"The song everyone sang? We're Not Gonna Take It? You remember that, right?"

"Oh, that. I don't know," she says. "Someone at one of the other events."

I wonder how many people in total sang "We're Not Gonna Take It" earlier this afternoon. It had to represent some kind of bizzaro world record for hairband singalongs.

"Daisy, can you put the phone down for a minute? We want to talk to you."

"One sec," she says.

Catelyn glares at her, ignored, and then punches me in the ribs.

"Hey…" I say to Catelyn. I look in the rearview.

"Daisy, now."

"Fine," Daisy replies. "There's just a lot going on right now."

"What's going on," Catelyn asks.

"Nothing, really. Dad, our CNN interview has like four million views on YouTube!"

"Awesome," I say.

"Daisy, if your father and I are going to continue to support this whole… movement, we're going to have to talk about it. All of it."

"Fine," Daisy says, reluctantly handing Catelyn her iPhone. "What do you guys want to talk about?"

"Oh, I don't know," I say. "Let me see… how's the school play coming along?"

"They gave all the good parts to the eighth graders. Again."

"Even with your celebrity?" I ask, digressing into my own sarcastic topic.

"Yeah, the school is trying to keep the whole celebrity thing separate from day-to-day activities. They talked about it in our morning convocation a week ago."

Smart, I think. Then I get back on topic.

"Daisy we don't want to talk about the school play, we want to talk about the giant event we just left where everyone treated you like Miley Cyrus or something!" I yell.

"Miley Cyrus?"

Daisy, Sam, and Catelyn ask, somewhat in unison.

"Hannah Montana. What?"

"I don't think anyone was treating me like I'm Miley Cyrus, Dad," Daisy says between fits of hysterical laughter with Sam in the back seat.

"Miley Cyrus kind of went off the deep end about four years ago, honey. She's in her twenties now," Catelyn says and gives me a sad dog, poor-daddy look. "And she's become very provocative if you know what I mean."

Weird, I think.

"Whatever, Daisy, you know what I mean. They were treating you like you were a huge Disney celebrity. Just tell us what went on when you were mixing with the crowds for, like, three hours?"

"It was really good. I mean, I didn't really say anything different than what I say in my blog posts, but it was nice to meet everyone and see how excited they are about what we're doing."

"And what is it you think we're doing?" I ask pointedly with a tone that makes me sound like a dissenter.

"We're shining a spotlight on the people who contribute to a corrupt financial system for their own gain. We're exposing the parasites who hurt other people. We're recognizing who gets hurt by the system and we're pointing a finger at the ones who benefited from that hurt and shouting 'bad!' at them. God, Dad, I mean, you came up with this whole format anyway. Before you got involved, I was just messing with you and mom, then writing about it. Why are you guys talking to me like I did something wrong?"

She's got a point. I'm all worked up. That was actually a very good summary. Daisy has a naturally eloquent way of putting things.

"Daisy, we're not trying to make you feel bad," I say. "I think you guys were great today. We're very proud of you. All of this is just… getting away from me a little bit. We'll figure it out. I'm sorry I got upset."

"It's okay," she replies. "I probably wouldn't be getting this much attention if I were just writing about you and mom, anyway."

"Dad, what's a communist?" Sam asks.

I knew it. This is what I was afraid would happen at the event. Put a bunch of discontents together, and they're going to start talking about communism and socialism. That's the trouble with mobs.

"Why do you want to know what a communist is, Sam?" I sigh.

"Because someone spray painted it on our house," Sam replies.

Catelyn gasps.

"Wow," I say, looking at the house.

Right there, beneath our bay windows, about a foot off the ground, is the word "COMUNIST" spray-painted in sloppy red letters across the white paneling. I'm assuming it was a banker since it's spelled wrong. And right in the middle of a Saturday afternoon. Go figure.

"Would you look at that," I say.

"You're taking this pretty well," Catelyn says as I pull into the circular driveway.

"It's just kind of funny, is all. I mean there's nothing communist about Daisy's doghouse or Stu-widdu," I reply, trying to pronounce the acronym correctly. "It would have been a lot more accurate to tag the house with something like COMPLAINERS. I mean, as far as I know, we haven't introduced any kind of alternative to the lopsided financial system. We're just talking about how wrong it is."

"I think maybe we should be more worried about the fact that someone defaced our house, no?"

"A little white paint and it will be fine," I say.

"So, what's a communist?" Sam asks again, as we get out of the car.

"It's a non-sequitur," I say.

"What's a non seq... What's that?"

"A non-sequitur is when someone says something that doesn't track with the sequence of a sentence or thought, usually the sign of someone missing the point or being out of context. And calling us communists is a non-sequitur."

"So why would someone spray paint it on our house?"

"Because they're confused. Or just stupid."

We walk into the house. Catelyn goes directly to the dining room and grabs a bottle of wine.

"Really, Dad," Sam says. You'd think he'd want to take a break from my rants.

Daisy's standing beside him, obviously also wanting to know why someone would call us communist. But she seems to be okay letting Sam take the lead on this one.

"Okay, sit," I say and take my own seat at the kitchen table. Catelyn brings me a glass of wine, and I thank her.

"I think you're going to need it," Catelyn says, knowing that I have enough opinions about communism to talk for hours. Not that anyone would ever want to listen to it but, I mean, they *are* asking...

"So... communism is a school of thought based on an idea that no one should own anything in society – that everything should belong to everyone. Actually, it's like the people own the state, and everything belongs to the state. So, nothing belongs to the individual." The kids nod uncertainly, and I continue. "Communism was a movement in the early Twentieth Century in response to some of the bad things that came out of capitalism."

"So, what does that have to do with us?" Sam asks.

"Nothing, in fact. But communism developed because people didn't like the fact that in a capitalist system, the rich get richer and the poor get poorer. So, communists tried to set up a government where this couldn't happen."

"That actually sounds like a good idea," Daisy says.

"Yeah, the idea is good, but the execution is impossible," I say, not at all wanting Daisy to start kicking the tires of communist philosophy on her blog. I wonder what Karl Marx was like as a twelve-year-old? I've got to shut that door, hard.

So, I go on to explain how any time people build a system, especially a governing bureaucracy that has the right to take from some and give to others, it's inevitably going to become overcomplicated and corrupt. How capitalism, with all of its flaws, is still much more in line with the Darwinist elements of human nature than some man-made governing system. It helps that both kids have learned about Charles Darwin in school.

"But there's got to be a better way than just survival of the fittest," Daisy says.

"Survival of the fittest always has to be a part of it," I respond. "That's how we're wired as human beings. But how the fittest live once they survive, that's what we need to work on. But you can't use rules to force people to be generous or to play fair – and that's where communism fails. People have to make the choice to be generous and play fair on their own."

"Makes sense," Sam says. Thankfully, Daisy appears to be on the same page as well. Which is a relief. Because if I'd handled that wrong, it could have jump-started another proletarian revolution within the blogging youth of America.

"Great, now Daisy, you can go write in your blog. And Sam, you can go play with your underground hacker friends."

They each give me a kiss as they leave the kitchen.

"Anarchy 101," Catelyn says and refills my wine glass. I put my forehead on the table, exhausted.

"It's their revolution. I just want to make sure they're grounded," I say. My lips are brushing the wooden table top. "What a day, huh?"

"Are you going to paint over that graffiti on the front of our house tonight?"

"Actually, I was thinking maybe we let it stay there for a while."

Chapter Twenty

On Sunday morning Daisy and I go out to breakfast while Catelyn sells cash cards for our kids' school after eleven o'clock mass. Catelyn didn't go to Catholic school when she was a kid. But I did, in the nineteen-seventies, and it was brutal. So, originally, I was not a big proponent of sending our kids to Catholic school.

But as a small child Daisy thrived on physical attention and, apparently, teachers aren't allowed to hug little students at the public schools these days. Combining that with the fact that it was 2009 and an indirect consequence of the prior year's financial crisis had been that the class sizes at the local public school had more than doubled, Catelyn and I had a reason to compromise. She agreed to let Daisy repeat kindergarten so that she was the oldest in her class, as opposed to the youngest, and I agreed to the small class size and a teachers' flexibility for physical affection at the local Catholic school.

So now, a couple times each month after Sunday mass, Catelyn helps supplement the school's modest tuition by selling cash cards for purchases at local businesses while I take one or both of the kids to breakfast at a diner by our house. Sam has opted out of both church and breakfast this morning, exhausted by yesterday's event, preferring to stay home alone and play Minecraft in his pajamas. Daisy and I make the short drive to the diner, and it looks like almost half the houses we pass are either toilet-papered or sporting a little red doghouse.

"Good post last night," I say after buttering and cutting Daisy's waffle, another tradition that will likely continue well into her twenties. Sam stopped letting me cut his food when he was four.

"Thanks," Daisy says. "Do you think I covered the communist thing okay?"

"Perfect," I answer. In addition to blogging about the fact that some toolbox had spray-painted our house, Daisy had brilliantly explained both the inapplicability of communism to our movement as well as the reasons that this type of ideological solution could never work in modern society. It made me proud to leave the graffiti on our house, a public testament to the stupidity of whoever perpetrated the vandalism. She also mentioned in her blog post that communist was spelled wrong, which must have made the perpetrator feel like a complete idiot.

"Daisy, honey, can we talk seriously about all of this for a minute?"

"All of what?"

The television mounted to the ceiling in the corner of the diner is playing highlights from yesterday's event, including my bad Stephen Hawkins impression at the first interview. I ask Daisy to stand up.

"Why?"

"Just stand up for a second."

Daisy stands up in the crowded diner. Eyeballs shift our way. There's a mumbling buzz. Then more than half the eaters begin to applaud. It's not like a rock concert roar, more like golf tournament applause, but it's heartfelt, and people are smiling broadly at my daughter. She puts on the same super-upbeat happy face she wore for the reporters, turns and waves to everyone for a few seconds, and then sits back down.

"All of that," I say.

"Oh, right," she says and stuffs a piece of waffle into her mouth.

"You're just handling all of this attention remarkably well."

"Thank you."

"But you've got to be feeling something about it. I mean, the reporters, being on TV, all of the crowds, all of the doghouses? That's a lot of celebrity in just two weeks. And I know you're a big girl, but you're only twelve. This amount of amped-up attention in such a short time would mess with Oprah Winfrey's head."

"It's not that big a deal," she says.

"Don't be ridiculous, Daisy. This is the literal definition of a big deal."

"I don't mean all this," she says, lifting her hand to the TV and the people eating breakfast. "The movement is a huge deal. I mean the celebrity part of it. It's just how I fit into the whole thing. I get that."

"How do you mean?" I ask.

"I mean, we're all doing our parts with this thing. You with the core message, Sam with technology, Mom helping to keep things in perspective, all of the moderators in the different regions... everyone has a part, and it's all important. I like to rant about things that I think are wrong with the world. I'm like you, except I'm good at being the center of attention."

"You always have been," I say. And it's true. Daisy was never one of those annoying kids that clamor for attention, but she's always had a natural confidence, as if she belongs exactly where she is at all times. Like the star of her own television show. I have no idea where she gets this.

Sam's childhood was a string of Daisy-inspired make-believe. *Cooking with Daisy* at the kitchen counter, *Body by Daisy* on the workout machines in the basement—which Catelyn purchased and used maybe once or twice—*Daisy's Super Dance Party* in the living room. I never really thought about the long-term damage this relationship might have done to Sam, living in Daisy's world as often as he was, but he seems confident enough so I don't stop to worry about it now.

"But this is different, honey."

"It's only different if I make it different," Daisy says. "This type of attention is useful when you want to change things. And don't get me wrong, I do like it. But don't worry, Dad. I've always known that I'm important. Nothing's going to change just because now other people think so, too."

At that moment a kid, maybe thirteen or fourteen, approaches the table and asks Daisy for her autograph.

"Sure," she says happily to the girl and then asks, "Can I have yours too?"

They exchange autographs on a couple of blank checks from the waitress, and I'm feeling pretty okay with how things are going.

After breakfast, and according to our normal routine, we go to Seven-Eleven for a cherry Slurpee and then Walgreens where we scout for the latest issues of whatever tween magazines are on the stand. Aside from a few random gawks and whispers from the Peanut Gallery, it's just a normal Sunday morning.

***

"We need a dog," Sam says when Daisy and I walk in the front door.

"We're not getting a dog," I respond. "I'm still ambivalent about having kids."

"Seriously, Dad. For protection, I mean. We need a dog."

"Why would we need a dog for protection in this neighborhood? We don't even lock our doors."

"We do when you leave Daisy and me home alone."

"And we will continue to do so," I say. "But why the sudden need for an animal to protect you?"

"Someone was out in the yard while you guys were at breakfast."

"Wait, really?" I ask Sam and feel a chill run down my spine. "At eleven o'clock on a Sunday morning? Someone was sneaking around our house?"

"Yeah," Sam replies.

"Did they try to come in the door?"

"No."

"Are you okay?"

"I'm fine."

"Do you have any idea who it was?"

"Yeah."

"You know who it was?"

"Yeah, I know who it was."

"Okay, then. Who was it?"

"It was Mr. Mahoney," Sam says dejectedly.

"Mr. Mahoney was sneaking around our house?"

"I guess he saw both cars were gone and thought no one was home. I know you guys say that we're not supposed to go outside when you leave us alone, but since it was just Mr. Mahoney, I thought it was okay to open the door."

"And?"

"And what?"

"And what happened when you opened the door?"

"I said 'Hi'."

"You said 'Hi'? Did he say 'Hi' back?"

"No."

"So, what did he do?"

"He ran away."

"He ran away?"

"Yes. Why do you keep repeating everything I say in the form of a question? Do you think I'm lying?" Sam asks.

"No, I don't think you're lying, I'm just trying to get my arms around what happened."

"I don't think Mr. Mahoney would be sneaking around our house if he knew we had a dog," Sam says.

"Let's shelve the dog conversation for a minute, okay?"

I step out the front door and look around our yard, not sure what I'm expecting to find. I walk to the end of our driveway and look at the Mahoney McMansion on the corner. Nothing. I'm eventually going to need to have a very awkward conversation with our neighbor.

Turning back to the house, I finally see Mahoney's work. He's added an undersized, slanted letter M to the word COMUNIST beneath our bay windows, correcting his original spelling mistake. I walk back into our house.

"Did anyone else see Mr. Mahoney writing on our house?" I ask Sam.

"I don't think so. We can check the video. Maybe see if any other neighbors were around."

"You have a video?"

"Yeah," Sam says. "I was playing Minecraft on the iPad when I heard something outside, so I turned on the camera. And then I saw that it was Mr. Mahoney. And, here, look…" Sam hands me the iPad, and I click play on a shaky video of his slippers casually shuffling to the front door, opening it, then panning to Mahoney in a full Adidas sweatsuit, crouched below our windows holding a red Sharpie with a hand-in-the-cookie-jar expression on his face. I hear a muffled 'hi' from Sam. Then I then watch Mahoney scramble to his feet in panic, dart from beneath our windows, trip over our shrubbery and sprint up our driveway towards his house. What a tool this guy is. Sam wraps up the video with a pan to his own smiling face.

"Nice camera work," I say.

"Thanks. I was thinking of submitting it to one of those TV programs that show the funniest home videos," Sam says. "So can we get a dog?"

"Please…" Daisy whines, finally joining the conversation.

"What, you're telling me that this situation would have been better served if you were able to sic a Rottweiler or pit bull on that moron?"

"I was thinking more like a smaller dog. Maybe a pug."

"You want a pug. For protection. Right. You should have just sprayed Mr. Mahoney with the hose."

"That would have been awesome, Sam," Daisy says enthusiastically. "You definitely would have gotten on TV if you'd sprayed Mr. Mahoney with the hose."

"Pugs were the imperial guard dogs in ancient China," Sam quotes Wikipedia, dejected at the idea that he could have improved the video by soaking Mahoney. "And anyway, a pug would just have to bark like crazy, and Mr. Mahoney would probably have run away."

"I'm not going to argue with you, since he obviously panicked at the sight of a ten-year-old boy," I say. "But none of this holds water as justification for why we need a dog. Especially a pug. Send me that video, will you?"

"Me, too," Daisy says to Sam.

"Why do you need the video, Daisy?" I ask.

"Because I'm going to *evizzerrate* Mr. Mahoney on my blog tonight, and I want to include the video. People like videos."

"All right, let's hold off on eviscerating Mr. Mahoney for now. Do you even know what eviscerate means?" I ask her.

"Not really, no. I just heard it somewhere."

"It means you want to scoop out his insides. That's a little harsh, don't you think?"

"He shouldn't be writing on our house," she replies. "Not to mention he's a corporate banker who lives in a McMansion, as if that's not reason enough to eviscerate him on my blog. Figuratively speaking."

Sam, Daisy and I once spent an entire ride to school in comic discussion about the meaning of literal and figurative. These kids are sponges.

"Yeah, but he's also our neighbor and has obviously gone off the deep end. I'd prefer this situation not escalate further until I've had a chance to speak with him. Okay?"

"Fine," Daisy answers, "but can you speak to him today? I want to know where we stand for tonight's post."

I'm so not looking forward to my pending conversation with Mahoney.

Catelyn comes home, and Sam enthusiastically reenacts the whole scene for her. She looks at me as if this were somehow my fault.

"We're not leaving them home alone anymore," Catelyn says to me once the kids have gone back to doing whatever it is they do.

"What? You're overreacting," I say. I want to protect our afternoon dates—a privilege allowed by the ability to now leave the kids at home alone—which we've enjoyed for less than a year. "Our kids are old enough to babysit other kids. Of course, we can still leave them home alone!"

"After what just happened?"

"What? Mahoney? He's harmless. A buffoon. Certainly not dangerous. Let's not lose perspective here."

"What if it were someone other than John Mahoney? What if it were someone dangerous? There are a lot of people who are not happy about this whole… movement thing we've got going on here. We should call the police," Catelyn says.

"We're not calling the police on our idiot neighbor."

"He graffitied our house. Twice."

"Yeah, but come on."

"Well, if we're not calling the police, then you've got to go over straighten this out."

"I will."

"When?"

"Later," I say.

"What are you waiting for?"

"Literally anything that might prevent me from having this ridiculously awkward encounter with our neighbor. Who we never liked in the first place, I might add."

"Fine. I appreciate your honesty," Catelyn says and opens the door for me. "Do you want me to come with you?"

"No. It's fine," I say.

I check my phone to make sure that Sam's video has downloaded. I walk out the door and down the driveway.

***

"Sullivan," Mahoney says, standing in his open doorway after answering the bell. John Mahoney is what you might call a fat-skinny person. He probably doesn't weigh more than one-hundred and fifty pounds, but he's got jowls and love handles and that kind of below-the-waistline belly that older women and flabby people sometimes get. I normally don't judge people by the way that they look, but his body type is a perfect match for both his personality and his profession as a corporate banker. There's a quiver in his voice, and I'm not sure if it comes from fear, anger, embarrassment or a combination of the three.

It's twelve-thirty, and I'm already exhausted on a Sunday.

"Mahoney," I answer, following the last name protocol that he's established.

"Is there something you want?" he asks in an even tone. I'm honestly impressed by his ability to stand here and look at me as if there's nothing going on between us. I'm tempted to ask for a cup of sugar or to borrow his lawnmower.

"I really don't have the energy for pretense right now, John," I say.

"I don't know what you're talking about," he replies.

"Dude, you misspelled 'communist' in red spray paint on the front of my house just yesterday. Then you came back this morning to correct the spelling, where you were happened upon by my son. He saw you. You were caught red-handed. So, let's talk about this, huh?"

"A lot of houses are being vandalized these days, Sullivan," he said and raised his palm to his trees, still draped with toilet paper. "Maybe you should look at your own family instead of trying to blame me."

"Seriously. This is how you want to play things? We both know it was your own kids who decorated your house."

"Vandalized," he says. "And I don't know what you mean. Why would my kids vandalize their own home? It was someone else in the neighborhood."

"Your son bragged about it to my daughter."

"I wouldn't put too much stock in what your daughter says. Or your son, for that matter."

"Jimmy bragged about it to my daughter, in writing, on her blog. Check it out for yourself. His user name is daisysneighborjimmymahony. Pretty specific."

"Anyone can create an online identity. You can't be sure it's him."

"Come on, man. He has a profile picture. And right now, we're talking about the illiterate graffiti on my house, not kid stuff like toilet paper and eggs on yours."

I hear giggling from inside the house.

"I don't know anything about that," he says, and now I'm starting to wonder if he isn't in a full-on state of denial. I don't think I've ever seen someone completely unravel before.

I pull out my iPhone, hit play on the video and hold it in front of his face. He obviously had no idea that Sam was recording their encounter on the iPad. He's still wearing the same navy-blue Adidas sweatsuit, Run DMC style, like a nineteen eighties misfit. He's lost so much color in his face that I'm afraid he's going to pass out.

The giggles from the stairs inside the house have erupted into howls of laughter. I look over his shoulder and catch the eyes of his ten-year-old daughter. Rather than ducking out of sight, she gives me a thumbs-up. This is getting too weird.

"Why are you doing this to me?" Mahoney whines.

He steps outside and closes the door on his kids. Did I just catch a glimpse of his wife on the stairs, too?

"What did I ever do to you?" he asks. "What, are you jealous because of my house? Because my kids go to good schools? Because I make a lot of money? Well, I hope you're happy now, because my kids are ashamed of me. My wife hates me. All because of your daughter's web site." I'm pretty sure his wife hated him before she started following Daisy's blog, but this isn't the time to mention it. "What did I ever do to you?" he whines again as if Daisy's blog and the entire country's reaction was somehow a focused attack on his own person. This type of narcissism just blows my mind.

"This might come as a huge shock, John. But aside from being a stereotypic example of the greedy, narcissistic parasite that is corporate banking, none of this has anything at all to do with you. You actually think this is an attack on you personally? Like you specifically are what's wrong with the world? As if you're relevant enough to warrant this type of nation-wide community reaction? Have you seen all the dog houses around the neighborhood? Have you watched the news? You're not the problem, you egomaniac. You're just a little speck of dust in a universe of filth. Other than a few dry heaves when I drive by your absurd McMansion, our family doesn't even know you exist. That's the problem with you money-people. There is a universe of distance between how important you think you are and how pathetically small you actually are to everyone else in the world. The only reason I'm even having a conversation with you right now is that you vandalized my house. Twice. So, here's what's going to happen. My daughter is going to crucify you on her blog tonight. And you're going to take it. You won't like it, but you'll just have to pretend you're a human being and suck it up. Because if there's any reaction at all, from anyone, regardless of whether you're involved, then I'm taking this video to the police. And if I do that, you're going to be brought up on vandalism charges like a freaking juvenile delinquent. How do you think that's going to play in the local papers? Or at the country club? You'll be more of a laughing stock than you already are. Because if there's one thing I know about social-climbing parasites, they never miss an opportunity to devour one of their own."

I stand there, looking into his eyes, waiting for some kind of reaction. But there's nothing left. He's climbed into some dark closet where he's watching all of this happen to someone else. Behind the closed front door, I hear cheers and the slap of high-fives from the eavesdropping kids.

I feel awful.

Daisy doesn't have to eviscerate Mahoney, I just did. In front of his family, no less.

***

"How did it go?" Catelyn asks as I walk in the front door.

"Not good."

"Not good how?"

"I went to a dark place."

"You didn't hit him, did you, Jack? I mean, he's built like an old lady. He's feeble. You couldn't have hit him?"

On a different day, I would let her run with this, the idea that I punched our chicken-boned neighbor to death and would be going to prison on second-degree murder charges. But I don't have the heart for comedic torture right now.

"No, I didn't hit him. I just went off on him, in front of his family."

"Oh..."

"I really lost it, Cat. He had this narcissistic idea that this whole movement was somehow about him. It's so typical of these people, that ridiculous self-importance. It makes me crazy. So, I kind of went black and really ripped into him. And like I said, his family was well within earshot."

"How did they react?"

"They cheered," I say glumly. "You know, I'd like to convince myself that he beats them. Or psychologically abuses them. Or maybe he's a serial pedophile or something. Like he deserves what just happened. But it felt like I was taking out all my hatred for the rigged-financial-system-people on him. I feel like I just used a fire hose to put out a match."

Daisy skips down the stairs.

"Dad?"

"Write about something else tonight, Daisy," I say.

"Aw, come on! Seriously? I don't have anything else to write about."

"Write about something else. It's only one o'clock. You can think of something. Mr. Mahoney's had enough for now."

"What'd you do to him?" she asks.

"More than he probably deserved."

"Give your father some space, huh, Daisy? He's having a rough time," Catelyn says.

Daisy says okay, walks back upstairs. She's clearly disturbed by the mood I've brought to the house.

I go sit down on the couch, and Catelyn sits down next to me.

"Don't beat yourself up, Jack. We're doing a good thing, here. Do you think all these people beat themselves up when they got their bonuses, or even when they kept getting paid after what the banks and money guys did to pension funds in 2008? Older people had to go back to work because their retirement money ultimately went to building McMansions and buying ultra-premium cars for people like John Mahoney. No matter how far they try to remove themselves from it, they're at fault. You don't get something for nothing in this world, Jack. And whatever happens, I'm sure these people are only getting what's coming to them. And that means they're going to get hurt. At least they will if anything is ever going to change. Just don't forget that you're one of the good guys."

She pats my leg, gets up and walks into the kitchen.

"I never realized how much I hate these people," I say, loud enough for her to hear. "It all just came out when I was talking to Mahoney."

"You don't hate the people, Jack," she calls from the other room. "You hate the system. The people are just collateral damage."

Chapter Twenty-one

Monday morning, I load the kids into the car for school and then brake immediately, fifteen yards from our house. I'm looking at the Mahoney McMansion. Beneath the second-story windows, in the same red spray paint that was used on our house, is scrawled MY FATHER BELONGS IN PRISON in a child's graffiti handwrite.

Beneath the chicken scratch are the names Jimmy and Annie, with an arrow pointing from each name to the windows of what I can only assume to be their respective rooms. Huh. I guess John Mahoney is going to have a hard time trying to pass this one off as neighborhood vandalism. At least all of the spelling is correct.

"Wow," Sam says, breaking my trance. Maybe stopping in front of the Mahoney house, with the kids in the car, wasn't the best idea.

"Daisy, did you know about this?" I ask.

"Jimmy was pretty upset that I didn't blast his dad on my blog yesterday, but I didn't know he was going to do this," she replies. She snaps a photo of the house with her iPhone.

"Stop that," I say and drive away from the corner. "This is serious. Mr. Mahoney was not in good shape when I left him yesterday afternoon."

"Dad, there are literally tens of thousands of kids doing this kind of thing to their money-people parents right now. Are you having trouble connecting to the Internet or something?" Daisy asks, sarcastically, but still kind of sweet.

I drive through neighborhoods of doghouses, toilet paper yards and several instances of suburban graffiti. My mind can't stop looking at John Mahoney's bloodless face in yesterday's doorway. How many other faces like that have we engineered?

I mindlessly pull up to the stop sign across the street from the kids' school and am startled when Sam leaps up from the backseat to give me a kiss. Daisy leans over and kisses me on the cheek before we start to move again. We exchange love you's and have a good day's when I drop them off.

Instead of turning towards home as I leave the school parking lot, I decide to drive through some different neighborhoods. It reminds me of Christmas or some other holiday, maybe Halloween. Maybe Mischief Night. Though it would be a Mischief Night from my childhood since things have toned down substantially over the last four decades. Until now, that is. It's mid-September, and nine-out-of-ten houses are decorated along common themes. A doghouse, or toilet paper and eggs, or spray paint.

I'm driving through an episode of *The Twilight Zone*.

When I get home, I turn on the TV. Catelyn watches television in the morning when she gets ready for work and has left it on a news channel. CNBC, I realize after a few seconds. The big story this morning is the decoration of America, a la Daisy.

Exterior Design with Daisy, I think.

News feeds from dozens of states, all of it the same scene I drove through after I dropped the kids off at school.

Anarchy with Daisy, I think.

There's a four-story building fire in the Bronx, and my heart drops, but that's just actual news from the local affiliate. Nothing to do with Daisy. At least as far as we know. The newscaster actually says this.

The doorbell rings. Every set change in this story makes my stomach drop.

"Uh, hi…" I say, after opening the door to a small blonde lady, mid-forties, as attractive as she can be, given what the doctors and salons had to start with.

"I'm Sandy Mahoney," she says.

Yes, Mrs. Mahoney. We've lived two houses down from you for the past ten years. I know who you are.

"Hi, I'm Jack Sullivan?" The question in my tone is less about who I am and more about why she's here, but I don't think it comes off that way.

"My husband's gone," she says flatly. "Have you seen him?"

"Have I seen him?"

"Yes. Has he been here?"

"Here?"

I sound like an idiot, but I'm bewildered by the fact that Sandy Mahoney thinks her missing husband might have come to my house. Two doors down from his own house. After I tore into him in front of his kids, and likely his wife, less than twenty-four hours ago. Like we'd be drinking beer together in my basement right now, playing foosball.

"I'm not sure I understand the question, Sandy. Did he run away? I mean, how long has he been gone?"

"He went outside with you yesterday, and he never came back inside," she says tonelessly. "Did he come here?"

"Sandy, I'm pretty sure your husband would have run off to Guantanamo Bay before coming to my house. Why do you ask? I mean, he's been gone less than twenty-four hours, right?" I ask, hashing some TV crime drama contextual reference point before I have a chance to think about what's coming out of my mouth.

"I don't know," she replies. "I just wanted to say…"

"Wait, Sandy. I can call you Sandy, right?"

"Sure."

"Great, you can call me Jack." This conversation is borderline ridiculous. "Okay, Sandy. I have something to say first. How I treated your husband yesterday—and I knew your kids were listening—how I acted was…"

"I just wanted to say thanks," she interrupts and looks at me like a principal would look at a nine-year-old troublemaker. Not exactly a traditional thank you look. I exhale, long and slow.

"I don't think we're having the same conversation, Sandy," I say.

"Do you know what I did before I married John?" she asks. Lady, you could have lived in a nuclear bomb shelter for the past ten years, all I know of you. "I got my Masters in social work. I went to Princeton. I was going to help people."

"They have a Masters in social work at Princeton?" I ask incredulously.

That just doesn't seem right. A lot of the parasitic banking community that I know comes out of Princeton. Maybe social work was a program for the betrothed wives and husbands of future robber barons? People killing some time before their better-half departs academia to destroy the world?

"Well, it was called Values and Public Life," Sandy says. "It was actually an undergraduate degree at Princeton. I got my Masters at Rutgers." Okay, that makes more sense. "The point is, I wanted to make the world a better place. And I met John at Princeton. And he's from a wealthy family. And I'm from a family that was up-and-coming – you know, trying to get into the wealthy set. And somehow it all just got away from me, you know? It's like Daisy says. Like I'm living my parents' dream. Following in their footsteps. Rich and empty. It's kind of funny because my parents hate John now."

I hesitate to tell this lady that she should not be taking life advice from a twelve-year-old girl before I recall that these are essentially my words typed from Daisy's fingers. And yet, I have no idea how to respond to her.

"So, John's missing, then?"

"Missing since he spoke to you yesterday. He just walked off, didn't even take his car."

John Mahoney drives a Hummer. He's such a tool. I have to keep bringing myself back to the conversation at hand.

"Well, he didn't come here. I'm sorry…"

"I was wondering if you could help me?"

"Help you find him?"

"Help me to make sure he doesn't come back."

"Are you asking me to kill him?" There's more than a hint of comedy in my voice, which is probably inappropriate. But I'm not sure, because I'm so not following this conversation.

"Oh, god, no!" she replies. "Why? Can you do that?"

"Uh… no. I was just kidding there," I say. "How would I be able to help you make sure he doesn't come back?"

"I just don't want to see him again. Like, ever," she says.

"Wow. Okay. Well, honestly, I can't say that I blame you, Sandy," I say in a back-peddling tone like I'm retreating from a crazy person. "But this whole Daisy thing is only a couple of weeks old, so, you know, we don't really have any kind of witness-protection service set up as yet."

I'm thinking about closing the door but haven't yet made any physical move.

"Oh, I don't want to go away," she says. "I want to stay in our house with the kids. I just don't want him to come home. Is there anything in your network that can help me with that?"

What does this lady think we're running here?

"You know, Sandy," I say, considering the scope of our network, "I'm sure there is. However, this network being only, what, sixteen days old, we haven't quite gotten around to organizing ourselves in terms of illegal activities. We're more like the Sinn Féin of this reformation movement. I'll give you a shout when our clandestine branches start to gain some traction, though…"

I now try to close the door, but she blocks it with her foot.

"I'm not asking you to do anything illegal," she says. "We have enough money for John to live on his own, get an apartment in the city. I just feel like you pushed him right to the edge yesterday. And with another little nudge, he would probably give me a divorce and stay away from us for good."

"Lady," I say, "he disappeared yesterday and hasn't been heard from since. You don't think he's already fallen off the edge?"

"Maybe," she says. "But the kids and I are behind what you guys are doing here. And we don't want him back. So anything you can do to help a fellow supporter would be much appreciated."

"Okay, Sandy. I'm going to be straight with you," I say. I seem to be getting exhausted by conversations with crazy people much quicker than I used to, back when I was running companies. "Throughout most of this conversation I've been talking to you much as I would an insane Mormon missionary who randomly knocked on my door. But let's level-set for a minute. Not only are you asking for our help keeping your husband out of your life for good, but you're also planning to keep the McMansion and probably half of his ill-begotten cash. Plus, I imagine some ridiculous amount of child support. Doesn't that seem a little, I don't know, unbalanced to you? I mean, considering what our cause it all about?"

"Didn't you just take money from these same people when you sold your company to private equity?"

Ouch. Knife to the heart. Touché, Sandy, very well played.

"Yeah," I say, defeated.

"Well, isn't that kind of the same thing?"

"Yeah," I sigh. "I guess it is."

"So, can you work with me here?"

"Yeah," I say. "What can I do for you? I mean, within the legal scope of things."

"I don't know. What are you going to do for yourself?"

"I'm doing what I'm going to do."

"So, help me, too. I mean, there's probably a lot of people like me who are sick and empty and disgusted with their lifestyles. You see what's happening around the country. Say we can separate from all the bankers and lawyers and other corporate sleazeballs? Say we can all figure out what we need to live a comfortable life and get our children started in a direction that will help make the world a better place? Say we take the money that's left over, our half in a normal divorce settlement, and we want to use it to help? To make the world a better place? What do you suggest we do if it comes to that?"

"Honestly, Sandy, I have no idea. I've never been in a position where I've had to help allocate a surplus of capital, from a do-gooder perspective."

"Well, you might want to start thinking about it," Sandy says, "because I don't think I'm the only one asking these types of questions right now."

She pulls her foot from the door.

"Wait, Sandy," I say and grab the door before it closes on her. "Wait a minute." What was it, thirty seconds ago, I was having a discussion with a crazy lady, and now I'm considering her advice? I settle down for a second, try to achieve a brief meditative state to clear my head. She's right, actually. Geeze, this whole thing is becoming such a hassle. "Okay, fine. You're right. It's your money, and you can do whatever you want with it. But if we're going to encourage people to use excess wealth to make the world a better place, I suppose we ought to at least provide them with some guidelines, optional though they may be. I hadn't thought about it. But we will. And I'll get back to you."

"I'm right up the street. Don't be a stranger."

She steps back and hands me a business card. The card has her name on it, embossed in gold, her phone, and address. I'm wondering who makes business cards to hand out when they don't have a business.

"And you're sure there's nothing you can do to keep John from coming back to the house?" she asks.

"I'll talk to Daisy and see if there's any way that we can tilt the pinball machine on that one, so at least your suggestion is clear to him. But generally speaking, no. You're going to have to take care of separating from your husband on your own."

She smiles and probably, for the first time since her Freshman year in college, looks like a person who will do something good in this world.

We wave goodbye, and she walks up the driveway towards her McMansion. I glance around our block, half expecting to see John Mahoney hiding in the trees, but it's just a beautiful autumn day outside. I sigh and enjoy the sun for a moment.

The discussion I just had comes back to me and disturbs my few seconds of peace. Guidelines for the voluntary distribution of wealth. What was I thinking? It's really not our job to tell people how to invest their money in order to make the world a better place, I tell myself.

But I feel a kind of pit growing in my stomach like I've opened a can of worms.

Chapter Twenty-two

"I have good news and bad news," Sam says and climbs into the back seat of the car. "Which do you want to hear first?"

Daisy gets into the front seat beside me. I ask her how was school, and she says fine.

"Good news or bad news, which first?" Sam repeats.

"Give me the bad stuff first," I say. "How was your day at school, bud?"

"Fine. Okay, the bad news first. Here it is. They hired a new music teacher."

"No!" I say in mock terror. My kids each have music once a week at their school. Oddly, they both hate music more than any other class. I guess a high percentage of music teachers are mean people, probably because they didn't make it as professional musicians and now have to teach throw-away classes to a bunch of kids that don't take them seriously.

The prior year's music teacher was a sadistic young woman who would torture parents by jamming up the entire car line while she made their disrespectful kids remain in class five or ten minutes after the dismissal bell. It's bad enough that the school forces parents to pick their kids up, instead of letting them walk or bike home like we used to back in the day. But to hold up the whole car line as well? By the end of the year, this practice of holding the kids after school stirred the parents up to the point that lynch mobs were beginning to form. So the principal fired the music teacher over the summer, and for the first month of school, the kids have been enjoying a substitute, which effectively meant an extra recess one day each week.

"Maybe she'll be good," I say. "Music is supposed to be enjoyable, you know."

"It's a he," Daisy says, "and he takes it too seriously. The principal introduced him today. You can tell by the way he talks about music that he's actually expecting us to learn something."

"God forbid," I reply. "Okay, Sam. What's the good news?"

"The good news is that we got the numbers from the events this weekend. We netted almost three million dollars, not including web sales, which are now at…" Sam checks his phone, "…oh, wow, about four-and-a-half million." My jaw actually drops. "And the hats and t-shirts aren't even on sale yet. Aw, man. We sold out of the small-sized doghouses. You'd think Amazon would be able to manage the stock better."

"Wait a minute. So, you're saying that over seven million dollars is going to be transferred into the bank account that we set up for Stu-widdu?" I'm getting better at pronouncing the acronym for Stuff That's Wrong with the World, Inc.

"Yeah," Sam says. "Wait, no. We only get half of the web sales after product costs and Amazon fees, so it's really just over five million dollars. I wonder if we get some kind of rebate since Amazon ran out of stock on the small doghouses?"

This is not a good thing, I think. Stu-widdu is a non-profit. It's actually just a hack-job of a company that we set up last week. I don't know anything about running a non-profit, aside from the fact that you're not supposed to make a profit. And we effectively have no costs. So, it's all profit. Which means we've got to figure out what to do with all this money.

***

"That's great, isn't it?" Catelyn asks and pours us each a Monday night glass of wine. The kids are upstairs double-screening TV and iDevices. I've spent the past four hours at the kitchen table on my laptop trying to get a handle on our situation.

"There are things that are great about it, sure, Cat," I say, my jaw resting on my palms as I stare at the screen in front of me. "I spoke to Bill Hartmann for over an hour this afternoon."

"Who's Bill Hartmann?"

"Our tax guy. He's an attorney, not an accountant."

"Oh," Catelyn says, not really caring to understand the difference.

"It means he understands the tax laws about non-profits."

"So, what did he say?"

"Technically, it's pretty simple. Anything we pay ourselves gets taxed as 1099 income, like a contractor, since the company doesn't have any full-time employees."

"You're not thinking of using any of that money to pay ourselves?" Catelyn asks. She's shocked at the thought.

"No, of course not. I'm just spelling out the rules. And any costs, like Bill's fees, can be paid using his tax ID, so that's another way that money can leave the account. But if we're going to donate money, it has to be to other non-profits that have registered as 501 (c) companies, which means they're recognized as non-profits by the IRS. Those are the only ways that the money can leave the bank account."

"So, what happens if the money leaves some other way?"

"Nothing, really. Whoever we give it to just has to pay tax on it, same as if we paid it out to ourselves."

"Okay, so we know the rules. What next?"

"So, here's what we've got." I pull up the Stu-widdu site, enter the administrator name and password that Sam reluctantly shared with me. "The good news is that everything is digital so it can all be tracked by region."

I pull up a list of the 453 local chapters of Stu-widdu which are spread across the country. The list has three header columns, MONEY IN, MONEY OUT and BALANCE. Each chapter has a total of the money earned from their event last Saturday in the MONEY IN field.

"This is where we track the money received by each chapter."

"Who built this?" Catelyn asks.

"Who do you think? Sam's clandestine hacker friends."

"But when?"

"Apparently today, after school."

"Wow."

"Yeah. So, tracking contributions by branch isn't a big deal. But the sponsorship money, just like the revenue from the web sales, comes in centrally instead of by region. It just comes directly to the Stu-widdu account. We track that here." I click on a link at the top of the page, and it shows a list of sponsors, with totals, as well as a total for the Amazon revenues. "You add up all the money coming in centrally, plus everything contributed by each region, and it should match what's in the bank account."

"Okay, so you can keep track of everything coming in. That's great. What next?"

"Well, I wrote up an explanation of the rules I just talked about with you, here," I click a link, "and I figure we let the moderators of each branch decide what to do with the money that their branches contribute. They can search for local 501 (c) registrations with this link," I say, pointing to the bottom of the page, "but we've got to figure out what to do with the money that comes in centrally, which is most of it. I didn't think we should just distribute it regionally, so we set up this page," I click another link, "where the moderators can vote on what to do with the larger sum donations. You just fill out this page," I click another link at the top, "to explain what you want to use the larger sums for, including the 501 (c) registration number and other information for the target non-profit, and the other users can check it out centrally."

"What if people want to use the money for things that aren't related to a non-profit, like with no 501 (c)?"

"We'd just have to add about thirty percent to the total donation and pay the taxes in advance of when the money is distributed. So anything that's not associated with a registered non-profit just increases the total—which should factor into the decision about whether to make the donation. And we can monitor exactly where all of the distributions go, here," I say, clicking another link that takes me to a blank page.

"And that's your problem," Catelyn says, pointing to the blank page. "What goes on that page, I mean. How to donate the money?"

Right when she says it, a line item appears on the distribution page. I look at Catelyn and raise my eyebrows, click on the line item. It's a donation to a Muslim organization with an address in our town. Four thousand dollars.

"Daisy! Sam! Come down here a minute!" I shout towards the stairs.

"One sec," Daisy shouts back. I look at Catelyn, roll my eyes.

"The small doghouses are back in stock," Sam says as he stumbles into the kitchen, eyes glued to the iPad in his hands. After two more shouts and "one sec" exchanges, Daisy finally graces us with her presence. She skootches me over, sits down next to me on my kitchen chair.

"What's up?" she asks innocently.

"What's this?" I ask and point at the pending distribution of four thousand dollars.

"It's a donation," she says. "See, they have a 501 (c) and everything, just like you said."

"I mean, what's it for? You didn't fill out the description."

"Oh, right. Sorry. I'll do it later."

"Daisy, you can't be making donations without talking to us first," Catelyn says.

"I talked about it with Dad and Sam when we got home from school."

"We talked about how we were going to set it up for people to make donations. We didn't say anything about making an actual donation," I say.

"I used the money we made from our own event on Saturday, like you said. I didn't touch the central money that you were talking about."

I click on the regional tally link, see four thousand dollars in the MONEY OUT column next to the Northwest New Jersey branch. The remaining balance for the branch is a little over two-hundred-dollars.

"But we need to talk before we start making donations," I say. "We don't even know what this Muslim organization is."

"It's a Muslim grade school," she says. "It's right down the street from our school."

"So why did you decide to give them four thousand dollars?" Catelyn asks.

"To rebuild their playground," Daisy replies. "I talked to them this afternoon, and that's what they think it will cost. They said they'd scan and input the receipts where they're supposed to on the site. And if there's money left over they'll give it back. They were really excited."

"But what made you want to rebuild their playground?" I ask. "I'm pretty sure you're aware that we're not Muslim."

"Dad, have you seen their playground? It's a death-trap. Probably a hundred years old, and little kids are playing on it. What does it matter if we're Muslim or not? This is something that will make the world a better place for the kids at that school. I thought that was the whole point, why we're doing this in the first place?"

She's right, of course.

"Honey, I think it's a great donation," I say. "And both mom and I would have supported it. But just talk to us before pulling the trigger, okay?"

She says fine, gives me a kiss on the cheek and walks around the table to hug Catelyn from behind. Sam's still fixated on the iPad. I reach over and tap him on the arm.

"What about you, bud? I'm surprised you're not arguing for a seat at the table when it comes to decisions like this."

"It was my idea," he says, his eyes still on the iPad.

I look at Daisy, and she nods.

"So why didn't you get involved in our conversation about it?" Catelyn asks him.

"I don't like drama," he says flatly. "That's Daisy's department."

My laptop beeps and I see three additional line items appear on the distribution tracking page. I click on each and browse the entries. Unlike Daisy, these moderators have done a good job filling out the information. Replacement computers for a Hebrew school in South Bend, Indiana. A new floor for the basketball court at a public school in Fargo, North Dakota. A stage curtain for the drama club at a Hindu community center in Camden, New Jersey.

I don't know why I was so frustrated trying to think of what to do with the money. These kids don't need a grand plan. They just see something that could make people happier, and they act on it. They live right now, not someplace wandering among future plans and priority lists.

I wonder why we feel the need to turn them into grownups.

Chapter Twenty-three

By Tuesday, late afternoon, all of the regional money in the Stu-widdu accounts has been distributed. Over two hundred individual donations, with several branches pooling their funds to work on common projects. Sam, Daisy and I set up a quick online meet with all of the regional branch moderators and vote to make half of the centralized funds available to support more local donations.

With the money that's continued to come in from web sales over the past twenty-four hours, it leaves us with a little over two million dollars in the central fund account. There have been some suggestions posted to the central fund distribution board, but nothing that's generated enough interest to necessitate a vote. It's generally been bigger picture stuff, like contributing to the cure of specific diseases or clean water projects or the Red Cross disaster relief fund – all very important causes—but we've buzzed with the moderators, and we all agree that we want to keep our movement operating on a grass-roots, community level. Keep it about right here and right now for everyone involved. Making the world a better place in ways that we can see, practically, in our everyday lives.

***

"What do you want, Dad?" Sam is lying on top of me on the couch.

"What d'ya mean, bud?"

"I mean, we're doing a lot of good stuff, right? But you haven't suggested any donations yourself."

"I'm old, Sam."

"What does that mean? I mean, I know you're old. But why does that have anything to do with it?"

"I'm actually not that old, Sam. But sometimes grownups get

weighed down by the world, you know. You don't know… how could you? It's hard for me to see things the way that you and Daisy do. It's like you grow up and you get world-weary and you start thinking more about why things can't happen as opposed to why they can. Everything gets a lot bigger and more complicated in an old person's mind, much more so than it really is."

"How can you be so bummed out when you're such a big part of everything we're doing? I think you should just relax. Think about what would make you happy. Use it as a starting point for what you'd like to see happen in the world. It doesn't matter how big or small it is."

"Stu-widdu makes me happy. So does watching you do impossible things on the technology side. And watching Daisy come into her own as a face and voice for a national movement. All to make the world a better place, that makes me very happy."

"Can you make it a little more about what you'd like to see happen, Dad?"

"I guess if I could make anything happen, I'd like to see the whole financial system collapse and be rebuilt with the bare minimum of rules. Where people who make stuff are the dominant species, rather than corporate bankers and traders and lawyers. Where companies aren't covered in red tape and personal guarantees and crippling interest payments. Where they can compete in a purer, more Darwinist-style environment. Where being a corporate banker or trader or private equity fund manager is considered a lower-level support job rather than the pinnacle of success."

"So essentially you want to help smaller businesses get out from under," Sam says plainly.

"Yeah, well if you're looking at what I actually would like to see happen—as opposed to the stuff I just want to complain about—I guess that's right."

"And what's the one thing that small businesses need the most?"

"Money," I answer. "That's why the banks and other-people's-money funds have so much control, why they're able to cripple a business with fees and interest and percentages and sway. And they make a ton of money doing it."

"So, there are non-profit companies out there, right? What about a non-profit bank?" Sam asks.

"That's a contradiction in terms."

"No, really," Sam continues, "Let's say there were a bank out there which does exactly what other banks do but isn't interested in making tons of money," Sam says. "Wouldn't everyone use this fantasy bank instead of the real banks that gouge people for profit? Wouldn't that help break the system you're talking about?"

"Well, yeah. I guess. But it would have to be a pretty big bank. It would have to drive down the rates and return expectations to the point where all of the other banks would need to match it in order to survive."

"A non-profit bank," Sam says. "That would make you happy?"

"Yeah," I say, closing my eyes. "Ask the Easter Bunny if he can arrange something like that next time he rides through here on his unicorn."

Sam climbs off of me. I apparently nod off to sleep for a bit.

***

I know I've been asleep because of the amount of drool that's on the front of my shirt when the doorbell rouses me. I look at the time on the cable box beneath our television. Six o'clock. Catelyn won't be home for another two or three hours. And I don't suppose she'd ring the doorbell anyway. So it's obviously not her. I shake the cobwebs from my brain, get up, walk to the front of the house and open the door.

Eesch. Not a pretty sight awaits me on the other side.

"Hello, Sullivan."

Mahoney. Still in the blue Adidas sweatsuit, white stripes down the side.

"Hi, John," I say, ignoring the last name protocol he always tries to establish. I don't think he's ever called me by my first name, actually. "Man, you look awful."

"My wife wants a divorce."

"I know, John. Wow, man, you look really terrible. Unhealthy. What have you been doing with yourself? You might want to go to a hospital."

"I've been walking around."

"For thirty hours?"

"I got drunk a couple of times. I think someone beat me up and peed on my sweat suit." I'm thinking that the pee probably came from inside the suit as opposed to outside, but I let that slide. He runs his hand over the top of his head. "Did someone cut my hair?"

"It looks that way, John."

His scalp looks like it got in a fight with a rogue lawnmower. A patchwork of bald, but with five o'clock bristles interspersed with puffy tufts of thinning blond. I'm figuring some of the kids got to him when he passed out. Probably his own kids since it wouldn't surprise me if he passed out somewhere on his own property. What they did isn't technically violence, but I don't think Gandhi would approve.

"Can I come in?" he asks.

"No, not a good idea." He really smells bad. "Let's talk here."

"Okay."

"Okay."

I wait. After a few seconds, he does a quick head shake that brings him back to the present moment.

"My wife wants a divorce."

"I know that already."

"How do you know that?"

"I know that because she came over to my house to tell me that you disappeared after our discussion yesterday. She told me that she and the kids are big supporters of Stu-widdu…"

"Stu-what?"

"Stu-widdu. It's an acronym for Stuff That's Wrong with the World. You know, the sister site to Daisy's doghouse." He looks at me blankly. "That Internet thing that has been calling out people like you for the past two weeks?"

"Oh."

"Right. So she told me that she and the kids don't approve of what you do for a living and she wants a divorce."

I've now kept my word to Sandy and communicated her wishes to John.

"Are you having an affair with my wife?"

"Don't be an idiot, John." Yuck. "Look, I hate to see any human being so down-and-out, even a parasite like yourself. But this really isn't any of my business. Your house is right there. Go talk to your wife or get your stuff or do whatever it is you're going to do."

He nods and starts to walk away. Then he turns back around,

looking a little more lucid and in control than he had looked under my yellow porch light.

"I understand it's wrong, you know," he says. "What I do, I mean. I know that people like me shouldn't be earning so much money when we don't actually do anything. No matter how busy we always are or how long we make our hours, we all know that we don't actually create anything." I look at him, and for the first time in ten years, he's a human being. "But my dad was a money guy," he continues, "and he wanted me to be a money guy. And you get used to the lifestyle. And it's so easy to look at other rich people and want what they have and to do the same things that they do to get it. It's so much easier to do that, to measure yourself that way than it is to try and figure out what you really need in life to be happy. I just want to make sure you know that we're not stupid. We're just caught up in a cycle that doesn't do the world any good. Well, I mean, spelling communist wrong on your house was pretty stupid, I guess." He smiles like a kid, "But what I mean is, we know it's wrong, what we do. But most of us are just caught up inside a bad system because we're afraid of being outside that system and actually having to live with ourselves."

People never cease to amaze me.

"You're going to be alright, John. I really think you are."

"Maybe," he says. Then he proceeds to vomit on his shoes and on my driveway. I flinch.

"Hey, man, can I get you a bottle of water or something?" I feel bad, but there's no way he's coming in the house after puking all over his shoes.

"No, I'm good. Can you… maybe can you call my wife, ask her to let me in the house? Tell her I won't stay. I just need to get some stuff together. Maybe I can talk to her for a couple of minutes?"

"Sure, I'll call her now."

"Don't you need our number?"

"Sandy gave me her card earlier today."

"Oh," he says, turns, steps directly into his own vomit and walks towards his McMansion.

I grab Sandy's card from the kitchen table and call her cell phone. I tell her that she might want to let John into the house, regardless of how he looks, how he smells. Tell her that I think it's worth her time to listen to him and then see where things go. Through the phone, I hear her doorbell ring. And then ring again. And then ring again.

John would be better served if he wasn't so annoying.

She hangs up, and I walk out our front door, sidestepping the vomit, stand at the end of our driveway. I see her open the door and see John walk into the house.

***

Daisy's Tuesday night blog post is directly addressed to the five wealthiest people in America, according to Google, she footnotes. It's the first time I've seen her use proper names on the blog, aside from her own. Three of the names are household. Two of them I've never heard before. She's asking them to pool their excess capital to start a non-profit bank focused on small businesses. Her argument is simple and direct, per the following six points that we came up with together:

First Point: Each of these people has so much money that they couldn't even spend one percent of it over the course of four generations.

Second Point: Donating huge amounts of money to things like curing diseases might make them feel good, but it's only going to make people live longer. And given the state of our retirement and pension funds, not to mention social security, living longer is only going to make a lot of people miserable and put a bigger burden on the taxpayer. For analogy, review the flawed logic behind the Right to Life movement.

Third Point: Businesses with fewer than twenty employees account for almost ninety percent of the Gross Domestic Product in the United States. Healthy small businesses mean a healthy US economy. So why not remove a giant, bloodsucking parasite from their backs?

Fourth Point: Bankers don't actually make or do anything. They don't deserve to make a profit. Moreover, they definitely don't deserve to make a ton of money, build McMansions and drive expensive foreign cars. See also: traders, brokers, and any type of fund manager.

Fifth Point: We're not asking anyone to lose money as a bank. We're just asking that these people not make money as a bank. Just asking them to break even on interest and other returns. Push the surplus back to their customers. Think of it as a zero-gain, zero-loss charity to revitalize the most important sector of the American economy.

Sixth Point: If these ultra-wealthy people don't work with us, we're going to talk to their children and grandchildren and great-grandchildren. Some of these kids are going to listen to us. So these ultra-wealthy people might want to think about Thanksgiving dinner next year.

She wraps by saying that it's obviously their money and they can do what they want with it. But, according to Spider Man's uncle, with great power comes great responsibility. And that might be true. And these five people are in a position to do more good for the American people than anyone else in the world. And they're all going to die, eventually.

She tells them that they probably don't want to risk whatever form of judgment might come, in whatever form of afterlife there is, by blowing this enormous responsibility to help the right people. Especially when she's spelled it out for them so clearly.

But that's just me, Daisy tells them. Do whatever you want, she says.

"Hey, Peanut!" I yell up the stairs.

"What?" she shouts down.

"Nice post!"

"Thanks!"

"Hey, Sam!"

"Yeah?" he shouts down to me.

"Thanks a lot, bud!"

"No problem," he shouts back. "Let's see how it plays out!"

My parents would totally not approve of this routine upstairs-downstairs dialog that's been established at my house. But they never had kids like mine, capable of changing the world.

So I cut myself some slack.

Chapter Twenty-four

"There's four million dollars in the central fund account," Sam says.

He's shoveling dry cereal into his mouth from a small Tupperware bin with a disposable plastic spoon. For some reason, neither of my kids put milk on their cereal. And it's always eaten with disposable crockery and utensils. As if we're trailer-park people every morning.

"We only had two million dollars' yesterday, after allocating two million to the local branches."

"I know. That's why I'm telling you."

"Did the hats and t-shirts come online?"

"Nope."

"So, where'd the money come from?"

"No idea. I didn't do the research," Sam says.

I roll my eyes to the ceiling and grab my laptop. He's right. We have two million extra dollars in the central account compared to yesterday. I click over to the sponsor page.

Ah ha!

New sponsors. Forty of them. Each donating amounts that range from ten thousand dollars to a hundred thousand dollars.

I click a contribution line item. It's from a regular person, not a company. A private citizen. In this case, a woman. A woman who apparently booted her sleazy corporate lawyer husband out of the house and now wants to help make the world a better place. I'm glad whoever designed the contribution input format added a text field for background and explanations.

People who are sick and empty and disgusted with their lifestyles. Sandy Mahoney said there were a lot of them. People like her. And everyone can see the grass-roots donations being made by the regional branches. It's all posted on the Stu-widdu home page. So this is where they want to put their ex's lopsided corporate winnings. Reinvest the newly estranged spouse's ill-begotten gains to make the world a better place and simultaneously tilt the scales further in their favor when it comes to the love of their children and the community.

Okay. All good with me. Money's money and we're actually doing something positive with it. I'm fully in favor of this cycle that's developing. I explain what's happening to Sam but don't get much of a reaction.

"Sam, can you have your friends track the last names and locations of new contributors against the names of the financial crisis beneficiaries from Dr. Greenburg's lists?"

"Sure. All of the people who robbed the pension funds are already in the database. That's how they're plotted on the map. I don't think it would be too hard to set up some scripts to match new contributor names and addresses. Is this afternoon okay?"

"Whenever it's convenient," I say. "Also, can we match incoming money, and its source, to outgoing money, and who it's being donated to?"

"I guess," he says. "I mean, it wouldn't actually be a real one-to-one relationship. We'd just need to set up a kind of a funnel tracking system. You know, newest money at the top and oldest money at the bottom. And we'd match the oldest money that came in with the donations as they go out. Maybe we do a little Tetris style bundle-blocking of the sources, so we're not splitting donations among web site sales and a bunch of different sponsors, but I don't see why it couldn't be done. Why?"

"I want the contributors to be able to see exactly what's being done with the money that they send us. I think that would sync up well with the primary motivation for a lot of these new, private citizen sponsors. That motivation being to win back the love of their children and neighbors. To get themselves out of the doghouse, so to speak."

"That's funny," he says, flatly. "Is it a pun?"

"Not exactly a pun, just a coincidental reference to Daisy's Doghouse."

"It felt like a pun," he says. "Didn't you tell me that puns were the lowest form of humor."

"Yeah."

"Hey," Sam says. "How about we do the funnel tracking on a

regional basis so that people from New Jersey can see their money allocated to projects in New Jersey – that type of thing. Hell, we could even regionalize it at the town-level, or by zip code, since there is sometimes more than one zip code in a city. That would probably make a big impact."

"That would be perfect, Sam. Don't say hell."

"Oops, sorry," he replies.

I wonder what he talks like on the playground.

Daisy walks into the kitchen, hands in her hair, still groggy from sleep.

"Here she is! Daisy!" I shout, a big smile on my face.

Ever since Daisy could walk down the stairs on her own, Catelyn and I have treated her morning arrival to the kitchen like the long-awaited homecoming of royalty. It's just something we do. Maybe it's one of the many factors that contributed to her handling celebrity so well. We used to do the same thing for Sam, too, but it seemed to annoy him, so we stopped the fanfare and just give him a silent hug and kiss in the morning. He's always up at least an hour before the rest of us, anyway.

"Hi," Daisy says, smiling, always happy with the elaborate greeting. She leans over my shoulder and kisses my cheek. "What are you doing?"

"We're getting contributions from private citizens now," I tell her. "Mostly moms or dads who are separating from their corporate swine other-halves and want to win over their kids' love by donating money to our site."

"Works for me," Daisy says through a yawn. "We'll put it to good use."

"And Sam is coordinating with his underground hacker friends to fix the site so we can track contributions to Stu-widdu all the way through to the donations made by Stu-widdu. So people can see how their money is helping their own community."

"It's kind of a shell game," Sam says, "but it will serve its purpose."

"Cool," she says sleepily. She's not a morning person.

"The coolest thing is, you know how we're tracking so many people who take advantage of the lopsided money system for personal gain?"

Ever since the event on Saturday, Dr. Gregory Greenburg has been staying up late at night and sending us data that extrapolates large financial windfalls in the corporate market and connects these giant gains to where the money ultimately came from, all with the appropriate public records. He's building a connection between the people who make out financially and the people who lose out financially, all under the assumption that the money-world operates in a vacuum, and you can't have a big winner without a big loser. I should pass this information along to Catelyn's brother, Jamie, whose phone calls have conspicuously stopped coincidentally to the momentum of our movement. Greenburg seems to have developed a pretty strong network of economics professors at other universities, all of whom have a keen passion to stick it to the banking and private-money bureaucracy. The data is vast and impressive.

"Yeah?" Daisy yawns again.

"Good, so you know how Dr. Greenburg's work helps us track the bad guys," I say, simplifying things. "Now we'll be able to track the good guys as well. Picture this... we can loosely track how greedy bureaucrats suck up a disproportionate share of money from the pension, retirement and college funds of unsuspecting citizens, and then we can track when the ashamed spouses separate from these corporate swine and donate a bunch of their shady wealth to us so we can use it to make the world a better place. We're closing the loop!"

"We're out of Rice Krispy Treats," Daisy says. Her name for Rice Krispies is Rice Krispy Treats. We don't let her eat actual Rice Krispy Treats, with the marshmallow and all, for breakfast.

"You'll appreciate all of this more when you see it in action," I say. "Eat something else. We'll get more Rice Krispies next time we go to the grocery store."

"I like it," Sam says enthusiastically.

"I know. Me too, bud. I like it a lot."

***

Catelyn comes in from an early morning run, looking slightly perturbed.

"Did you guys know that there are news vans outside?" she asks and kisses Sam on the cheek as she passes by the kitchen table. Sam nuzzles into her sweaty face, never bothered by situations of questionable hygiene. Catelyn bends down to kiss Daisy, who shields her face, looks sweetly at her mother, and then blows her a kiss. "Nice, kid. You're aware that you came out of my womb, right?"

"I'm aware," Daisy says, "and I love you for it. Dad, can I go out and talk to the news people?"

"Finish your… what are you eating?"

"Chips," Daisy says. "I told you we're out of Rice Krispy Treats."

She's filled a Tupperware bowl with potato chips and is eating them with a plastic spoon. I didn't even see her get up.

"Nice, Jack," Catelyn says, giving me a sweaty kiss on the cheek as well.

"Not for breakfast, Daisy," I say wearily.

"What am I supposed to eat?"

"Let's start with not potato chips and move from there. You're making me look like a bad parent in front of your mother, and you know that's supposed to be our secret."

Catelyn puts a few strips of bacon in the microwave for Daisy, although I'm not sure if that's a healthier breakfast than a bowl of potato chips.

As we walk out the front door for our drive to school, the news people shout for Daisy's attention. I look back, and she's turned into the full-on, public Daisy. Huge smile and her trademark wave, arms fully extended about halfway above her head, shaking her palms excitedly at the reporters.

"Two minutes, Dad?" she pleads.

"Fine," I say. "Have at it."

She walks to the end of our driveway.

***

"What did you talk about?" I ask as she climbs into the front seat five minutes later.

"Nothing, really."

"Daisy, I'm going to watch the news later. Just tell me what they asked you."

"It was mostly about last night's post, the one where I asked those rich people to start a bank."

"I'm familiar with the post," I say. "What was their angle?"

"They were asking me if I thought the rich people would listen to me. If I thought they'd set up a bank for non-profit. How am I supposed to know if the rich people will listen to me? I just told them I hope so. I said that we were just trying to figure out how to make the world a better place, and I thought that this non-profit bank thing could really help. Are we going to be late for school?" she asks anxiously.

"We have plenty of time," I say while making a left turn at the disgraced Mahoney McMansion.

I decide I'm going to paint over the erratically spelled graffiti on the front of our house when I get home. Maybe go over to the Mahoney place and see if Sandy wants me to paint over her kids' second-story scrawl clamoring for their father's incarceration. It might start a clean-up trend. Right now, our little suburban community looks more like it belongs to a former Soviet Bloc country than to North Jersey.

***

When I get back home, I decide to turn on the news before going outside to clean up the house. And there's Daisy's upbeat, smiling face, making ultra-positive statements about the non-profit bank, addressing the reporter by his first name.

They bring the camerawork back into the news set, and I'm about to flip the switch when I hear the word terrorist. As in, a watchdog group of concerned citizens in South Florida has recently made allegations that Daisy in the Doghouse and Stuff That's Wrong with the World, Inc. popularly referred to as Stu-widdu, is engaged in the funding of terrorist organizations in different parts of the country.

They flash to a local Florida affiliate and an interview with a man who could be John Mahoney's older twin.

"We're not saying that they've done anything definitively wrong, here," the man says, looking at the reporter's face as opposed to the camera, "but there has been a lot of money, moving in small amounts, to Muslim organizations that have been linked to radical Islamic groups."

I should be more upset than I actually am. But this just seems way too absurd to get a rise out of me.

"And how have these Muslim groups been linked to radical Islamic factions?" the reporter asks.

"Uh…," the man pauses, "because they're Muslim."

"Oh," says the reporter. "Is that all?"

"Isn't that enough?" asks the older Mahoney twin.

"Okay. And how did your watchdog group obtain this information about Daisy's group making donations to these organizations?"

"It's on their website."

"So, it doesn't seem like Daisy and her group are trying to hide this information then?"

The screen flashes to the Stu-widdu site, scrolls through our list of hundreds of donations which includes the names of recipient non-profit organizations. They flash back to the interview.

"No, it's right there for everyone to see. They're shoving it right in our faces. We've got our eye on you people," the man says angrily and finally addresses the camera. "And if you think you're going to pull any Nine-Eleven type nonsense, you've got another think coming. It's not going to happen on our watch!"

"Ohhh-kay. Well, Steve, obviously not a happy man we've got here in Fort Lauderdale," the reporter says, also addressing the camera. "Now I understand we're going to switch over to Sam Evans in the neighboring community of Hollywood, Florida, to what we think is one of the Muslim organizations that has received donations from Stu-widdu. Sam?"

"Thanks, Rob," Sam says. "I'm standing inside the Muslim Community Center and Mosque here in Hollywood, Florida, with Ahmed Abad, a leader in this Muslim community. Hi, Ahmed."

Ahmed is a thin, mid-thirties man, darker skin, wearing a nervous smile for the camera.

"Hi, Sam," he makes a small wave at the camera.

"Ahmed, we understand that your Community Center has received donations from Stu-widdu recently?"

"Yes! We did," he says, excitedly. "They are helping us rebuild our pool!" The camera pans to a wide shot that includes an empty pool behind Ahmed and Sam. "This pool has been empty for three years because of the cracked bottom. Look, you can see it there. So, a few of the kids in our community are involved with Daisy's make the world a better place initiative, you know? And they came up with the money to fix our pool."

"Did Stu-widdu just cut you guys a check?"

"No, no, no. We have to post the contractor receipts on their website, show before-and-after pictures, that kind of thing."

"What would you have used the money for if they had just cut you a check?"

"I don't know. There are a lot of families that need help in our community, and we have a lot of programs that need funding," Ahmed says. "But Daisy's people gave us the money specifically to fix the pool. So, we're fixing the pool. And the kids are going to be really happy when it gets so hot during the summer. We're even talking about joining a swim team league."

"Ahmed, are you aware of allegations that your community is somehow related to Radical Islamic terrorist cells?" Sam asks, cautiously.

"Why, because we're Muslim?"

Sam hesitates and then answers, "I think that is the reason, yes. There's a watchdog group in a neighboring town that is alleging the money from Stu-widdu is being funneled towards these radical groups."

"What's radical about fixing our pool? Other than it's going to be radically fun for the kids when it gets hot! Wait. Is this that group of old people in Fort Lauderdale?" Ahmed asks.

I get the impression that Sam nods his head, even though he's off camera, and Ahmed looks at the sky and then addresses the camera as if he's speaking to the watchdog group in Lauderdale.

"Come on, man," he says into the camera. "Not every Muslim is a terrorist. We're just trying to fix our pool here. Why do you people have to turn everything we do into some kind of subversive plot? Not you, Sam. I'm talking to the haters in Fort Lauderdale."

"Thanks for the clarification, Ahmed."

"How about this," Ahmed says. "Even though you people hate us because of our religion, I invite any of you to come here and enjoy our new pool when it's fixed."

"That's a very generous offer, Ahmed."

"Not really," Ahmed says. "The people who hate us in Lauderdale are all rich and have their own pools, so I don't think we'll have any takers. Not just because they have pools, I mean. But the offer still stands."

"Thanks, Ahmed. Back to you, Steve." Sam says.

The camera cuts back to the news desk. I turn off the television, exhale, and walk to our garage to get some white paint.

***

It takes four coats to cover up the scrawl beneath our bay windows. I try just painting over the letters, but since the new paint doesn't blend with the siding well enough, from certain angles, it ends up looking like a COMmUNIST watermark. I end up painting a rectangular section over the entire area. It still doesn't look great—the paneling on our house was not designed for graffiti clean-up—but hopefully, the weather will eventually help to blend it.

I step over our shrubbery and walk, paint can and brush in hand, towards the Mahoney McMansion.

"I don't remember calling for a contractor," Sandy says wittily after she opens the door and looks me up and down.

"I work cheap. I just finished our house. Do you want me to do something about that stuff?" I ask, pointing up and around to her second story.

"Wouldn't it be dangerous, climbing onto the roof, I mean? It's very steep."

"That didn't seem to pose a problem for your kids. I don't think it will be an issue."

"I think I'll call a professional. Maybe leave it there for a little while."

"Suit yourself," I say. "How did it go with John last night?"

"He took some things and is staying at a hotel."

That's not really what I asked. "The guy's a mess, Sandy."

"You think? Anyway, he deserves to be a mess. Give him a few days to recover from his hangover. He'll turn right back into the same arrogant, greedy sleazeball I've been married to for twenty years."

"Harsh."

"Let him change his life. Let him hop on the bandwagon and do something good. Then maybe I'll have a little compassion for him. Otherwise, he's just a casualty of war."

"Okay," I say and turn back in the direction of my house.

"Let me know if you need any help with Daisypallooza!"

"What?" I ask, still facing the opposite direction, not really wanting to turn around.

"Daisypallooza," she repeats. "The concert? I saw it on the website."

"When?" I still haven't turned around.

"October, I think. A few weeks away still."

I'd actually meant, when did she see this on the website, but I let it slide. Daisy must have posted something from school.

"Okay, I'll let you know," I say and walk back to my house.

Chapter Twenty-five

"Hi, Dad. We've decided something we can do with a bunch of the central fund money," Daisy says brightly as she climbs into the front seat.

"Daisypallooza," I say.

"You read it! What do you think?"

"I think we really need to talk before you commit to these things. Where's your brother?"

"No idea."

I hold up the car line for another thirty seconds and then drive around the corner, park and walk back to the front of the school. Daisy stays in the car. I look around at the kids waiting for pick up. No Sam. I walk into the school. To the right of the front door is the nurse's office, where I see Sam's profile. He's sitting on a couch.

"Hey!" I say, walking into the nurse's office.

"Hey," Sam says and turns to face me.

Whoa! He's got a huge black eye. Like the kind you'd see in a Rocky movie.

"Oh my God, bud. What happened?"

"I got punched."

"By what?" It looks like someone pounded his face with a sledgehammer. Catelyn is not going to be pleased.

"By an eighth grader. Billy Prescott. He's a bully. He was mad at Daisy's blog."

"So why did he punch you?"

"He said he wouldn't hit a girl."

"Well, that's noble of him. So he hits a fifth grader instead?"

"I guess."

"So where is this Billy Prescott, now?"

"Nobody knows."

"What do you mean, nobody knows?"

'They think he's hiding in the woods somewhere in Randall's Park. His mom and dad are in with Dr. Hennessy, I think."

Dr. Hennessy is the school principal.

"Why is this kid hiding in the woods?"

"Self-preservation."

"Please, Sam. Just tell me what happened."

"Okay," Sam says, seeming to gear up for what promises to be a very long and elaborate explanation, per his typical style.

"Just the Cliff Notes, bud. You can tell me the whole story when we get home."

"Fine. So this kid Billy is mad about the blog because his father's some kind of fund manager and has been filling Jimmy's head with all kinds of lies about us. So he comes up to me at recess, and he pushes me up against a tree at the edge of the playground, and he punches me in the face."

"What did you do?"

"I fell down and started to cry," he says matter-of-factly. "But the kids on the playground, they saw it. And I guess a lot of them are involved in our stuff because they went nuts. I mean, outhouse rat crazy." Outhouse rat is a euphemism that we use at home. "It was like the whole playground started yelling and cursing and running towards us. I thought they were gonna rip him to shreds."

"And then…"

"And then Billy wet his pants and screamed and ran away. I actually saw him wet his pants. It was disgusting. So, he had about twenty yards on the rest of the kids, and he's a fast runner. They chased him as far as Strumpner Field, I think, and then lost him in the woods."

"Where was your sister?"

"She has recess before me. My class has recess with the second grade and the eighth grade, not the sixth grade. It was the eighth graders who acted like they were going to kill Billy. The second graders didn't do anything except watch."

"Fine. Are you okay?"

"Yeah," he says. "It looks worse than it feels." I call Daisy's cell phone, tell her to come back to the school and meet us in the nurse's office. Not in one sec. Now.

"What's up," Daisy says, walking into the nurse's office. "Oh my god, Sam! Your face. What happened?"

"I got punched."

I take Sam and Daisy by the hand, walk across the hall and open the closed door of Dr. Hennessy's office. As I enter the office, a fat man in a suit, who looks like a shorter version of Chris Christy, and a thin, unattractive lady who looks like she's trying to look like a modern version of Jackie O, both turn around from the wooden chairs in front of Dr. Hennessy's desk. They stare at me and the kids.

Dr. Hennessy, a small-boned woman in her early seventies, sits behind her desk with an expression of controlled panic. The poor lady obviously has no idea how to handle any of this.

"This is all your fault!" the fat man bellows at me. He twists his large frame further around towards us. The arms of his chair are wedged tightly against his huge hips, so the chair lifts with him as he tries to stand up. He glares at me in a half crouch, the chair stuck to his bottom. He looks ridiculous.

"Are you an insane person?" I lift both of my hands, palms upturned, to Sam's face.

The fat man remains indignant as he shimmies his hips to release himself from the grip of the chair. I think he's desperately trying to hold on to the idea that he's actually the victim here, but he's also aware that he looks like a buffoon with that chair stuck to his giant bottom, and that's not making him any happier with the situation.

I glance at Daisy who's holding her iPhone in front of her face and wearing a pleasant, far-away expression. I assume she's capturing all of this on video.

"You started all of this!" he screams and points at me. "You and your stupid daughter and that stupid website!"

"Mr. Prescott!" Dr. Hennessy shouts in an admonishing voice.

Prescott looks like he's ready to charge us. He's finally removed the chair from his hips and appears to have gone completely bananas. I glance protectively at Daisy. She's lowered the iPhone about six inches, still capturing the video, and on her face is the most enormous, genuine smile that I think I have ever seen.

She is absolutely beaming, right at Prescott. And I realize that her smile is born of a deep understanding that if Prescott approaches her with even a hint of violence, Daisy's followers will be auctioning off his body parts on eBay before the day is out.

She continues to beam at him, confident as a queen bee, very comfortable in the knowledge that she's got an enormous hive of killer drones ready to protect her from any kind of harm. Prescott looks at her, holding the iPhone, and seems to wake up from an angry dream as he realizes the situation that he's in.

The room is icy silence.

"Billy shouldn't have hit my brother, Mr. Prescott," Daisy says in a slow, creepy voice.

She pans the camera over to capture Sam's face. Counterproductive to the mood Daisy's trying to create, Sam gives her a cheesy smile. She pans the iPhone back to Prescott, who slowly sits back down in the chair, his butt thumping against the seat as his hips finally wedge themselves past the arms again.

"I, uh… I know," Prescott says to Daisy, his voice shaking like he's talking to a ghost or to Darth Vader. Or to the Angel of Death.

"You should apologize to my brother, Mr. Prescott," Daisy says. She's still using that creepy voice, still videoing the scene, still with that laser beam smile fixed on Prescott's deadening white face.

"I, uh, yeah. Okay, you're right. I'm sorry… boy."

"My brother's name is Sam, Mr. Prescott," Daisy says slowly.

I want to nudge her because she's starting to ham it up. But Prescott doesn't seem to notice. He's still shaken up, still looking at the camera. I don't think his wife has turned around again, even once, throughout this entire episode.

"Yeah, okay. I… I'm sorry, Sam. I'm sorry this happened. I'm sorry Billy hit you."

"That's not good enough, Mr. Prescott…" Daisy continues.

"Daisy, enough, okay?" I say.

"Fine," she says and lowers the phone, turning back into my twelve-year-old daughter.

"You're going to handle this," I say to Dr. Hennessy.

"Yes, I will," Dr. Hennessy replies automatically, obviously freaked out by the past few minutes.

"Then we're gonna go."

I'm on the verge of saying something to Prescott about threatening my family, but I look into his eyes and see that he is deeply and truly frightened. Of Daisy. Of what would happen if people were to get the impression that he threatened her. He's thinking about all of the doghouses in the neighborhood, all of the doghouses around the country.

I have a feeling that, over the last couple of minutes, whatever narcissistic fantasy world he's been living in has collapsed. Or at least it's severely shaken. I don't think he's ever going to be the same fund manager that he was before he walked into Dr. Hennessy's office.

***

"Does it hurt, Sam?" Daisy asks as we walk around the corner to my car.

"Not really. It did at first."

"You totally look like a bad dude," she says, and Sam smiles. "So, Dad, about Daisypallooza?"

"Let's put that on the back burner for a minute, Creepy McGee. I want to talk about that spooky little scene in Dr. Hennessy's office."

"Oh, right! I know! I like, totally crushed him. It was like an out of body experience, what I turned into."

"What you turned into," I say flatly.

"Oh, come on, Dad. I'm a method actor. I saw a part taking shape, and I just ran with it. No big deal."

I guess she didn't do anything wrong, actually. Other than acting like a child of the damned in front of her principal and a couple of adults. Two adults who seem to be, frankly speaking, worthless as human beings.

"It was really cool," Sam chimes in. "I got goosebumps when you told Mr. Prescott to apologize. It reminded me of a movie."

"What movie?" she asks.

"I don't know, just a scary movie," he says.

"Dad... Daisypallooza?"

"Okay," I say. "I saw it mentioned on the site. Go ahead, pitch me on the idea."

"Okay, you're going to love it! So, my people have been talking to other people's people, right? And some of these people are the people for the people at MTV. And they said the MTV people think we can get a bunch of bands to come and put on big concerts at these outdoor, open spaces. You know, like have a bunch of concerts at the same time, one in each major region, so everyone has a chance to come. And the concerts would last, like, three days."

"MTV?"

"You know, Music Television, the network."

"I know MTV. I'm just a little taken aback that you've been talking to MTV."

"My people have been talking to their people, like I said. And MTV loves what we do."

"Do they?"

"Yeah. MTV hates the corporate types. Even their corporate types hate the corporate types. Have you watched MTV lately? You should check it out."

I'm forty-seven years old. I haven't watched MTV since *The Real World* in the Nineties.

"I will. You know this type of thing has been done before," I say, though I'm not exactly sure about simultaneous concerts in different regions of the country.

"Not like this. And it could be, like, a fundraiser. We'd get a whole mess of national sponsors and local vendors, make a lot more than what we made at the events last weekend. And—I'm just saying—the money that we brought in so far is almost used up already. We need to do something big to keep the momentum rolling."

"Who's going to plan this nation-wide extravaganza?"

"Not us," Daisy says. "We can just show up, like last weekend."

"Okay, but who's going to do the actual planning? Who's going to coordinate with the sponsors and the vendors and the field space and the bands and all that?"

"I guess it would be MTV. Or they'd contract it out, like we did for last Saturday, to local event planning companies. Only these would probably be super-deluxe event planning companies."

"Okay. Let's talk about it with your mom when she gets home."

"Dad! I already said that we would do it!"

"Well, maybe you ought to stop saying we'll do things before you talk to your parents."

***

Catelyn comes home around seven-thirty. Sam is at the kitchen table, on the iPad, wearing a pair of Catelyn's oversized zyl frame sunglasses. He looks like a small version of Sir Elton John in the seventies.

"What's with the shades?" Catelyn asks.

"Glare," Sam replies.

"Sam."

"Okay." Sam lifts the sunglasses, now looking like Sir Elton John gay-bashed by a bunch of rednecks outside of a hillbilly bar, in the seventies. "It's not dad's fault."

"Oh, my god! Jack, what the hell happened?"

"Come on, Cat. He just said it's not my fault. It happened at school."

"Everything's your fault," Catelyn says to me briskly, without the slightest hint of sarcasm. Then she walks over to inspect Sam's busted face.

I need to get a job. There's too much ambient blame surrounding people who stay at home all day.

"You should have seen Daisy," Sam says.

Catelyn pours us wine, something that's become a nightly routine over the past two weeks. Sam tells her the long version of his story, his arms flailing as he talks. He wiggles his butt, imitating the chair stuck on Prescott's hips. He glares when he describes Daisy in the principal's office, which is not descriptively accurate, but I assume that's how he remembers it. He mentions Daisypallooza as he wraps the story, precipitating raised eyebrows from Catelyn and opening another can of worms with which I'll need to deal. When he finishes the story, he exhales, looks at the iPad and says, "Hey, Dad. There's six million in the central account now."

"Really, it was just four million this morning. How much of it is web sales and how much new sponsors?"

"Only a half million in web sales," he replies. "Three and a half million in new sponsors."

"Is that half million after Amazon fees and costs?"

"Yeah, it's all clear."

"Would the two of you please stop with the Stu-widdu talk and let's get back to this afternoon?" Catelyn says, exasperated. "Actually, Sam, why don't you go upstairs and get into your pajamas. Brush your teeth, and you can watch TV in our room. Mom needs some alone time with your father."

"It's okay with me if Sam wants to stick around," I say.

"Yeah, I bet it is. Sam, go," she says.

He gets up from the table, comes over and sits on my lap. Puts his face in my neck. Tells me he's sorry. This kid gets popped in the face and then tells me he's sorry. I was never this magnanimous as a child. I give him a kiss on his unbusted cheek, tell him everything's fine. He walks out of the kitchen and up the stairs still wearing the oversized sunglasses.

"Our son was attacked," Catelyn says when Sam has cleared the stairs.

"Come on. He got into a fight on the playground. It's not that bad."

"He got punched in the face by a kid twice his size."

"How do you know the kid is twice Sam's size?"

"I've seen Billy Prescott. He's got a full-on mustache. I think he even shaves it. And he's in eighth grade. He must have a problem with his pituitary gland or something. He's huge. And he made Sam look like a battered wife."

"Or like Rocky, maybe? I mean, seriously, Cat. A battered wife? He's a dude. Let's keep these descriptions at the dude level. At least when he's in the room."

I'm super protective of Sam's masculinity when it comes to his mother.

"He's not in the room."

"Yeah, but when he is, I mean. It would probably be better if we just talk about all of this in very masculine, tough guy terms – even just between ourselves – so we don't slip when he's actually here."

"Jack, this isn't a joke. I was okay with all of this stuff as long as I felt like the kids were safe. Now I don't know."

"Safe? Are you kidding me? Half the playground was ready to posse up, hunt this kid down and hang him from the nearest tree after he hit Sam. And Daisy went head-to-head with a three-hundred-pound Manhattan fund manager. Manhattan fund managers, by the way, are known for being very tough guys. And when she was done with him, he was a puddle on the floor. Our kids have never been this safe."

Catelyn takes a sip of her wine, looks at me as if I'm the guy responsible for bringing all of this weirdness into her family. Which, I guess, is at least a partially fair judgment.

"I don't know, Jack," she finally says. "This has gotten very big, and there have been more than a few instances that I think are dangerous to the kids."

"And we've also done a ton of good. Look at the money that we're donating. This stuff we're doing is making people's lives better. Not in a curing cancer type of way, but in an everyday, ray of sunshine, the-world-can-be a-more-beautiful-place type of way. That's important. Not to mention the fact that we are seriously undermining the delusions of corporate money people who pretend that they're upstanding members of society. That's hugely important, even if we're just chipping away at it. And look at how engaged Daisy and Sam are. Look at what they've done. No school in the world could give them the kind of confidence and life experience that they've gotten in the last sixteen days."

"Can't we just slow down a little bit?" Catelyn asks.

"No, we can't," I reply. "We are way, way past the point of no return with this thing. The only way to get through it is to come out the other side." She nods slowly. "Sure, there's a lot of dangerous stuff, but our kids are really living right now. They're in it. There's world-changing stuff happening around them, and they're directly involved. Hell, they're leading it, not just observing it. People are born and die never having the kind of engagement that our kids have experienced over the past couple of weeks. We've got to embrace this, not slow it down."

"Okay, fine. I'm with you. I'm trusting you on this, Jack," she says and takes another long sip of her wine. "So what's Daisypallooza?"

Chapter Twenty-six

On Thursday morning Daisy enters the kitchen to the typical morning fanfare from Catelyn and me. We don't realize that she's on the phone.

"No, it's okay. I'm not walking into any kind of speaking engagement. That's just my parents," she says into her phone, walking over and resting her free ear against my chest in lieu of a hug. She's using her public voice.

I look at Catelyn and shrug. Catelyn does the same, assuming it's some kind of news interview and goes back to cutting strawberries. Although our trailer park plastic bowls and cutlery at breakfast might imply otherwise, Catelyn is actually a big advocate of well-balanced meals for the kids. Every home meal, not just breakfast, is accompanied by a small side of fruit or vegetables, served mornings in Tupperware, afternoons and evenings in small ceramic chaffing dishes.

Sam loves this routine. He has gotten mad at me when his mom isn't home, and I give him a reheated slice of pizza which isn't accompanied by an appetizer portion of fresh fruit or vegetables. Conversely, I have never seen Daisy eat a single thing from these small serving dishes of greens or fruit. For Daisy, these side dishes are prepared, ignored and thrown into the garbage with a regularity that makes you think about skipping a step or two. Not that this has any impact whatsoever on Catelyn's routine.

"Daisy," I stage whisper, "who are you talking to?"

"One sec," Daisy says, covering the microphone slot and whispering to me, "It's one of the rich people."

I take a breath and try to let this situation settle for a second. Maybe I'm missing something here, sitting at the kitchen table in my boxers at seven-fifteen in the morning, but I think there's a good chance that my twelve-year-old daughter is having a conversation on her iPhone with one of the five richest people in the United States, according to Google.

I tug on her uniform skirt.

"Who is it?" I ask.

Daisy gives me a dramatic shrug and a wide-eyed I-don't-know look.

"Yeah, okay. One sec," she says again into the phone.

"I didn't get his name when he said it," she whispers to me. "I think it's like Greek or Russian or something." She resumes her conversation with the phone.

"What's up," Catelyn says from the sink, turning on the garbage disposal.

"Ahhhgh! Off, off, off!" I whisper-scream at her, my arms flailing big and wide like a referee signaling a missed field goal.

"Fine," Catelyn says in a normal voice and flips the switch on the garbage disposal to turn it off. It grinds down slowly. I hang on Daisy's every word, which is difficult because she's hardly speaking at all aside from an occasional uh-huh and yeah.

"Look," Daisy says into the phone, "this whole non-profit bank thing was really my dad's idea. He might understand what you're saying better than I do. Do you want to talk to him?" I gape at her, my palms outstretched in front of me like she's some kind of rabid dog. "Okay, great. Let me get him."

I am entirely unprepared to have a conversation with one of the five wealthiest people in our country this early in the morning.

"Hello?" I say.

"Hello. Mr. Sullivan?"

"Yeah, speaking," I say. He introduces himself. It's one of the three household names on Daisy's Google list. His last name is not even close to Greek or Russian.

"Mr. Sullivan, you've got quite a daughter there."

"I know. Uh, thanks."

"Let's cut to the chase, shall we? Mr. Sullivan, Disney put his head in a freezer."

I have no idea what he's talking about. I mean, I know about the rumors that Walt Disney wanted to be cryogenically frozen, but I think he was actually cremated. Beyond that, I have no contextual idea as to what he's talking about.

"I don't believe in cryogenics," he continues. "I think you've got to do what you're going to do while you're here on earth the first time."

"Ah, okay."

"I'm a rich man, Mr. Sullivan. Your daughter's right. I couldn't possibly spend enough of my money to ever change the lifestyle I've got, or my family's lifestyle, for several dozen generations. For all we know, the sun could blow out by then."

It seems highly unlikely to me that anything would happen to the sun over the course of several dozen generations of people, but I don't contradict him.

"Okay."

"Mr. Sullivan, I want to explore this idea of a non-profit bank."

"Okay. I mean, great."

"So, talk to me," he says like he's expecting a pitch.

"It's a pretty simple concept," I say. "You just do everything that a normal bank would do, but the goal is not to make a profit or return on investment. For the bank, that is."

"Okay, so a question," he says. "Why would anyone do that?"

The question annoys me, which is good because it puts me back in my element.

"Alright," I say. "Let me try and spell this out for you a little more. If you think about it, the financial world is like a vacuum. Nothing is created, nothing is destroyed, money just changes hands. Are you with me?"

"I am."

"Good, so every time banks or financial institutions make a big profit, every time executives take home huge bonuses and shares of that profit, it has to come from somewhere. It's not as if the financial system just creates money to reward bankers and fund managers for being so clever. What I'm saying is, any time money-people win, there is also someone who loses. It's coming out of someone else's pocket, so to speak. There might be a lot of distance and layers that separate the winners from the losers, but ultimately no one can win unless someone else loses. Are you still with me?"

"Yes. But that's capitalism, Sullivan. There are winners, and there are losers."

"Well, of course. In capitalism, there are always winners and losers. I totally agree with that. But we're not talking about companies competing on the strength of their product here. We're talking about banks and financial institutions, which are parasites. These are firms that don't actually make anything or do anything. They don't provide any inherent value to humanity from their brains or hard work. These firms just manage other people's money to provide necessary capital to the companies that are competing on the strength of their product or service."

"But banks are necessary for these companies. Without banks, they wouldn't survive."

"Yes, I agree. Banks are necessary. Companies couldn't survive without credit lines and loans. But my point is that banks don't need to make so much money providing this necessary service. Do you get me? Money is a commodity."

"I don't know if I'd call banking or fund management a commodity, Sullivan. You're talking about a lot of smart people who are very good competitors."

"I didn't say that banking is a commodity. I said that money is a commodity. And bankers or fund managers are really only smart at finding ways to leverage their position as commodity providers in a way that generates maximum personal gain."

"I think I see your point."

"I'd assume so because you got wealthy by actually making and selling technology products. Banks and financial institutions don't actually produce anything. They exist only to make profits using other-people's-money. I mean, can you think of anything that these firms actually create that makes the world a better place for anyone but themselves?"

The phone line is silent for a moment.

"No," he finally says.

"Okay, so what if there was a bank that provided the same commodity, with the same level of expertise around it, but that bank doesn't make a profit? Because it's funded and run by people who have so much wealth that they can afford to do something with their money other than using it to make even more money. That's what I'm talking about in terms of a non-profit bank. A commodity management company where the would-be profits are reinvested to allow for lower interest rates and distributed returns – therefore allowing its customers to be much healthier and better equipped to compete in the free market. And, as an added bonus, it would totally take the legs out of other banks and financial institutions in the market because they'd be forced to compete with the lower rates and higher customer returns—assuming the non-profit bank were big enough. Am I making any sense here?" I ask.

"Oddly enough, it does make some sense. Even though you're almost manic in your explanation."

"I'm sorry about that. It's just, I've lived on the other side of these parasites for a long time, and they've all but sucked me dry. Emotionally speaking, I mean."

"That's fair. But just so we're on the same page... we're talking about setting up a banking institution that is funded and run by experts who are specifically trying not to make a profit or huge bonuses? Is that right?"

"Trying not to make a profit for the bank, or huge bonuses for themselves, yeah. So it can only work when people with so much disposable wealth decide that their priority is not to use their money and brains to make even more money than they already have. Instead, they would commit to using their money to give smaller companies a stronger opportunity to succeed. I know it's a long shot."

"It is a long shot. But maybe less so in my circles. I think I follow you, but you're going to need to shape up your presentation if we're going to sell this thing. Let me talk to some people and get back to you. Is this number okay?"

"This is actually Daisy's phone. Let me give you my cell number."

I give him my number, we exchange pleasantries, he hangs up, and I allow my upper body to collapse on the kitchen table.

***

"Great, you're done," Catelyn says. She pats my head, which is lying sideways across a placemat. "You need to hurry, or the kids are going to be late for school."

Changing the world is nothing like what I thought it would be. Not that I'd ever given it much practical thought. I walk out to the car and Sam is sitting in the front seat. Daisy, pouting, looks at me from the back.

She doesn't think it's right when Sam takes the front seat.

"So?" Sam asks.

"So, what?" I ask back.

"How did it go?"

"Fine, I guess."

"Anything else?" He asks, annoyed at my lack of response.

"You know, this is how you always answer me when I ask how was your day at school. Frustrating, isn't it?" I say.

"I guess, but let's keep this about you. Is this guy gonna help make a non-profit bank?"

"I have no idea. I get so wound up about this financial system stuff that I think I might have blown it." I've really got to figure out some way to control my soapbox rants.

Sam sits beside me, silent, like a Buddha. Like a Buddha who's been the victim of domestic abuse. A wise little man with a giant black eye. He puts his hand on my shoulder, his head against my arm.

"So, enough about banking," Daisy says from the backseat. "What say we talk about Daisypallooza?"

Chapter Twenty-seven

When I get home from dropping off the kids, I check the site. The web sales are still rolling in at about a half million clear income every twenty-four hours. They're obviously going to level out once we've saturated the plastic red doghouse market, although the hats and t-shirts might represent a strong uptick.

I click the link to the sponsor list and... wow. The sponsorship contributions are continuing to climb, another five million since yesterday morning. All of it coming from what I've termed "private citizens." Sandy Mahoney's compatriots. People—I assume mostly spouses in the process of separation—who are sick and empty and disgusted with their lives. Part of me instinctively wants to dwell on all of the hurt that's happening in the world right now. Families being broken. Confused, unsuspecting wealthy people who are suddenly being held in harsh judgment for the same stuff that once warranted a pat on the back, at least from themselves. All of the John Mahoneys out there lost and ridiculed and alone. Their soon-to-be ex-wives and ex-husbands pulling big chunks of money out of the greedy black holes that are their bank accounts. Sending it to us so we can use it to help rebuild pools and playgrounds and church roofs. Helping to bring a little happiness into the world.

To keep myself from dwelling on the unhappiness of the recently dispossessed, I click over to the home page and play with the interactive map. I click on menu icons and submenu icons, scroll through thousands of major financial transactions. Seeing which institutions and individuals are making the big money, where that money comes from, noticing especially the places where normal people save their money – pension and retirement and college funds. Big money indirectly siphoning huge windfalls from the unsuspecting little money.

Dr. Greenburg and his team of university night owls have certainly been burning the midnight oil. It occurs to me that I should give him a call, but before doing so, I click and scan the sponsor contributions, filtered to see only the private citizens, pushing us chunks of their soon-to-be-estranged spouses' ill-begotten wealth. The money being sucked out of the system by the ultra-wealthy is incomparably enormous relative to the tiny trickle of money being contributed to our site. But at least there's a trickle starting, and it's coming from the right place, and hopefully, it will continue to grow.

I close the site, pull my cell phone out of my front pocket.

"Dr. Greenburg? Jack Sullivan."

"Mr. Sullivan, call me Greg."

"And you, me, Jack," I say awkwardly.

"Okay, Jack. Nice work on the site. I could never have imagined seeing all of our data in an interactive graphic interface. Your programmers are amazing. Where did you find them?"

"They're kids. At least I think they're kids, probably, mostly anyway. They're friends of my ten-year-old son, Sam."

"Remarkable. Say, do you mind if I use screenshots of the site for something that I'm working on?"

"Of course, do whatever you want. We wouldn't have the whole money flow without your data. Do you mind if I ask what you're working on?"

"Well, me and the guys," he's referring to his network of professors, "are trying to put together a presentation template. Something really simple and layman – we might even use cartoon graphics and animation. Stuff that real people can understand. And we want to tell the story of how our top-heavy financial system has exploited and siphoned funds from the places where normal people save their money. Like pension funds, retirement and college savings funds, that kind of thing. But we want to make it very localized, and that's why we're trying to build a plug-and-play template. Because it's the same story everywhere. And we want to give each town something that will let them know very specifically how they are being abused by a broken system. And we want to identify the actual perpetrators on a company and individual basis. And then we want to sit back and watch what happens."

Dr. Greg Greenburg giggles like a kid.

"Very cool," I say. "Let me know if you need some development help, and I can have Sam try to hook you up."

"That's exactly what I was getting around to asking for your help with."

"I'll set it up when Sam gets home."

"That would be really great. Thanks. And, so, you called me, right? What can I do for you?"

"I'm working on a project that you and your friends might be interested in."

"Hit me," he says.

I tell him about my conversation this morning, try to give him the details regarding my idea for a non-profit bank without sounding too stupid or sophomoric. Talking to an economics professor about economics is a humbling experience. I'm kind of expecting him to give me some simple reason why it would never work, so I'm surprised when he seems intrigued by the idea.

"So, it's just a regular bank, but the corporate mandate is that the bank doesn't make a profit," Greg says.

"It doesn't make a profit, and it doesn't give out big bonuses to its executives."

"And you think you can find a way to fund this thing with money from ultra-wealthy people?"

"They're the only people who could possibly make it happen. People who have so much surplus wealth that they can afford to operate with a motive that isn't profit," I say.

"What about the actual workers? The ultra-rich aren't going to do any grunt work."

"The workers will get paid a fair salary. They're part of the operation, and the bank can make enough interest and investment return to cover the cost of operations, just not any more than that. So workers are not only involved in a banking system that's actually making the world a better place—which seems like a contradiction in terms, I know—but they're also getting a ton of experience. I see it as the banking equivalent of how fresh lawyers earn their chops at the District Attorney's office. Maybe the pay isn't as good as they'll get somewhere else, but there are other motivations."

"Sounds reasonable. I mean, the whole thing's obviously a long shot, but at least it makes sense. So how can I help?"

"You know banks, right?"

"Intimately," Greg says.

"Well, I've worked with banks, but I don't know anything about the actual banking world. I figure if you and the guys understand what we're trying to achieve, you might be able to color inside the lines and come up with an operating structure that's feasible."

"Consider it done, my friend," he says. "I'll get back to you within forty-eight hours."

I figure there's no way that my new uber-wealthy friend is going to respond to me any sooner than that, so I thank him. We exchange pleasantries and hang up.

I open a blank WORD document and start on a pitch outline for the non-profit bank, pending a call back that might never happen. But I don't come up with anything more than what I explained to Greenburg, so I ditch the effort and take a nap instead.

***

"Your eye looks better, bud," I say as Sam climbs into the backseat at four-thirty.

"Yeah, it's starting to look normal," he says glumly.

"Hey, Peanut," I say as Daisy slides into the front seat.

"Hi."

"How was school?"

"Fine."

"So, Sam, did they ever find Jimmy Prescott?" I ask.

"Yeah, I heard he snuck home last night when he got hungry. He's expelled."

Quick work, Dr. Hennessy.

"The kids were talking about going over to his house today to beat him up," Daisy says, "but I went all Gandhi on them, and everyone decided to let Sam take one for the team, passive resistance style."

"Good work, Peanut. You too, Sam."

"My people texted me that MTV is fully onboard to plan and help sponsor Daisypallooza. It's going to be on October 11th," she says.

"That's only two weeks away," I say.

"I know. They're cutting it pretty close. But they want to do it before the weather turns bad in the Northern States."

I guess that makes sense.

"How are they going to promote and market something so big in such a short amount of time?"

"They're not. We are," she says.

"We are," I say, flatly.

"No big deal, Dad. We're just going to tell people about it on the site."

"Aren't they a little concerned about turn out?"

"Dad, did you see how many people showed up last weekend? More than four times what the organizer had originally estimated. And we have almost fifty million followers across the country now."

"Some are international," Sam says.

"Not enough to make a real difference to Daisypallooza attendance," she replies snippily.

"I know," Sam says. "I'm just saying it's cool that people in other countries are following us now, too. Some of the programming guys want to set up a branch in Bangalore. Can we do that, Dad?"

"I supposed we could," I say. "I don't know anything about non-profit laws in India, but we could float the idea to some of our people."

"So, it's apparently going to be forty concerts in twenty-eight States over the course of three days. And MTV wants to fly me to three or four of the biggest venues," Daisy says. "Please, can I, Dad?"

"What? Where are these biggest venues?"

"One's in upstate New York. Another's in the desert outside of Las Vegas. And the last one is somewhere between Los Angeles and San Diego. MTV still isn't sure if trying to fly me to the one outside of Austin is going to be too rushed."

"How are you going to get to all of those places in three days?"

"They have a private jet."

"Awesome," Sam says. "Can I go too?"

"Maybe," Daisy replies.

"Tell them we'll consider it, but only if all four of us go together – Sam, you, your mom and me."

"I don't know if there's enough room in the jet."

As if she knows anything about how much room there is in a private jet.

"If there isn't, they'll just have to get a bigger jet. Put your foot down on this one. It's the only way you're going to get to go," I say.

I'm already feeling guilty that I appear to have committed to this concert hop before I've even spoken to Catelyn.

***

When Catelyn comes home, I ask everyone to join me in at the kitchen table.

"Did we do something wrong," Sam asks, carrying his iPad.

"No, Honey," Catelyn says and then pauses, "Wait. Jack, did they?"

"No, nobody did anything wrong. Where's Daisy?"

"One sec," she yells from the living room. We wait. As usual.

"Look, guys," I say when everyone has taken a seat, "we're up to almost ten million in the central accounts, so we've got to make some sort of…"

"No, we're not," interrupts Sam.

"No, we're not what?"

"We're not at ten million in the central account. See?" he holds up the iPad. "Now it's almost thirty-three million."

Good lord.

"When did that happen?"

"When was the last time you checked?" Sam asks.

"Late this morning."

"So, I guess it happened sometime between late this morning and when I checked now," Sam says.

I roll my eyes, open my laptop and head to the Stu-widdu site.

"The t-shirts and hats are online," I say.

"Finally," Sam says.

"We did thirty million in t-shirt and hat sales?" Catelyn asks.

"No," I say, "but they are selling well. We'll probably clear a million in web sales overnight, after cost and fees. No, the extra thirty-million came in through sponsorships. It looks like it's still mostly contributions from private citizens."

I browse the list. There are contributions that range from ten thousand dollars to two million. No, wait. I see one for three point five million. Holy cow.

"Daisy, did you post anything today, from school or home, calling for contributions?" I ask.

"No. I mean I always thank everyone and call out some of the local branch donation projects, but my post this afternoon was about Daisypallooza."

"Maybe the message is just gaining momentum, Jack," Catelyn says. "Anyway, this is a good thing, right?"

"Yeah, I mean, of course, it's a good thing," I say, "but we need to keep the outbound donations in some kind of balance with the incoming contributions. I mean, we've got a regional tracking system to show contributors what we're doing with their money, which in retrospect might not have been the best idea, I guess. Because we can't let the money just pile up. If we do, people will get frustrated and it's going to slow the momentum. I'd originally called us all down here to talk about what to do with the central account when I thought it was only at ten million dollars. Now it's getting critical. We need to find some good to do with all that money. Like fast."

"We've got Daisypallooza coming up," Daisy says.

If I hear Daisypallooza come out her mouth one more time... But she's excited. I get it. What twelve-year-old wouldn't be busting out of her skin about an upcoming series of concerts named for her?

"Daisy," I say, "Daisypallooza isn't going to use any of the central fund money. MTV is covering all of the deposits and set-up costs. We're just taking a share of the profits, which means even more contribution money. No, we've got to think bigger. Bigger things to do to make the world a better place."

"Why do we have to be the ones to figure this out?" Daisy asks.

"Who else is going to do it?" I respond.

"How about we let the people that follow the sites come up with ideas, too?" Daisy asks. "I mean, so far we've been letting branch moderators decide where to make donations. What if we set up some kind of interface that lets everyone that follows the sites submit requests for donations?"

"And we put in a process to qualify these requests on the front end like they need to be associated with a 501 (c) company or something, so we don't get flooded with a bunch of idiots 'can you donate me a million dollars' requests," Sam adds.

"I guess that could work. Sam, I assume there's no problem having your guys set this up?"

"Easy," he says.

"So where do we start?" Daisy asks.

"First, let's post something to the moderators. We want their buy-in before we start talking about this with the whole follower base. Sam, run the concept by your developer friends, too. Once we've rounded up some initial feedback, assuming there are no hitches, then Daisy can do a blog post with a simple explanation of the idea and outline the rules."

"So, what? Like, tomorrow night?" Daisy asks.

"Why tomorrow night? Don't you think we need a little more time to get our heads around this?" I ask.

"Plan, plan, plan," Daisy says. "That's the problem with grownup people. You just can't seem to let go and run with anything. And didn't you say that the money in the central account is piling up and we need to get started on a solution fast?"

I did say that, yes. I don't bother protesting further. I know Sam and Daisy will get feedback from their respective groups within hours. We might as well go full steam ahead.

"So, tomorrow night?" she asks. "It's Friday tomorrow so people will be able to come up with suggestions over the weekend."

"Fine. Tomorrow night."

The kids get up and go back to their stuff.

"Fifteen minutes, then pajamas and brush teeth," Catelyn shouts after them.

"Wine?" I ask Catelyn.

"We've been drinking at least a bottle of wine every night for the past three weeks. Do you think we're drinking too much?"

"I don't think we're drinking nearly enough. I really didn't think taking time off from work was going to be this busy," I say.

"And weird," Catelyn replies and opens a fresh bottle of Cabernet.

"Yeah, weird too. A whole lot of weird."

Chapter Twenty-eight

"All my guys think the whole thing about opening up donation requests is a good idea," Sam says, scooping dry cereal from a Tupperware bowl with a plastic spoon.

"The moderators, too." Dry Rice Krispies drop from Daisy's overfull mouth when she speaks.

"Sounds good," I say. "Daisy, I'll outline the stuff like we talked about, and we can discuss it before you write your post tonight, okay?"

"Okay. Did you see any news vans outside, Mom?" Daisy asks.

"No. Why? Do you have something to say?"

"Not really," she says glumly. "I was just wondering."

"Honey, don't get sad," Catelyn says. "The national news can't cover you every morning. Think of all the poor kids who didn't have any reporters scrambling to talk to them – twice – in the past six days."

Catelyn looks at me, some variation of I-told-you-so, like it's my fault that Daisy's becoming a media junkie. I hold my hand up and nod a few times, nonverbally communicating that I'll have a talk with her.

Our ride to school reinforces what was indicated by all of the private citizen contributions over the past thirty hours or so. There is obviously a colossal rift developing within the families of people who capitalize on the broken financial system for personal gain. It's possibly coincidental, but the Mahoney practice of spray-painting intra-family slurs on the fronts of McMansions seems to have caught on. There's been progressively less toilet paper and more graffiti as the week has moved forward.

We see MY MOTHER LOVES MONEY MORE THAN SHE LOVES PEOPLE scribbled across the side of a huge house on a corner lot. Then more doghouses. Someone with a flag of a doghouse, which I haven't seen before, making me wonder if another website is trying to horn in on the money-making potential of our logo. Whatever. We can figure it out, and Daisy can eventually shame them back into trying to make money off of their own ideas.

We pass YOU CAN'T TAKE IT WITH YOU, BUT I STILL WANT YOU TO GO on our right. And more doghouses. As we approach the street before the school, we see MY WIFE IS A SLUT scrawled in thick white letters across a red brick house by some idiot who has obviously missed the point of what's actually happening around the neighborhood.

***

After dropping off the kids, I park in front of a local coffee shop around the corner from their school. It's not one of the big chains. In addition to a doghouse on the sidewalk outside of the entrance, there is a poster taped to the front window with a hand-drawn, green dollar sign in gold trim on it, nested inside one of those red circles with a line slashing diagonally through the center, indicating NO something.

Now, what does that mean? We don't take money? I walk in the door and up to the counter.

"What's with the poster on the window?" I ask the barista.

"Are you corporate?" she asks, ignoring my question in lieu of her own.

"Am I corporate what?"

"Like, do you exploit the rigged financial bureaucracy for your own personal gain?"

Now, who would ever say yes to that? It feels like she's asking if I've accepted Jesus Christ as my own personal savior. Same kind of creepy.

"No," I reply. "Why?"

"Because we don't serve corporate swine. That's our new thing," she says and adds sweetly, "Now, what can I get you this morning?"

Not all micro-businesses are intelligent.

"Hold up. You don't serve rich people? Your lattes cost six dollars. Poor people can't afford to get their coffee here."

"We serve rich people. We just don't serve corporate slime. Like corporate bankers and lawyers, investors, people on Wall Street... those kinds of rich people."

"How do you know the difference?"

"We ask."

"How do you know people are telling the truth?"

"We expect people to be honest."

"Do you think corporate swine are honest?"

"Uh, no. I don't think so, no."

"Well, who else would lie when you ask if they're corporate swine?" The girl thinks for a minute.

"Look, it's not my policy. I just work here."

"Hey, I'm kind of vested in everything that's going on, like, in the country right now," I say in a disarming tone, "and I'm trying to keep my finger on the pulse of a few different things. So, is it okay if you tell me whose policy this is?"

"Jack, the owner."

Did she just address me directly, using my first name? I don't know her. Does she maybe remember me from the news clip?

"Excuse me?"

"What? I said it was Jack's policy. Jack. That's the owner's name. He came up with the policy."

"Oh. That's my name, too," I say. Kind of a surreal moment there. My nerves are definitely shot.

"Oh," she looks at me for a few seconds, kind of like I'm damaged. "Well, it's a very nice name. Do you want a coffee or something?"

"Yeah, I'll have a large black coffee, please." I'm still curious, and since there's no one behind me in line, I figure she has no way to avoid it when I try to continue our prior conversation. "Do you have any idea what Jack the owner was thinking when he decided to make this coffee shop a no rich people zone?"

"Corporate."

"Sorry, a no corporate people zone."

"I guess he was thinking that it would help differentiate us from the chain shops, you know?"

"By excluding people with enough money to buy your expensive coffee? Isn't that kind of, you know, stupid?"

"Jack's my boyfriend."

"Sorry, no offense to Jack. I'm just trying to figure this out."

"We don't exclude people with money. We exclude corporate parasites. There's a difference." She walks back to the counter, puts my

coffee down in front of me, looks me in the eye. "Let me put it this way —
in case you're not up to speed with our changing market — every wife
who leaves her banker husband, every husband who leaves his
corporate attorney wife, every kid who hates their financially-myopic
parents, that's our target market. We want to give those people a reason
to come to our shop rather than one of the big chains. Stupid? Our sales
have almost tripled over the last few days."

"But we're the only ones in here right now."

"The next yoga class doesn't let out until nine. And you should see
how packed we are after school."

"Okay, I get it. Clever. I'm thoroughly impressed," I say. I mean it.

"We do what we have to do to survive," she says, also meaning it.

"That's exactly what I love about small business," I say and put a
dollar into her tip jar. "But do you, you know, give anything back?"

"What do you mean?"

"I mean, you're really capitalizing on what's happening in the
neighborhood…"

"Across the whole country," she corrects me.

"Right, across the country, but you know what the whole message
is about, right?"

"Sure, ostracizing corporate scum."

"I think it's more about shifting the social mindset from self-interest
to helping other people," I say.

"Sure," she says.

"So, you're leveraging the message. Are you doing anything to help
other people? Anything to make the world a better place?"

"You'll have to talk to Jack," she says. "I just work here."

***

By the time I get home, Greenburg's brief on the non-profit bank has
made it to my Inbox, delivered in less than half the time promised. I
skim the eight pages, and it seems to confirm my original premise that
a non-profit bank needs to do everything that a for-profit bank does,
only without making any money. I guess the pitch to the friends of one
of the richest people in the world, if he ever calls back, needs to focus
on the magnanimity and market impacts of a bank that doesn't make a

profit, as opposed to any structural limitations.

Sometimes I think I'm off my rocker, all the counterintuitive things that I seem to be asking people to do. But, taking a cue from Daisy, I decide not to overthink or over-plan this potential conversation and instead just to think on my feet and let whatever's going to happen, happen. Ten minutes later, right after I closed my eyes on the couch, my cell phone rings.

"Jack Sullivan," I say drowsily.

"Jack, I'm glad I caught you. Look, I've got a few friends on the line. We want to talk to you about this non-profit bank thing." Like all uber-rich people, I imagine, he doesn't bother to introduce himself. But I think everyone in the country would probably know his voice, so I let it slide. And he's using my first name now, which I try to take as a positive sign.

"Sure," I say, yawning inappropriately, as I often do when I'm nervous. "Hi, everybody." There are no replies to my "Hi."

"Okay, so let me set the stage here. We all read Daisy's post. Hell, aside from me it was directly addressed to two of the people on this call. And we know all about your Stu-whatever website – what it's tracking. Candidly, we don't really like what it's tracking, about where all the wealth goes. But, anyway, we also see what you're trying to do for the country, which we all do really like. Or, at least our children and grandchildren like it. And, look, we've also got some bankers on the line here. And your daughter's been shoveling out some pretty harsh words about how bankers make their money. How bankers have made us all a lot of money. So, it's not all roses and sunshine on this side, you understand. But the fact is, we've all made ten times more money than we would ever need to continue our lifestyles for the next fifty generations, and we recognize that fact. And we all struggle with how to give back, you know, in the right way. Not just handouts, but something that's going to make a practical difference in the world. Teach a man to fish, that kind of thing. A way to invest in real change. The way we made a practical difference in our respective markets when we were in business. And I think, deep down, we all agree with you that money is a commodity product. And people who lend it, or use it to buy and sell companies, or trade on futures and derivatives markets, really don't deserve to be the rich ones in this country. And we sure as hell agree that corporate law firms and accounting firms shouldn't be making the kind of profit that they do."

"Hey!" says someone on the line.

"Come on, Frank. You know it's true. So, what I'm saying is we've made our wealth, and we recognize the problems in the financial system. And we're open to hearing about ideas that can change that system, despite how good it's been to us personally. And if the ideas are good, then maybe we can help make them happen. Make sense, Jack?"

"Sure."

"Does anyone on the call object to anything I just said?" Silence. "So, Jack, the floor is yours."

"Okay, thanks. So, I assume everyone knows how a bank works?" Silence. "I mean practically, like taking in other people's money, then lending and investing that money at a profit that's greater than the interest or returns that they pay to the people who supplied the money." Still nothing but silence on the line. "Well, what I'm suggesting is that we create a bank that does exactly what other banks do. But instead of making a profit on the delta between interest and returns paid versus the interest and return on investment generated, our bank breaks even. No profits, no bonuses to the executives. All of the money that would typically go to profit and executive compensation is essentially reinvested in the bank so that it can maintain lower interest rates and greater returns for its customers."

"Why the hell would we do that?" asks someone on the line.

"Mostly because ninety percent of America's gross domestic product comes from small businesses, I mean companies with less than twenty people. And banks have a stranglehold on these small companies. Between interest on credit lines and mortgages and other financial devices, they're sucking the lifeblood out of these companies. And if we don't find a way to reinvigorate these companies so that they can thrive, then there's no way that we can count on our country to survive. In the long run, I mean."

"Are you part of some radical nationalist group?" asks another voice on the line.

"What? No. What? Look, our country, someone else's country, it doesn't really matter to me. My point is, there are a lot of little companies out there struggling every day to survive. And they need a break. And it's not charity. It's just getting rid of a bloated, bloodsucking parasite that these small businesses should never have had to deal with in the first place. Banks are absolutely necessary, parasites though they may be. Lend money, make interest and returns, sure. But how about we don't let them get filthy rich off of it? It's only gonna kill the host. And that's just short-sighted."

"One non-profit bank isn't going to make enough of a difference to change the way things work," says another nameless person on the line.

"No, but a big enough non-profit bank can take the legs out of all the other banks. Make them non-competitive, steal the people who give them money in the first place. Steal the people who they lend money to. You all know how much infrastructure these banks have, how much profit they make. Properly executed, the right non-profit can create a freefall in the banking market. And ultimately what's the damage? That banks don't make huge profits? That executives that don't make huge bonuses? That's the only thing that changes. Not as many McMansions. The sales figures for expensive foreign cars drop. That, and small companies have a better chance to survive. Which is something that you can all be proud of."

"You know, if this worked," says another nameless voice on the line, "I bet we could also design a different type of market to trade stocks and commodities, one that eliminates the huge profits that go to traders and brokers."

"I bet we could do the same thing for corporate law firms and accounting firms. Break the market from a competitive perspective and suck the profit out of those guys, too," says another nameless voice.

"Hold it." Yet another nameless voice. "Are you talking about socializing legal and accounting services?"

"This has nothing to do with socialism, idiot," says the immediately prior nameless voice. "We'd be the ones funding all of this, and we'd be doing it voluntarily. If we don't like it, we take the funding back. We're in complete control. Nobody tells us what to do. We're just doing it without the motivation to make a profit. Like a charity."

"The voluntary distribution of wealth," I say.

"What?"

"The voluntary distribution of wealth. When people voluntarily distribute their excess wealth, they retain all of the control. It's just that they decide to use their wealth to make the world a better place, rather than using it to generate more wealth. It's the only way to rebalance how capitalism leads to concentrations of excess wealth. It's the capitalistic solution to what socialism and communism have never been able to accomplish."

"What are you, some kind of dime store philosopher?"

"I'm the guy that back-room engineered the massive social revolution that's happening in our country right now. I assume you've seen all the doghouses in your neighborhood. You might want to listen to me."

Sometimes these uber-rich people appreciate a little moxie, I tell myself.

"Alright. Settle, everybody. We can talk about this offline." I assume by offline he means without me on the phone. "Jack, we appreciate your time. We'll circle up on this stuff and get back to you, okay?"

"Sure," I say and hear their discussion start up again as he drops my line.

It's possible I could have handled that last part better.

***

After I pick the kids up from school, Daisy and I sit in the living room talking about the rules for allowing followers to submit donation requests. It's pretty simple, but I want to make sure she explains everything correctly when she writes her post, so we don't get flooded with inapplicable requests that jam up the lists. We're midway through the discussion when her cell phone rings.

"Who is it?" I ask.

"I don't know," she says. "I don't have any contacts stored in my phone except you and mom. Can I get it?"

"Be quick," I say, and she answers the phone.

"Hello? Oh, hi, Bruce!"

She's public Daisy again, on a comfortable first name basis with some MTV executive or a reporter.

"Um-hum, no. But my mom and dad do," she says. "I will! What? Oh, I don't know. One sec," she turns to me, covers the handset, "When are we going to be at the upstate New York concert?" she asks me.

"I have no idea."

"We have no idea," she says into the phone, pauses. "Okay, let me check. One sec." She turns to me. "Do you think we can go out to the other venues first and finish up in New York?"

"Again, I have no idea. I mean, I don't see why not, but maybe you should talk to the MTV people who are going to be flying us around. They might have some kind of plan we don't know about."

"Good idea," she says to me and uncovers the handset of her cell phone. "Bruce? Hey! Listen, I don't think that will be a problem, but can I talk to the MTV people first to make sure they don't have other plans? I know… I know… I know… Yeah, I know, but they're flying me around the concerts for a couple of days so I probably ought to check with them… Yeah, I know… I know… I understand… Sure, I'll check with them right away. Can I call you back on this number? Sure… super, thanks. Bye!" She turns to me again. "Sorry."

"No problem. Where were we?"

"You were telling me about the rules for opening the floodgates on donation requests from the follower base."

"Right. Who was that on the phone?"

"Bruce Springsteen."

"Seriously?" Whoa.

"Yeah, he wanted to be at the concert when I'm there, so he was asking about my plans for the upstate New York show."

"Oh," I say. Wow.

"Hey, Dad? Can I make a quick call to the MTV people to see if they know when I'll be at the upstate concert? Bruce seemed pretty worked up about the schedule so I should probably get back to him sooner than later."

"Yeah. I mean, he's the boss."

"Is that sarcastic? I mean, are you mad that I'm interrupting our talk? It will only take a minute."

"No, Peanut," I say. "Absolutely not. The Boss is what old people like me and mom call Bruce Springsteen. Go ahead and square up your plans."

I'm thinking about how much money someone could probably make selling Bruce Springsteen's private phone number, which is stored in Recent Calls on my daughter's iPhone. Daisy walks into the kitchen to make her calls and Sam walks in from the other direction.

"Amazon is on the phone," Sam says.

"What, like Jeff Bezos?" I reply, and then I realize that Jeff Bezos might actually have been on my call this morning.

"Who's Jeff Bezos?" Sam asks.

"The guy who made Amazon."

"Oh, yeah. Well, I don't think it's him."

"No?"

"No. It's a girl. She wants to talk about expanding the apparel assortment for Daisy's Doghouse and Stu-widdu."

"Well, let her talk to Daisy."

"I think Daisy's on the phone, probably with someone like Taylor Swift or Vladimir Putin or Jesus. Maybe we shouldn't interrupt her."

"Okay, give it here," I say and take the phone, "Hello?"

"Hi. Who am I talking to, now?"

"Daisy's father. Also, the primary holder of our Amazon account. How'd you get my home number?"

"It's the only contact number that we have for the account."

"Oh, yeah. I was worried that you guys would cold call me if I added my cell phone to the account. My bad, that's obviously not Amazon's style."

"Yeah, I'm not really on the consumer sales side of the business. I just wanted to talk about expanding your product assortment."

"Why?"

"Well, Mr. Sullivan, your unit sales have broken pretty much every record at our company in terms of volume. But you've really only had one product in three sizes. The red doghouse, I mean. And yesterday we launched one hat, in one size, and one t-shirt, in male and female cuts, three sizes each."

"Okay."

"Well, we sold out of all of the apparel in seven hours. But don't worry. It was back in stock this morning."

"Okay. This is all good, right?"

"Sure, it's awesome. But it seems like your brand commands a lot of selling power, right?"

"So it seems."

"Yeah, well frankly, you need more stuff if you're going to take advantage of all that selling power, don't you think?"

"I guess that would help."

"So, my team sources the fashion merchandise sold by Amazon to consumers — or to other companies like you — who resell it on your own sites. And there are a ton of us here who really love the whole Daisy and Stu-widdu thing, you know?"

"Really?"

"Totally, I mean your movement is the biggest thing to hit Seattle since Grunge. There are doghouses everywhere."

"I'm happy to hear it."

"Yeah, so me and my team, we'd love to come up with, like, a whole bunch of Daisy and Stu-widdu merchandise to put on your website. Actually, we already have come up with it, and I was just looking for your approval."

"Do you have product shots yet?"

"We have some merch images with your logos photoshopped in. And we've got some design sketches from the factories, some CAD drawings, that kind of thing. And, you know, you're sourcing this stuff through us, and it's our responsibility to manage the inventory, right? So, more styles aren't actually going to cost you anything, it will just give you more to sell."

"Yeah, I hear you, but we've got to make sure it's brand appropriate," meaning Daisy has to approve everything or she'll have a tantrum, "so can you send over whatever representations you have of everything you want to sell so we can approve it?"

"Sure, that's not a problem. I think we've got about two hundred and fifty alternatives, and we'd love to get the item count on your site up to at least one hundred, optimally two hundred. Is the e-mail associated with the account okay to send a Dropbox link?"

"Yeah. Send it as soon as possible, and we'll try to turn around the approval by later tonight or early tomorrow."

"That would be awesome, Mr. Sullivan. We look forward to hearing from you. And thanks for being an Amazon client. Oh, and can you thank Daisy from all of us, too? For making the world a better place?"

"Will do. Oh, and can you send samples of everything that we approve?"

"Do we have to wait for final approval until you see the physical samples?"

"No, I just want Daisy and my son to get some free merchandise."

"Not a problem. After you approve the styles, we can turn them around in about twenty-four hours and then send them to you overnight," she says. "You should have them by Monday."

I thank her profusely and say goodbye. By the time I pull up Outlook, her e-mail is sitting in my Inbox. I guess there was a pretty strong assumption that we'd be moving forward with this expanded product line idea.

"Daisy," I shout and forward her the link. "Can you hop on the family computer and click through the link on an e-mail I just sent you?"

"Why?"

"Because I need your help with something," I say. She is going to be thrilled.

"Can I do it on my phone?"

"No, you need to open the link on the computer. You need a bigger screen."

Seriously, what does it take to surprise this girl?

"Sam's on the family computer."

"Well, can you ask him to give you a turn?"

"I'm right in the middle of something. Can I do it later?"

"Sure," I say, deciding to forfeit the surprise factor in order to break her inertia. "Our apparel vendors just need your fashion input to make final decisions on a bunch of new Daisy clothes that we're looking to sell on the Stu-widdu site. It can wait."

I hear her jump up, run into the den and quickly plead Sam off the computer. I get up and walk in behind her.

"Oh, my god, this stuff is too cute! They're going to make this? Can we buy some of it?"

"You have to select about two hundred styles. Do you think you can do that tonight? If so, this stuff can be on the web site sometime next week. And they're sending samples."

"I'm on it," she says happily. "If we launch these this week, people can get them delivered before Daisypallooza!"

An hour later she's approved two hundred styles, having asked for Sam's help on the male products. She gives me the thumbs-up, I log-in and e-sign the release, and she goes up to her room to write the blog post inviting donation requests from the entire follower base.

Chapter Twenty-nine

A couple hours later Daisy wakes me up on the couch with a shove.

"Did you read my post?"

"When did you finish it?" I ask groggily.

"Just now."

"Yeah, it was great. Nice work."

"You didn't read it. You were asleep."

"So, why'd you ask me?"

"Can you just read it, please."

I get up from the couch, shamble over to the computer.

"It is great," I say. "Did Sam get the donation request interface working?"

"I don't know."

"Well, if he didn't, and you just released this, then there's going to be some frustrated people clicking on the link in your post."

"Sam!" she yells.

"What?" Sam yells back, from the den.

"The donation request interface?! Is it live?!"

"We could have just clicked on the link," I say, and we do. We're taken to the donation request interface, which appears to be working since there are already twelve, no fifteen, no twenty requests, and counting.

"Yeah," Sam shouts back from the den, and Daisy tells him to never mind, then thanks him.

She and I look at the donation requests coming in at maybe twenty or thirty a minute. The post's only been live for like fifteen minutes. But they're all small donation requests—three hundred dollars for art supplies, eight hundred dollars to fix a broken heater, five hundred dollars for textbooks, that kind of thing.

"Are you seeing a trend, here?" I ask Daisy.

"Yeah, there's a lot of requests, but they're all pretty small. I don't know how we're going to put fifty million to work on the back of this stuff."

"Right. Good point," I say. "But did you also notice that nine out of ten of these requests are coming from teachers or social workers? And it's all stuff for the people who they help on a day-to-day basis."

Wow, I think. Education and social welfare budgets look pretty tight from where I'm sitting.

***

By noon on Saturday, we've had a little over ten thousand requests. The protocol that we put in place automatically approves all but a couple hundred, based on simple criteria like valid non-profit registration numbers, non-duplicate request names or URL's, donation size... that kind of thing. Of the requests rejected by the automatic approval system, we push through all but a few dozen. And the ones that don't make the cut are either typos – like I don't think anyone was really asking for a million dollars for hot breakfasts at a private school – or ridiculous – like I don't think ten thousand dollars for new basketball sweat suits is a reasonable request.

All in all, it's a pretty good hit rate. Not as many people trying to take advantage for personal gain as I'd originally expected when we opened up donations to the public. Still, it hasn't yet been twenty-four hours since Daisy' last post.

The other thing that's hard not to notice is that over fifty percent of these requests seem to still be coming from teachers. And social workers are coming in at a not too distant second. These people, who struggle to make enough money to live a normal life in today's society, are asking for money that can be used to help other people. If only we could find a way to make this grassroots passion for helping human beings contagious within the wealthier circles. But I suppose that's exactly what we're trying to do with the sites. Still, it blows my mind that people with so little material wealth – inadequately compensated, likely strangled by student loans and mortgages – are the same people who care so desperately for others in need.

My reverie is broken by the buzz of my cell phone.

"Jack, it's me." My uber-rich friend.

"Hey," I say.

"Okay, right to it. If we were to set up this kind of non-profit bank that you explained, you don't have any silly ideas that you're going to run it, do you?"

"Well," I say, "since you're asking me so nicely, sure, I'd be happy to run it."

"Errr, no," he says, sounding genuinely awkward, which is probably a first for him, "What I meant was…"

"I know what you meant," I say. "I was making a joke. In no universe would I ever want to try and run a bank. That's not my thing."

"Ah, funny. Nice work. You got me," he says, clearly relieved. "I'm very glad to hear you say that, Jack. We were a little worried."

"I'm happy you're happy," I reply. "You do realize that none of this conversation is particularly flattering to me, right?"

"Sorry. But I had to make sure there were no misconceptions about your involvement in this thing."

"It's your money. You're voluntarily using it as a bank. You guys are obviously in complete control."

"Good. We're on the same page. Once we made the decision to move forward, everyone was concerned that we didn't vet your expectations," he says.

"Wait a second. You're saying that you guys are actually going to do this thing?"

"Not all of us. Some of the people on our call yesterday think you're an idiot."

"Thanks. I appreciate your sharing that with me."

"But enough of us like the idea to more than make it happen. No one needs bankers getting rich. And that whole banking market could use a major correction for the betterment of the world. Also, there are a few other markets that we think would benefit from a non-profit presence as well," he chuckles. "So, look, now that we've cleared the air regarding the fact that you don't have any delusions of managing this thing, we'd like your input. Maybe you could head up an advisory board?"

"Sure, that's fine. I've got some people in mind who might be good for this type of advisory board," I say, thinking of Professor Greenburg and his cronies.

"Good. Just make sure everyone realizes that it's only advice. No compensation, but we'll cover your expenses for the meetings and such. Oh, and we want to make Daisy the honorary chairperson of the bank. Good for publicity and to reinforce the fact that we're on the right side of things. Do you think she'd be up for it?"

"I'm sure she'd love it," I say, still dumbfounded by the conversation that I'm having.

"Great, great," he says. "So, it's Saturday now, funding isn't an issue, but there's a lot of legal and administrative red tape if we're going to be FDIC insured. The lawyers are working overnights, so we can probably be in a position to operate by late Monday."

"You're setting up an FDIC insured bank in two days."

"Correct. We know the right people. We don't really need FDIC insurance, but it's good cosmetics."

"Sounds reasonable," I say. "What about all of the workers?"

"We're not going to have any branches. It's going to be completely online and automated. There have been banks doing it this way for almost two decades. We're using a template site, so it just needs to be customized a bit. And we're sourcing the help desk overseas. A big group in Bangalore that does all of the banks, so they should be solid and ready."

"Okay." I think it might be nice to keep the work stateside, but don't say anything. Gift horse and all.

"So, we can confirm on Monday, but let's plan for the press releases to go out on Tuesday, so we've got some buffer."

"Press releases?"

"Of course, we've got our PR people on it now. They can reach out to Daisy to confirm some quotes, right?"

I shudder at the thought of public relations people trying to put words in Daisy's mouth. Good luck with that.

"What's it called?"

"What, the bank? Oh, right. I never told you. We want to call it the Daisy Federal Saving and Loan. That's not a problem, right?" he asks, and I nod into the phone. "Jack?"

"Sure, that's fine. I'll tell Daisy," I reply.

I guess it's just a drop in the bucket, really. More Daisy celebrity, this time helping small businesses get out from under the oppressive weight of the banking system. Suddenly I have an idea. A big idea to move money from the Stu-widdu central accounts and actually do some real good.

"Excellent. It has kind of a Fanny Mae, Freddie Mac, sound to it, no?" he asks.

"Yeah, it sounds great. Hey, before you hang up. Since you asked about this whole advisory board thing," I say, "can I run something by you? A project that I think the bank would be interested in…"

It only takes me about sixty seconds to explain.

"You know those are about the riskiest loans in the country right now, Jack," he says.

I tell him that I'm aware of that fact, tell him we can take it piecemeal, tell him that contributions from Stu-widdu can work as side collateral to mitigate the risk of bad debt. We go back and forth on a few points, but by the end of the conversation, he's fully on board.

After we hang up, I go back to my laptop and look at the site. Another couple hundred small donation requests in the past thirty minutes. I link over to the contributions page, and the money from dispossessed spouses and angry children continues to roll in at a brisk pace. I smile and think that with the new bank we can make this idea of mine work as an inside job. No need for outreach, just make it happen. That's so our style. I round up our family, and we sit down at the kitchen table.

***

"I've got some good news, some bad news, and some more good news," I say to the assembled Sullivans.

"The bad news first!" shouts Sam, enthusiastically, like he loves bad news.

"No, in the order I just said."

"Which good news first?" asks Daisy.

"What do you mean?" I ask.

"Well, you said there were two bits of good news, right? So, which bit are you going to tell us first?" Daisy asks playfully.

"But you don't know what either bit of good news is until I tell you, so what would it matter?"

"Give us the second bit of good news first!" Sam shouts.

"How about you guys just let me say what I'm going to say, okay?" The kids settle, and Catelyn looks at me with a curious grin. "So, the first bit of news is that a few of the wealthiest people in the country are going to make the non-profit bank happen."

"Yay," Daisy says in an enthusiastic, albeit room-temperature, voice. She means it, but this is just her standard level of excitement for surprises that end up being not directly about her. Sam, on the other hand, is beaming.

"They want to call it the Daisy Federal Savings and Loan," I say.

That cranks up the temperature on Daisy's response some.

"We did it, Dad," Sam says, his eyes welling up.

"We did it. They did it, I mean, the people who have the money to make it work," I say. "I'm just really, really glad that this is happening."

"So, what's the bad news?" Daisy asks.

"So, right, the bad news," I say. "And it's really not actual bad news, more of a luxury problem..."

"Just tell us!" Catelyn yells, more rapt than I'd noticed.

"Okay. It's just that contributions and donation requests are both pouring in at a very fast pace."

"Is the system working okay?" Sam asks.

"Bud, the system is amazing. It's working so much better than I ever thought it could," I say, and Sam nods his head. "The only problem is that the amount of money coming from contributions is out-pacing the amount of money needed to fulfill donation requests by about a hundred-to-one."

"So, it's the same problem we talked about this morning," Daisy says. "It's not really bad news if we already know about it. It's not really news, I mean."

"Fine. I just added it for context to set up my next piece of good news." I drum my hands on the table, dramatically. "I've got an idea. Something that we can do with the central account funds. Something that will move the money at a pace that's more in line with the contributions."

And I explain it to them, just like I explained it to my uber-rich friend. How it impacts the people who are asking for the donations.

How we can use the contact information that they provide when they make their requests. How we can associate it on an individual level with the people making contributions.

They get it. No major questions. This weird Sullivan family is fully on board. I list out specific jobs for Daisy and for Sam concerning their respective areas of expertise, and they excuse themselves, get to work.

"This is going to change a lot of lives, Jack," Catelyn says.

"I hope so," I say.

Chapter Thirty

The next morning Catelyn doesn't have to sell cash cards, and as we're not every Sunday church-going folk, we decide to have a family outing.

We drive about an hour west into Sussex County, towards the Pennslytucky border to an outfit called Astro Farm. It's a zoo, and it is awesome. Or at least Daisy and I think so. Sam is ambivalent. Catelyn is tolerant, especially when it gives us the excuse for a half-day road trip.

I discovered Astro Farm on a weekend eight years earlier, when the kids were two and four. Catelyn was on a yoga retreat in Cape May, part of her certification as a yoga instructor. My acquiescence to Catelyn's yoga instructor certification being one of the more controversial exchanges in our marriage. Only after she'd signed up, I'd found out that program cost was twenty-five hundred dollars and required her to do two hundred hours of yoga class, including four weekend retreats.

Sadly, dropping my two and four-year-old kids at their grandparent's place every time Catelyn was doing yoga was not an option. Subsequently, I was left to devise creative ways to entertain and exhaust my toddler children over several intermittent weekends. Astro Farm was one of the only good things that came out of the whole fiasco.

And Catelyn's certification, too, I guess. Whatever. Anyway, I was totally hoodwinked.

So, eight years ago, I Google "things to do with kids in New Jersey" and start checking through the lists. And, side note, there are some pretty awful "things to do with kids in New Jersey." At least for a single parent father with childcare skills that would rank on a par with the distant-single-uncle set. But Astro Farm was one of the good ones. We arrived expecting some sort of Star Wars theme zoo, but following a conversation with a worker, I found out that the family of ownership sports the surname "Astro." So, it's really just the Astro family's farm. No interstellar theme. But that took nothing away from the experience.

Deep Northwest New Jersey definitely has a mild *Deliverance* vibe. Same as South Jersey. But walk into Astro Farm, and you could be so many fathoms below the Mason-Dixon line. I imagine that a conscientious vegan would turn spastic fits if they happened to enter the lobby that so thoroughly celebrates taxidermy and the skeletal remains of slain animals.

And the fun doesn't stop there.

For a very reasonable price of admission, you can see a huge variety of dangerous wild animals, at remarkably close range, lounging in their natural habitats – if their natural habitats happened to be chain-link fence cages. But, seriously, I'm not knocking it. There's a generous amount of space in the cages, and the animals don't seem to know the difference. They're obviously fed well, and there's much more animal diversity within roaring range than they would ever experience in the wild.

And there's this concrete snake pit, also surrounded by chain link, where there are like several hundreds of live and likely venomous snakes squirming all over each other and around this hunk of dead tree in the center. Like something out of an *Indiana Jones* movie. But so incredibly real. Not the type of experience you get at a typical zoo.

The weekend after our first visit, the kids and I insisted that Catelyn join us for a second. Interested, though not necessarily in a good way, Catelyn walked with us through grounds that resemble a high school campus, but with basketball and tennis courts housing terrifically dangerous beasts instead of uncoordinated kids. But it was sunny, not too hot, and made for a pleasant, if not a little bit creepy romp, before the kids' naps. So, Catelyn became a fan as well.

Since then, Astro Farm has been a go-to for impromptu Sullivan day trips despite the fact that the kids are now almost a decade older.

We buy each of the kid's a flavored honey stick — blue for Daisy, yellow for Sam — as well as a bag of cracker-feed for the smaller animals. Then we set out on a long walking loop around the circumference of the zoo. It's almost October so the snake pit is empty, prompting a discussion about what happens to the snakes during the winter.

"They probably kill all of the snakes and freeze the eggs, then hatch them in the spring for a whole new mess of snakes each season," Daisy says.

Though obviously a very sweet girl, there has always been a certain heartlessness about Daisy when it comes to some types of animals. Like she's missing a very tiny piece of her soul. Maybe it's the carnivore in her.

"I think by the end of the summer, most of the big snakes have already eaten the smaller snakes. So they probably organize some kind of single elimination death match for the survivors, and let the last one live," I say.

"Two snakes enter! One snake leaves!" chants Daisy.

"Don't listen to them, Sam," Catelyn says, taking his hand and intentionally lagging behind us.

We continue to walk among the chain-link fenced lawns. As we pass a small and somewhat incongruous cage of metal bars containing a black panther, Daisy and I hear a harsh, cracking sound. As if the black panther were crunching on very loud Grape Nuts or gravel or something. I look over and then grab Daisy by the shoulders. I turn her to face the cage, point at the carcass of a hedgehog or warthog or other stiff-backed hog, the size of a housecat, which the panther is literally tearing to shreds with its claws and teeth.

I'm amazed this is really happening.

Daisy and I look at the cage, then at each other, and then break into wild hysterics. What an efficient system! They feed the dead animals to the live ones. Or at least that's what seems to be going on in this case.

Sam lets go of Catelyn's hands and sprints over to see what we're laughing at, and he is not amused. He's a much more conscientious child than his father and sister, a trait apparently inherited from his mother, who walks over and reacts similarly. She gives me a judgy look, takes Sam's hand, and they walk towards the hyenas twenty yards to our left.

"What kind of animal is that?" Daisy asks when we've calmed down.

"I think it's a panther," I say.

"Not the panther," she replies, rolling her eyes and pointing to a small sign that says 'Panthera Pardus, The African Black Panther.' "I mean, what kind of animal is the panther tearing to shreds?"

"I don't know. Maybe a hedgehog?"

"Is it weird that I'm thinking about bankers and lawyers right now?" Daisy asks with a giggle. I tell myself that a twelve-year-old sense of humor hasn't evolved to the point where it can discern boundaries.

"Yes. And don't go turning into a sociopath, Daisy," I say. I take her hand and steer us towards the hyenas. "Your mother would be furious with me."

We catch up with Sam and Catelyn and, in addition to it somehow being my fault, the scene with the panther has dampened the family's enthusiasm for the day trip. Though I'm unclear whether Catelyn is more disturbed by the panther's mangled animal corpse take-out or by how eerily funny Daisy and I consider it.

Regardless, we're only at the park another fifteen minutes before Catelyn and Sam vote to leave.

"What?" I ask as the kids buckle themselves into the back seats.

"We'll talk about it when we get home," Catelyn says. The ride home is no fun.

***

As the kids clamor out of the car and head into the house, Catelyn puts her hand on my arm, asks me to wait.

"Oh, come on. That was not my fault," I say.

"You encourage her. She's twelve, Jack."

"Seriously? You can't blame me for the panther thing. It's not like I threw a small animal into its cage for lunch. And it was hysterical. Did you see what was happening? It was like a Quentin Tarantino movie, what went on behind those bars."

"Would you take Daisy to a Tarantino movie?"

"Well, no," I say, conceding her point. "But Daisy has a special sense of humor, Cat."

"She has your sense of humor."

"Okay. I'll give you that. But she's a good kid. So what if she thinks that controlled scenes of ridiculous violence and gore are hysterical? Would you rather she be traumatized, like Sam?"

"I think that's the healthier reaction for a child, yeah."

"Let's not make such a big deal of it. It's not like she saw a person being eaten."

I don't share Daisy's comment about the scene making her think of bankers and lawyers. It made me cringe a little when she said it at the cage.

"Daisy is going through a lot right now. Obviously," Catelyn says. "Can you imagine what all of this celebrity is doing to her head? Do we really need her exploring the dark humor of nature, too?"

"We talked about this. She's handling it well—so much better than I could ever have imagined. Not that I ever imagined this."

"You don't know how she's handling it," Catelyn insists. "She doesn't even know how she's handling it. It's too big to get our arms around. And that means we've got to be careful, as parents, that she doesn't go off the rails. And encouraging a laughing fit in front of a living thing being torn apart isn't being careful."

"I've got to imagine the hedgehog was dead when they threw it in the panther cage, Cat."

"This isn't funny, Jack."

"Look, I hear you," I say. "Really. I'll talk to her. I'll keep an eye on it."

"Please do," Catelyn replies coldly and gets out of the car.

***

"The contributions are at one hundred seventy-two million," Sam yells from the den as I walk into the house.

"How about the donation requests?" I shout back.

"Just counting the ones that were auto-approved, we're at six-and-a-half million."

"Okay, thanks. How are the guys doing with building contact lists from the people asking for donations?"

"That was done before we left for the zoo," Sam shouts.

"Great. How many contacts have we got so far?"

"A little over a thousand!"

"And you guys were able to sync up the loan exposure for everyone on the list?" I ask Sam.

"Yeah. Did you want me to personalize the amounts on each letter?"

"No," I say. "I'm not exactly sure it's legal that you guys were able to dig up all of these outstanding loans so let's just keep it internal and use it for matching the contributions, but all on the down-low. We don't need that information going public."

"Okay!" he shouts.

"Thanks!" I shout back and walk upstairs to Daisy's room. She's sitting on the floor at the foot of her bed, pecking away at her iPhone.

"How are you doing with the message?" I ask.

"I'm finishing it now," she replies, not looking up. "You wanted it to be real simple?"

"Straight to the point," I say. "You're writing on the template Sam gave you, right?"

"Yeah," she says and hands me the phone. "Here. You can read it."

"Send it to me. I'll read it on my laptop."

"Okay."

"Hey, Peanut?"

"Yeah?" she asks warily.

"That whole thing at the zoo?"

"What about it?"

"Well, you weren't laughing because the hedgehog was getting eaten by the panther, right? I mean, the funny part wasn't the fact that the body of the hedgehog was being mutilated, right?"

"Geeze, Dad, I'm not a psycho. I thought it was funny because we were walking through a public zoo. And there's a bunch of little kids around. And here's this cute, fuzzy animal getting ripped apart by a giant panther. Like a Disney movie gone berserk. Which is exactly why you thought it was funny, too. Don't read too much into it. Has mom been talking to you?"

"Okay, good," I say. I ignore the question about her mother. "Just checking. Send me the file."

She says it's already been sent and I head downstairs.

I open the document and try to imagine myself receiving the e-mail. As if I were a teacher or social worker or similar type of generous person who recently submitted a donation request to Stu-widdu over the past few days. As if I were the one who asked for art supplies or winter coats or money to fix a heater, despite the fact that I am probably drowning in my own student loans or mortgage payments. As if I were one of those people who seem to care so much about everyone else, except themselves. It's a little hard to do, not only because these are better people than I am, but also because the letter is in a format designed to accommodate the personalization program:

Dear <INSERT DONATION REQUEST, USER FIELD, FIRST NAME >,

We would like to thank you for contacting STWWTW and asking that we make a donation to <INSERT DONATION REQUEST, TARGET RECIPIENT FIELD> for <INSERT DONATION REQUEST, TITLE FIELD> in the amount of <INSERT DONATION REQUEST, AMOUNT FIELD >. We are happy to inform you that <INSERT DONATION REQUEST, TARGET RECIPIENT> has received the donation that you asked for.

We have received thousands of donation requests from people just like you. People who have dedicated their lives to teaching, social work and other helpful fields. People that always seem to care more about others than they care about themselves.

And now we would like to do something for you.

We recognize how difficult it can be to keep contributing to the welfare of other people when so much of America is struggling under the weight of high loan payments. We don't think that a person like you should have to bear that burden alone.

Daisy Federal Saving and Loan, a newly formed, FDIC insured, not-for-profit banking organization would be honored to refinance all of your outstanding loans at a zero percent interest rate with a payment schedule that can be adjusted to your convenience. Please click on the below link and fill in the necessary information regarding any outstanding <Fx% INSERT \$'STUDENT LOAN'\$ OR \$'HOME MORTGAGE'\$ OR \$'STUDENT LOANS AND HOME MORTGAGES'\$ Fx%> loans applicable to your household. This is not a joke. <INSERT DFSL SITE LINK>

Additionally, we are happy to inform you that one of our contributors, who actually lives in your neighborhood, would like to further help you by providing the funds to pay down fifty percent (50%) of your current outstanding loans. The contributor's name is

<Fx% INSERT FIRST NAME, LAST NAME, SEQUENTIAL ZIP CODE MATCH CONTRIBUTOR, ADJUSTED TO WHOLE Fx%>. You are welcome to thank <Fx% INSERT FIRST NAME, SEQUENTIAL ZIP CODE MATCH CONTRIBUTOR, Fx%> by posting a message via the following link <INSERT 'THANK YOU' BOARD LINK>.

We hope this gift will help make every day a little happier for someone who has obviously given so much to the people around them.

See you at Daisypallooza!
Much Love,
Daisy and the gang at STWWTW

P.S. No givebacks. Just enjoy it and let someone else do something nice for you for a change. Geeze!

"What did you think?" Daisy asks as she walks into the kitchen.

"That'll do, pig," I say, reciting a movie line that made both of us cry a few years back. "That'll do."

She and Sam, who has appeared out of nowhere, each hug one of my shoulders from behind.

"Wait a second," Sam says. He runs upstairs and comes down with Catelyn a few seconds later.

"What's this about?" Catelyn asks, looking at Daisy's cheek still pressed to mine.

"Group hug," Sam says. He's often the coordinator of group hugs in our family.

"What's going on?" Catelyn whispers to me during our family embrace. I see she's noticed the tears on my cheek as her face presses against mine.

"Nothing," I say, sniffling. "I just feel like it's going to be a really good week."

"Don't think you're off the hook about that hedgehog thing," Catelyn whispers sweetly.

Chapter Thirty-one

Monday morning feels to me like the day before a major holiday, which is odd given the fact that I haven't worked in over eight months. We drive through the neighborhood, yards sporting doghouses, McMansions scrawled with graffiti. We don't talk much on the way to school. After dropping off the kids, I drive around the corner and park in front of the zero-corporate-tolerance coffee house.

"Are you corporate?" A twenty-something longhaired kid asks when I step up to the counter. He's wearing one of our original red doghouse logo hats as well as a matching t-shirt. Once again, I'm the only one in the shop.

"I was. Not anymore. Are you Jack?" I ask.

"Yeah," he replies, eyeing me like I'm from the IRS or something.

"This is your place?"

"Yeah. Look, mister, is there something I can do for you?"

"Just a large black coffee," I say.

"You're not corporate?"

"No," I say.

"Do I know you?" Coffee Jack asks, his back turned to me as he fills a cup with drip from a push-top vat.

He's probably seen my CNN interview clip from the event, but I'd need to contort my face into a knot for him to properly recognize me.

"I was talking to your girlfriend the other day. About this whole marketing campaign you've got working."

He turns around and places the cup in front of me. My expression is flat, and he adjusts his face to match.

"What about it?"

"Nothing. I think it's a good idea. How's business?"

"Look, man. You're creeping me out, here. What's the deal?"

"No deal. I'm just asking how your business is doing with the whole

Daisy's Clubhouse vibe you've got going on."

"Business is great. For the first time since we opened, business is great. What's it to you?"

"Are you donating any of the proceeds?"

"What?"

"I mean, you seem to be riding this 'Daisy train' pretty hard. I was just wondering if you're giving anything back."

"Dude, last week was the first time we ever turned a decent profit. We're crawling out of a hole here," he says.

"I get it," I say. "I'm just wondering if you're ever going to remember some of the ideas behind this movement you're leveraging to differentiate yourself in the market. Maybe do some good… when you're in a position to make it happen."

"What are you, the Daisy police?"

He walks away from the counter and pretends to rearrange some pastries on the glass-fronted shelves.

"It's about balance," I say and put three dollars on the counter because he forgot to charge me for the coffee. I turn to leave. "It's a dangerous thing, exploiting this type of a movement solely for personal gain. Seems pretty corporate, actually."

"Whatever, man," he says as I walk out the door.

As I walk to my car, I notice a woman wearing a yellow t-shirt with a red doghouse logo on the front. Not one of our original red shirts. And Daisy's extended line of apparel doesn't launch on the Stu-widdu site until tomorrow. It amazes me that some online vendor would try to hijack a brand like ours.

Well, I think, at least Daisy will have something to write about when she gets home from school.

***

Daisy's play practice ends a half hour later than Sam's cross country again, so I pick him up, and we head downtown to the smoke shop for Pokémon cards. It's unseasonably mild, so we sit at a table on the sidewalk outside of Smart World Coffee, me with a large black Mud, him with an apple juice. He picks a deck, and I open it, hold up one of the cards, back facing him, spin it quickly.

"Weedle," he says, naming the Pokémon. "Hey, one of the Scatch guys who helped with the personalization algorithm for the letter that Daisy's sending out tonight, he had an idea."

"Really," I say, pulling another card from the deck and flashing it in front of his face. "What was it?"

"Bulbasuar," he says. "He says we can take the same kind of list personalization that we used for the letters and do personalized printing with it."

"Okay. So?" I flash another card.

"Caterpie. So we can make personalized gifts for the people making contributions to Stu-widdu. He's got some cool ideas about what kind of personalization, too."

"Like…" I flash another card.

"Pidgey. Like bumper stickers."

"Bumper stickers?" Flip.

"Rattata. Yeah, they're cheap to make and cheap to send, and the contributors can stick them on their cars to show people that they're making the world a better place. You know how important it is for contributors to let everyone know that they're part of the solution. And you can put cool words on them."

"Like what?" Flip.

"Nidoran. Like 'MY OTHER CAR IS A JUNGLE GYM AT AN INNERCITY PRESCHOOL' or 'MY SUMMER HOME IS A KINDERGARTEN TEACHER'S STUDENT LOANS'. That kind of thing."

"Sam," flip, "that's an awesome idea."

"Vulpix. Thanks. I'll go ahead and set it up when we get home. Hey!" Sam shouts, pointing, "Is that guy wearing a green t-shirt with our logo on it?"

***

Daisy climbs into the back seat and, as expected, is furious when we tell her about the counterfeit Doghouse merchandise. I laugh, tell her to calm down.

"Are you kidding? Why aren't you more upset about this? These people are stealing money from our donation pool!"

"Easy, honey. It's not a big deal."

"Not a big deal?!"

"Daisy, who buys Doghouse merchandise?"

"What do you mean?"

"I mean, they don't carry our stuff at Target. It's not geared for consumption by the general public," I say.

"So, what does that have to do with it?"

"So, I'm saying, who is it that buys our stuff?"

"The people who go to our site. The people who believe in what we're trying to do. The people who read my blog… oh, right." She smiles broadly, an impossibly evil glint in her eye. "Those counterfeiters are dead meat."

"Send out the loan forgiveness letters before you eviscerate the counterfeiters," I say. "Oh, and you need to talk to the PR people at Daisy Federal Savings and Loan before you do anything else, so the press releases can go out in the morning."

I'm doubting that other parents make this type of laundry list for their twelve-year-old girls.

Chapter Thirty-two

On Monday night everything goes off pretty much without a hitch. There are a few dozen mismatches with the personalization letters, which are rejected by the system and need to be fixed manually. And the team moderators, who agreed to perform the final proofread, find a few incongruities that need to be revised, but the system is able to send out over thirteen hundred e-mails before eight pm. I'm impressed. I click on one of the letters to read the actual copy that the recipient will get, as opposed to just the template:

Dear Mary-Anne,

We would like to thank you for contacting STWWTW and asking that we make a donation to The Immaculate Heart Catholic School, for repairing school windows, in the amount of $1,250. We are happy to inform you that The Immaculate Heart Catholic School has received the donation that you asked for.

We have received thousands of donation requests from people just like you. People who have dedicated their lives to teaching, social work and other helpful fields. People who always seem to care more about others than they care about themselves.

And now we would like to do something for you.

We recognize how difficult it can be to keep contributing to the welfare of other people when so much of America is struggling under the weight of high loan payments. We don't think that a person like you should have to bear that burden alone.

Daisy Federal Saving and Loan, a newly formed, FDIC insured, not-for-profit banking organization, would be honored to refinance all of your outstanding loans at a zero percent interest rate, with a payment schedule that can be adjusted to your convenience. Please click on the below link and fill in the necessary information regarding any outstanding student loans applicable to your household. This is not a joke. Click here for link to DFSL website

Additionally, we are happy to inform you that one of our contributors, who actually lives in your neighborhood, would like to further help you by providing the funds to pay down fifty percent (50%) of your current outstanding loans. The contributor's name is Margaret Hennibalm. You are welcome to thank Margaret by posting a message via the following link: click here for link to the THANK YOU! page

We hope this gift will help make every day a little happier for someone who has obviously given so much to the people around them.

See you at Daisypallooza!
Much Love,
Daisy and the gang at STWWTW

P.S. No givebacks. Just enjoy it and let someone else do something nice for you for a change. Geeze!

Not bad, I think. I click over to the donations page. Paying down the student loans and mortgages has already moved a little over forty million dollars from the contribution pool in the past three hours. But this is just catch up. The numbers should regulate with donation requests as things even out going forward. We'll need to put in a bunch of new diligence protocols once the word leaks that people requesting donations are getting their loans paid down by half.

I let myself enjoy the magnanimity for a moment. These people, who were kind enough to reach out to Stu-widdu to ask for donations to make life a little better for whoever it is they help every day, who probably never ask for anything personally... these same people, so suddenly and unexpectedly, are going to be relieved of a huge financial burden.

It feels almost wrong to enjoy this so much.

QuickMule, the user name of the guy with the idea to send personalized thank-you bumper stickers to the Stu-widdu contributors, has already set up auto-pay from our central account. We're expecting the first batch of bumper stickers to be mailed tomorrow. He's now talking to Sam about personalized hats and t-shirts for the larger contributors, which I think is also a great idea. Anything that can be used by contributors to show everyone in their neighborhoods that they're on the side of making the world a better place is going to be a huge help in continuing to build momentum on the giver-side of our online community.

"Admiring your work?" Catelyn asks and sets a glass of Cabernet on the table in front of me.

"It's not my work," I say. "I just can't believe this is actually happening."

"People can surprise you, sometimes," she says. "It's amazing, really. The more wealthy people become, the more they seem to silo off their lives in these vacuums of twisted motivations. Make more money, buy a bigger house, get a nicer car. Keep up with the Joneses. And the people who get paid so much less, who spend their time helping other people on a grassroots, day-to-day basis – these are the people who are connected enough to recognize what's actually going to make other people's lives better. Able to recognize it enough to ask Stu-widdu for something specific to help. And now we've finally helped to put together something that can make life happier for these grassroots givers. I think it'll make life happier for the wealthy contributors, too. It's a good cycle, Jack. Maybe the wealthy people, they just needed something to care about."

"I think a lot of them still care more about distancing themselves from their estranged greedy spouses or their corporate-world parents than they care about where their contributions go," I say, "but that doesn't really matter as long as the money is moving. I just hope we can keep this giving trend going, regardless of how it's motivated. Some really good stuff is happening here, Cat."

We click glasses, walk over to the couch and turn on the television.

***

After dropping the kids at school on Tuesday morning, I see Sandy Mahoney hurrying across the street towards our house.

"Hi, Sandy," I say guardedly.

"I just got a call from a woman who works with autistic kids at the Lakeside school..."

"Kids with autism," I correct her.

"What?"

"The correct term is 'kids with autism', not 'autistic kids.' The latter makes it sound like the developmental disability part is more important than the kid part."

"Whatever," she says, waving me off. "I thought it was a prank call. This lady couldn't stop crying, I hardly understood anything that she said. How did she get my home number?"

"Is it listed?" I ask.

"Yes, I think so."

"Then she probably looked you up."

"This isn't funny," she says. "Why was she calling me?"

"Didn't you get an e-mail last night?"

"I get a lot of e-mails."

"Well, check your Inbox for something from Daisy's Doghouse," I say. "I think you just paid off half of that woman's student loans."

"I did?"

"Yeah."

"When?"

"Last night," I say.

I really thought people were more on top of their e-mail, especially with smartphones and all.

"Oh," she pauses, confused. "Why did I do that?"

"You made a contribution to Stu-widdu, right? So, Stu-widdu used some of the contribution money that it's been receiving as a donation to help pay down the woman's student loans. Ergo, indirectly, you paid down that woman's student loans. We just made it look a little more direct since we thought it would make both sides feel good."

"But why pay down that woman's student loans?"

"Because she helps people, Sandy. Christ, she works with special needs children, do you know how hard that is? And she must have asked Stu-widdu for a donation to help the kids she works with, something specific for the school or a family. So, Stu-widdu tagged her as a selfless person and wanted to do something nice for her as well. So, we paid off half her student loans. And because you're both in the same zip code, we allocated your contribution to paying down those loans. Make sense?"

"I should call her back," Sandy says, sheepishly.

"What did you do?" I ask, wide-eyed.

"Nothing. I mean, the lady identified herself on the phone and then started crying so much that I couldn't understand her. And I was worried that maybe Jimmy did something wrong. You know, accidentally. Like maybe Jimmy killed a special needs kid or something. So, I yelled at her and hung up."

"That's your response to the idea that your son might have accidentally killed a special needs child?" I ask incredulously. I wonder what kind of world Sandy lives in where this would be her first assumption. "What did you yell at her?"

"I told her she'd be hearing from my lawyer. And I called her a bad name," she says.

"Why—in addition to a hundred other questions I have—would you call her a bad name?"

"I don't know. I was upset. My nerves are fried. With everything that's happening – John moving out to an apartment in Manhattan, graffiti on my house, the whole town going nuts – I freaked out at the thought of someone taking Jimmy away from me, too. I couldn't stand the thought of him in some juvenile delinquent school."

Wow.

"Okay," I say. "Well, thankfully, I don't think this has anything to do with Jimmy killing an autistic kid..."

"Kid with autism."

"Thanks, kid with autism. But, just a side note, if that's the first thing that popped into your head, then maybe you want to get Jimmy in front of a therapist," I say "And, yes, you need to call the woman back."

"Can you call her for me? Please?" she asks.

These rich people never cease to amaze me.

"I could," I say, "but I think it would be better if you called her yourself. Just tell her there was a mix-up. You were confused as to who you were talking to. You were drunk or something."

"At ten-thirty in the morning?"

"It's more believable than you think," I reply. "And say how happy you are that your contribution could be used to make her life a little easier. Go ahead. You'll be happy you did it." She nods and turns back towards her house. "And make sure you make it very clear that DFSL is still refinancing her loans and that you're still paying down half of them. Tell her that first. I'm sure she's very confused right now. And apologize for calling her a bad name."

You idiot, I say under my breath. But I'm wondering how many of these little mix-ups are occurring across the country right now. Probably a good idea for Daisy to write a post when she gets home from school, just to clarify the situation for everyone.

***

On my way to pick up the kids from school, I pass the zero-corporate-tolerance coffee house. It's empty. But it's been empty the last two times I visited, so I can't attribute this lack of business to Daisy's seething indictment of counterfeiters—and other like-organizations—trying to capitalize on the Doghouse brand exclusively for personal gain. Like-organizations being organizations like Coffee-Jack's shop.

On the brighter side, I don't see a single piece of knock-off Daisy apparel on my drive to or from the school. Last night's post seems to have been effective.

When we get home, Daisy is quick to blast out a clarification post telling everyone that, regardless of any confusing interpersonal contact yesterday or this morning, each recipient is still getting their loans refinanced and paid down by half. She reminds contributors to please check their e-mail.

The DFSL press releases go out at four pm. By five there are a half-dozen news vans in front of our house.

"Can I, Dad?" Daisy asks from the downstairs bathroom where she's applying lip gloss.

"Sure," I say. "But try to mention the mix-ups you just posted about. Oh, and sneak in something on the counterfeiters and people trying to profit from our brand, if you can, to reinforce last night's post. And go easy on Daisypallooza!"

"Will do!" she shouts and walks out the door, still in her plaid school uniform. An hour later she walks back towards the house, beaming her usual public smile. Catelyn and I turn from the window and meet her at the front door.

"How'd it go, Peanut?" I ask.

"Good," she replies. "Stephanie, the CNBC reporter, was all shocked and disgusted when I told her about the counterfeiters trying to funnel money away from our sales… like they're stealing from the people who we're trying to help."

"Great. What else did they want to talk about?" Catelyn asks.

"Mostly the DFSL," she says. "They just wanted to know how I felt about the launch of a major not-for-profit bank, the historical significance and all that. I just told them that banks shouldn't be making huge profits when people who actually do some good in this world are suffering under the weight of enormous amounts of debt."

We're talking in the doorway, and I'm watching the news vans drive away. When the last one leaves, I notice John Mahoney standing at the end of our driveway. I sigh, excuse myself from Catelyn and Daisy, and walk towards him.

What a downer.

"Sullivan," he says as I approach.

"John," I reply. Sober and cleaned-up, he's looking much more like the flabby, stoic banker I've lived next door to for the past decade.

"What I want to understand is, what do you expect us to do?"

"I'm fine," I say, rolling my eyes. "How are you?"

"Seriously, Sullivan! What is it you expect us to do? You've turned us into pariahs. Mission accomplished. So, what now? Do you want everyone in corporate America to quit their jobs? You want to turn this whole country into some kind of Kibbutz or something?"

"First of all, John, I liked you a lot better when you were drunk and drenched in pee. Seriously. Think about that. Second, we didn't turn you into pariahs. It's not like everyone didn't always know that corporate America is greedy and self-interested. You even said it yourself the other night. We just brought it to the surface, made it a public thing, gave the other side some motivation and solidarity. The whole pariah thing happened naturally from there. And third, how am I supposed to know what you're supposed to do now? What? You all wanted to suck an unfair share of wealth out of society and simultaneously be treated like fine, upstanding citizens by the same people who you took from? Well, there's not a market for that anymore. Deal with it. Find a way to do some good."

Mahoney deflates, the robot banker being replaced by a petulant child.

"I don't know how to do any good," he whines.

"That's pathetic," I say. "You've got money. That means you've got more potential to do good than most people. You're just stuck in a world where all you care about is yourself."

"And what other people think of me," he adds with uncharacteristic insight, a little bit of the human being I talked to last week sneaking out of his psyche.

"Well," I say, not without some sympathy, "it looks like we took that part away."

He nods, shaken. And then he literally bursts into tears. Like an explosion of this deep-seated sadness and regret, coming up from some buried depth that I don't even want to think about. Our house can't be the only place in the country where this type of scene is playing out. I stick my head inside the front door, yell for the kids to go upstairs for a while. I actually yell straight into the faces of Sam and Daisy, who've been standing beside the half-opened door listening to the whole scene.

"Come on, guys," I say, now in a normal voice. "We need some grownup time."

They scamper up the stairs.

I take Mahoney by the shoulder and walk his uncontrollably sobbing body into the house, down the hall and over to the kitchen table. I sit him down in one of the chairs.

Catelyn goes to the Keurig to make him a cup of tea. She doesn't bother to ask what kind of tea he wants since he's still wailing like a professional mourner from the Middle East. She sets the cup in front of his heaving body and takes a seat opposite him, beside me. We wait.

After a few minutes, he calms down and looks at us.

"I don't know what to do," he says calmly, exhausted by his emotional outburst.

Catelyn puts a hand on his forearm, gives him a kind look.

"We're sorry you're in so much pain," she tells him.

"It's your fault," he says quietly. He can't help himself, so many years of being a jerk.

"No," Catelyn says with more compassion than he probably deserves. "It's your fault. I think the first step towards turning things around is to admit that. And not just to yourself. I think it would help for you to admit that to the people who you care about."

"They hate me."

"They're not going to hate you any more than they already do. If you try, I mean," Catelyn says.

"I can't quit my job. I don't know how to do anything else."

"We're not telling you to quit your job," I say. "Maybe just try to think more about other people when you're doing it."

"I'd get eaten alive."

"Then just do whatever you can, if the banking world is so cutthroat. And nothing's stopping you from giving back some of what you earn to make the world a better place."

"I think my wife has already given enough," he says, cough-laugh-sob.

"Extend yourself," I say. "You don't have to radically change your lifestyle, but you can give until you actually feel something. If people see you extending yourself, they're going to be more inclined to welcome you back. Believe me. And it might feel good after a while, too."

"Thank you, Jack," he puts his hands on his knees and shoves himself up from the seat. He extends his hand, and I shake it. "Thank you, too, ah… Mrs. Sullivan," he says awkwardly.

Seriously? Ten years next door and he doesn't even know my wife's first name? Way to ruin a moment.

Catelyn evens things up when he tries to give her a kind of half-hug, and she instinctively pulls away as if he has head lice. But she does grasp his shoulder, a combination move that provides a modicum of moral support and simultaneously keeps him at a distance. After only a few seconds—as awkward as if it could have been an hour—she drops her hand, and he walks out of our house.

"That fills up my quota of weird for the day," she says to me when he closes the door.

She walks into the dining room and yells that we need more wine. I ask her how much is left and she tells me only two bottles. I say I'll pick some up tomorrow. We watch a couple of Tuesday night television programs with the kids that night, and then Catelyn puts them to bed.

Before going upstairs, I check the Stu-widdu account balances. $175,743,200 in the Contributions account, negative $53,750,000 in the Donations account, $11,409,868 in web sales, ending net balance of $133,403,068. A little over one-hundred-thirty million difference, income and contributions versus donations. We're catching up.

My cell phone rings.

"Jack, it's me." My uber-rich friend. I wonder if he ever identifies himself on the phone.

"Hey, everything seems to be humming with DFSL. Nice work."

"Yes, thanks. Might turn out to be the best thing I ever did." I'd resent the fact that he doesn't say "the best thing we ever did," but since he's funded this thing with eleven digits of his own personal wealth, I figure I can let it slide. "Look, on that note, we're putting together non-profit legal and accounting firms focused on the small-to-medium sized business market. Smart guys, Ivy League, you know. Lots of rich kids graduating who are looking for an alternative to what their parents wanted them to do with their careers. Oh, and by the way, they can also be available pro-bono for your debt forgiveness people if they have questions about refinancing their student loans and mortgages. Nice thing, using the contribution money to pay down half of those loans. We'd like to do our part too."

"Cool. Great. I'm sure small businesses, as well as everyone involved in the loan forgiveness program, will be really happy to have access to that kind of resource," I say, not quite able to process the fact that wheels are now also in motion to take a crack at the parasitic legal and accounting side of the broken financial system.

"Indeed. So, we need Daisy to do a couple of posts, let her followers know about the legal and accounting firms."

"Okay, we're on it."

"Great. I'll send you the details, and you can work out the messaging with her," he says. "Next—and this will take some time and connections—I'm thinking about launching a whole new stock market. One where everyone gets a fair shake, not just the institutional investors."

"Wow."

"You betcha, wow. It will take some time, but in the long run, this could take the legs out of all the traders, brokers and fund managers who suck so much money out of the system. Fair deals for the little guys, you know? Shake off the parasites. Make the world a better place."

"It's a great thing, what you're doing. You know that, obviously."

"I'd say it's about time we correct this whole bastardized system that we've built. From the inside." I notice the "we" instead of "I" when he says it. "You give Daisy my best, you hear?"

I tell him I will, and we hang up. I'm going to sleep well tonight.

***

On Wednesday I drop the kids at school, pull around the corner and walk into the zero-corporate-tolerance coffee shop. Taped on the storefront window, very large, is a sign that reads "50% of all profits donated to STWWTW."

Coffee-Jack had a bad day yesterday, I assume. I walk in the front door, the shop empty aside from me, not unusual at this time. Coffee-Jack is behind the counter. He gives me an icy stare.

"Hey, man!" I say with an inordinate amount of cheer. "Just a large black drip."

He turns to pump the coffee into a cardboard cup.

"That was you, right? The Daisy post about people capitalizing on her brand," Coffee-Jack says, back still turned. "You really screwed me, dude."

"Explain," I say.

"I recognized you from the CNN interview after you left on Monday. I knew I'd seen you before. Stroke guy, right? From a week ago, Saturday. Daisy's father? What, did they find a cure for muscular dystrophy in the past nine days?"

"I like the new sign," I say.

"I'm so glad. It's not doing anything for me. Once I got tagged as the enemy after Daisy's post, I might as well be selling leprosy. A heads-up would have been nice before you, like, totally submarined me."

"Wow, man. Really?" I think about John Mahoney a couple weeks ago, before he spiraled. How he had this weird perspective that Daisy's site was an attack specifically targeted at himself. I guess small business people can be as blindly narcissistic as the greedy rich. "You seriously think Daisy's post had anything to do with a speck like this coffee shop? I know it can look tricky sometimes, because of the angles and all, but our world doesn't actually revolve around you. All over the country, we're trying to make the world a better place. And all over the country, I'm sure there were parasites like you trying to capitalize on our momentum to take and not give back. This had nothing to do with you personally, you idiot. You're just one of a million tiny little parasites."

"So, what? I'm not big and important, like the national coffee shop chains? Sure, I'm just a little guy, trying to make a buck on his own instead of working for the man. I thought that's what you guys were all about. And now you call me a bug?"

I pull back, not wanting to go off on him like I did Mahoney. This guy doesn't deserve the type of emotional dress-down I could give him. And he's already shot himself in the foot.

"Listen," I say, "you've got it all wrong. You're not a bug because you're a small business, you jerk. That's not what makes you a little person. You're a little person because you can't think about anyone but yourself."

"I was just spreading your message, man! It was brand exposure for you guys."

"And… you delude yourself. That makes you a bug too."

"You delude yourself!" he shouts incongruously.

I turn and walk out of the shop, leaving both the coffee and money on the counter.

***

When I get home, I check the accounts, see a huge spike in the donation requests, and it looks like a couple thousand have been flagged by the system for review. Word has obviously spread about loan forgiveness for people who make donation requests. Now everyone wants a piece of that action.

I click on one of the rejected requests. It's from a guy named Bill Waters in Cleveland, Ohio. He's asking for fifteen thousand dollars to be donated to a battered women's shelter so that it can be repainted. The shelter is registered as a 501 (c). I Google Bill Waters, Cleveland, Ohio. He is, of course, a painting contractor. I click on another rejected donation request. Sarah Ingham, asking for five thousand dollars to be donated to a community center in Kansas City, Missouri. Another 501 (c) nonprofit. The description of the donation just reads "Toys."

This is going to be a problem.

"Why can't people just be good?" Daisy whines from the front seat after I've picked the kids up from school and explained the issue we're having with questionable donations from seemingly self-interested parties.

"Unfortunately, this is pretty typical, Peanut. Every time someone tries to do something good on a large scale, there are going to be people who will try to cheat the system for personal gain. That's why systems get so complex. Look at what happened to capitalism. You've got a playing field that's about fair competition, right? And people try to cheat – they don't keep their word, they don't do what they say they're going to do – and so now you need rules. But people try to get around those rules so that they can continue not keeping their word or not doing what they say they're going to do, so then the rules get more complex to stop the cheaters. And then the cheaters try to come up with more ways to get around those more complicated rules, and the system of rules gets even more complex. It's a bad cycle. So that's how we end up with a system of rules that is so big and complex, parasites like corporate attorneys and accountants can get rich by just telling people how to get around the rules, or by defending people when someone else tries to break them."

"Whatever," she says, frustrated. "We're just trying to make the world a better place. Don't these people realize that they can bring the whole thing down by doing this kind of stuff?"

"I think a big part of the problem is that people don't look at how their cheating impacts the bigger picture, especially when they're cheating a large organization. Some little painting contractor in Ohio makes a deal with a battered women's shelter, right? The shelter gets a new paint job, the contractor gets paid to do the job, and it's only fifteen thousand dollars. We donate tens of millions. So who really gets hurt, he thinks? There's a million ways to delude yourself and try to justify it when you're doing something that, deep down, you know is wrong. That, unfortunately, is the world we live in."

"So what do we do?" Sam asks from the backseat.

"We put a stop to it."

"How?" Daisy asks.

"Well," I say, "just like we did to the greedy people capitalizing on the lopsided financial system, just like we did to the parasites who tried to leverage our brand and divert the money into their own pockets. We're going to ostracize them, publicly."

"How do you mean?" asks Sam.

"I mean we're going to call them out. Shame them. Let the user community know that this is a problem and publish the unapproved donation requests within each region so people can check up on their neighbors... and then let them police the situation themselves," I say. "Daisy, you can rip into this situation with a post this afternoon, right?"

"I can't wait."

"Well, wait a bit, because before you post anything, we've got to make some adjustments to the Stu-widdu site. Sam, can you have your guys break out donation requests within each zip code? Or better, by towns within the same zip code?"

"But don't some towns have multiple zip codes? Aren't there, like, a hundred zip codes for a city the size of New York?"

"You're right," I say, surprised that he would know this. "So let's just sort the donation requests by zip code, if you can do it."

"That shouldn't be a problem."

"Good, have your guys set that up. We want people in every zip code to be able to look at the donations that other people are requesting, especially the cheaters. And we'll need some kind of interface that lets people flag donations that they think are suspect."

"What kind of people are going to flag cheater requests?" Daisy asks.

"People who work at the nonprofits targeted to receive the suspect donations. People who might know the users who are requesting suspect donations. We're not going to start overcomplicating the process by layering in a bunch of new rules for making donation requests. A lot of the donation requests rejected by the system protocols are probably legit. We just expose everything and let the communities that would benefit from these donations take care of it on a local level. They're the ones who should be responsible for confirming the validity of these requests as well as identifying donation requests from people trying to cheat the system – like a selfish person who's just trying to get their loans forgiven, or anyone with some other kind of personal interest angle. And these local communities will also be the ones who treat the cheaters the way that they deserve to be treated on a day-to-day basis. We give everyone the ability to keep their own backyards clean. But, Daisy, in addition to ripping on the cheaters and explaining the format, you've got to reinforce the whole Gandhi thing. We don't want communities forming any lynch mobs. Most of all, it's really important that people understand that what these cheaters are doing—no matter how small—can collapse everything that we've been trying to build here."

"Got it," Daisy says as we pull into the driveway. "Sam, let me know when you can get the site changed."

"I'm on it," Sam says, walking into the house, heading straight for the den.

***

When Catelyn comes home, I'm asleep on the couch, television off.

"Busy day?" she asks with a hint of sarcasm.

"Busy enough for me," I respond, shaking out the cobwebs, getting up and walking over to kiss her hello.

"Anything go on?" she asks.

"Nothing that we couldn't handle," I say.

Sam's guys have the new site format up and running by seven pm. It's awesome. I don't know who's doing the interface work, but the intuitive user-friendliness of the site is truly remarkable. I tell him as much.

"My guys do good work," Sam says.

Daisy's post goes out at seven-thirty. It's scorching. She tears mercilessly into the people making questionable donations as only a twelve-year-old could. She references the site links where people can see the questionable donations within their own communities, asks the communities to help police themselves. She makes a clear statement about our position on violence. And she wraps up by bringing it down to the fundamentals – asking people to do the right thing, no matter how easy it is to delude themselves that the wrong thing is too small or harmless to make a difference. She tells us that it's the only way we're ever going to make the world a better place.

"Great stuff, Daisy," I say and give her a hug and kiss.

"I do good work," she replies.

***

Before going to bed, in what is becoming my nightly ritual, I check the Stu-widdu account balances. $195,622,400 in the Contributions account; negative $83,505,000 in the Donations account, not including another $44,985,000 in donations pending approval or, more likely, rejection, $49,409,868 in web sales, obviously reflecting the launch of Daisy's new apparel lines, ending net balance of $161,527,268, not including pending requests. I feel like we're in pretty good shape, given the fact that almost fifty million of that balance is web sales, and we're only at a delta of one-hundred-twelve million between contributions and donations.

We're putting a lot of money towards some very good work.

Chapter Thirty-three

By Thursday morning over forty million dollars in pending donation requests have been removed by the users who made those requests. Daisy's post and Sam's systems changes have effectively plugged the holes.

Apparently, no one wants to play chicken with the wrath of an honest community.

As we drive to school, I notice some new graffiti jobs on a few normal-person houses, instead of McMansions. I TRIED TO RIP OFF DAISY'S DOGHOUSE, HATE ME! scrawled in blue paint across a single-level ranch. MOVE SOMEWHERE ELSE, WE DON'T WANT YOU in red on another. GREEDY PERSON LIVES HERE in white shaving cream on a black macadam driveway.

I'm not sure how to handle these after-hours vandal anarchists. Nothing burned or bashed, though. And teenagers will be teenagers, I guess. Plus, it's a good punctuation mark on publicizing the donation lists, so I choose to turn a blind eye from a Stu-widdu perspective.

***

"Can I contribute money to pay down loans for specific people?" John Mahoney asks as I get out of my car, back from the school. He's standing by the front door when I pull into the driveway.

"Morning, John. How's your day going so far?"

I wonder why he isn't at work.

"I'm taking the day off," he says, as if in answer to my mental question. Then he remembers to be civil. "How are you doing?"

"I'm doing great, thanks," I say. "Now what did you want to know about contributions?"

"Can I contribute money that will be used to pay down loans for specific people, you know, individuals who I want to help."

He stares, and I think about it for a moment.

"We're not set up for that. It's more like gifting than donating, isn't it? Why don't you just contact whoever it is and pay down their loans directly?"

"Because I wouldn't get a tax break?" he says in a squirrely way. I give him a look. "And, I want it to be visible, on the site, you know? I want my family to see it."

He's embarrassed to add this point, which is ridiculous considering how humiliating his behavior has been the past two times we've spoken. In my mind, though, I'm playing out the implications of adding this type of feature to the site. Whether there's a positive element to allowing contributors to assign their donations. After a moment, I realize that it doesn't fit, unfortunately for John.

"Who are you trying to help?" I ask, avoiding the original question.

"Sandy's parents. I want to pay down their mortgage. They got slammed in 2008 and never really recovered. I know the mortgage payments on their house are killing them, but my mother-in-law refuses to sell it."

"Absolutely not. Have you been following what's going on with the donation requests over the past twelve hours? If you make a request to use Stu-widdu money to pay down a family member's mortgage—even if it's ultimately from your own contribution—you're going to get put into the cheater camp. That's pretty hot right now."

I point down the street at the word CHEATER scrawled in spray paint on the side of a white house. He raises his eyebrows.

"And anyway," I add, "your family will know if you help them out directly, so what's the problem."

"My in-laws don't want my money."

"That's just silly. What do you mean?" I ask.

"Sandy's parents. They said they'd rather live in a box on the street than let me help them with the mortgage."

"When did they say this?" I ask.

"In 2009, when I got my bonus after the government bailout. Their attitude towards me and the banking community kind of did a one-eighty after that fiasco."

"About how much is the mortgage?" I ask out of sheer curiosity.

"Two-point-five, give or take. Two-point-five million, that is."

"That's a pretty big mortgage."

"It's a pretty big house," he says.

"You know, John, I don't think there's any way we can help you out with Stu-widdu. First of all, I'm not sure how you think that Sandy and the kids would know where the money came from, while still keeping her parents in the dark."

"My in-laws aren't big on the Internet," he says.

"Okay. Well, aside from the fact that Stu-widdu doesn't work in a way that can accommodate your request, maybe instead you should reach out to your in-laws? You know, let them know what's going on. How you're trying to change, I mean. Maybe you can mend some fences. That might help a whole lot more than all this tomfoolery you're talking about."

"Are you sure?" he asks.

"Am I sure you should reach out to them?"

"No, are you sure you can't work the site so that Sandy and the kids know about the contribution, but I can keep it anonymous to her parents?"

"Yes," I say. "Of that, I'm sure."

"Fine. I'll try reaching out to them," he says and walks away without a thank you.

"You have a good day now, John," I call to his back.

He lifts his hand and gives me a weak wave. Sometimes I wonder why I bother with these people at all.

***

That afternoon, when I'm getting the kids, I pull up to a light behind a silver Mercedes with a black-and-white bumper sticker that reads MY OTHER CAR IS A NEW SECURITY SYSTEM AT A METHADONE CLINIC. At the stop sign before the school, I'm behind a black BMW Five Series with a bumper sticker that reads MY SUMMER HOME IS A BATTERED WOMEN'S SHELTER.

That one seems open to misinterpretation.

The kids pile into the car, and according to them nothing happened at school that day, nothing new learned. On the drive home, we notice evidence of Daisy's new apparel line. A red hoodie with a black doghouse logo, a black t-shirt with Stu-widdu's white globe beneath a drizzling cloud. Daisy confirms that they were on her select list.

"What's next?" Sam asks, looking at the sidewalk people wearing our clothes.

"Let's take some inventory," I say. "From the start. So, we've done a good job of exposing greedy corporate swine, identifying who got hurt as a result of them abusing the lopsided financial system to get rich. We've helped families and communities to recognize what selfish parasites these people actually are, and to treat them accordingly."

'Check," Sam says.

"On the back of these social shifts, we've built a system that lets people contribute their excess wealth towards specific, grass-roots donations that are requested mostly by people who spend their lives doing good things in their own communities. The contributors are motivated because they're recognized by the communities and distanced from the corporate parasites. The people who request donations are just happy that the money goes to something that will help others in a practical and visible way. And, more importantly, we've helped a lot of these same generous people by unburdening them from the stranglehold of student loans and mortgages."

"Check," Daisy says.

"And we've helped motivate the ultra-wealthy to establish a non-profit banking system, with non-profit legal and accounting services not far behind, all to help small businesses better survive without being strangled by a rigged financial bureaucracy. There might even be a new stock market in the works, which will play by different rules. At the very least, there's a group of high-powered individuals out there who are now self-motivated to fund stuff that's going to help even the playing fields for capitalism in this country. Help give the small guys a fair shot."

"I didn't know about any stock market. That's cool," Sam says.

"I just found out. Must have forgot to mention it yesterday."

"You should make sure you tell us about this stuff," Daisy says. "Do they have a name for it yet?"

"I'll try to do a better job next time something comes up," I say, ignoring Daisy's question about the name. "And, getting back to the summary, we've launched effective counter-attacks on counterfeiters and companies trying to siphon funds away from our cause and into their own pockets."

"Check." Sam's smiling.

"And we've exposed cheaters trying to take advantage of the donation system for personal gain and put them under the harsh glare of society as well."

"Check," Daisy says. "And don't forget about my blog numbers. Almost a billion followers."

"Yes, and we've increased Daisy's Internet celebrity substantially."

"And don't forget about Daisypallooza, either. It's less than two weeks away," she says. "And it's gonna be awesome."

"Yes, and there's Daisypallooza, too. So, now the money coming in for contributions is only a little bit ahead of the donation requests, which is where we want it," I say. "All of the wheels seem to be turning in the right directions. All of these plans continue to gain momentum. It's not all going to happen overnight, and I'm sure there will continue to be some bumps in the road, but if everything keeps moving the way it's going now, every day the world should be a better place."

"So what next?" Sam asks again.

"I think we can take a breath," I say.

"Isn't there anything else to fix?" Daisy asks. "What am I supposed to blog about? I need a constant stream of fresh material."

"We'll figure something out," I say.

"So, does that mean you're finally going to start writing your book?" Sam asks.

"Maybe. But the world's turning into something very different from what I'd originally wanted to write about. Maybe I'll just start another company. See what this brave new country is like from the inside."

Epilogue

A couple weeks later MTV flies Daisy, Sam, Catelyn and me to three Daisypallooza shows over the course of about ninety hours. Sam loves to fly, and the pilot lets him sit in the cockpit for a good part of each trip.

The first show we hit is outside of Las Vegas. Daisy has no problem whatsoever getting on stage in front of hundreds of thousands of people, her face huge on the giant screens erected throughout the park site. No planned speech, she just riffs. And the crowd loves it. Loves her. Loves what we're doing. What we're all doing.

In between sets, roadies ready the stages for the next bands, and the huge LCD screens show measured clips of Dr. Greenburg's video series, cartoons that explain simply how the lopsided financial system works. All of the dirty secrets of corporate America, simplified so that it can be understood by a child. It's good.

After the Southern California stop-by, we're exhausted. We sleep on the plane to upstate New York. Daisy and Sam make an appearance at the Woodstock concert for an hour or so when we arrive, and then we head to the hotel to crash. We order room service and a ridiculously expensive pay-per-view movie that none of us stays awake to see end.

Daisy and Sam are tired, like three sleepovers in a row tired. I'm worried they're not going to be able to handle the final day of the concert.

My worry is unfounded. Eight hours later they are tugging Catelyn and me out of our beds like it's Christmas morning. We order room service again for breakfast, which the kids think is awesome. The whole room service thing, I mean. Like they would be happy ordering room service for every meal of their lives. We clean ourselves up and are at the concert by ten-thirty.

I'd never been to Woodstock before, but the prior two concerts have clued me as to the enormity of the event, so I'm less surprised than I would otherwise be with both today's turn-out and the setup. There's only one main stage at the foot of a slight incline a half-mile away from where we enter. But the giant LCD screens are everywhere.

Dr. Greenburg's cartoons are already playing, different loops on different screens, as the roadies set up the main stage. What looks like a few hundred thousand people are milling around, hopping from group to group, guided by Twitter feeds, same as the event at Strumpner Field.

Was that really only five weeks ago?

Sam has already disappeared to find his hacker friends, proudly carrying his own phone, which we purchased for him prior to taking off on the Daisypallooza adventure. Police and security are everywhere. Sam knows not to leave the concert grounds, so we're not as worried about the thousands of Internet predators who must be in attendance. We walk with Daisy to a bunch of news vans so that she can do her interviews before diving into the crowds.

We see Martha Chase, the CNN reporter who obviously gained a huge reputational boost from Daisy's first interview at Strumpner Field. The one where my jaw was all cramped up, where the world first came to know me as Daisy's disabled father. Martha recognizes me, gives me a look that says "shall we go again?"

I shake my head slightly, nonverbally declining her offer, and gently push a solo Daisy towards the clamor of microphones and cameras.

After five hours of following Daisy at a distance as she darts among different groups in the crowd while we simultaneously and hopelessly try to keep track of Sam, the headline acts are announced. We head to a special area backstage, roped off for the bands and the MTV people.

Bruce Springsteen announces Daisy, and she walks out onto the main stage. Our little twelve-year-old girl – beaming, smiling, waving like she was birthed for this specific moment. Not a hint of fear or shyness. She riffs an unprepared speech for a couple of minutes, same as the prior two concerts, thanking people and distributing all kinds of credit to everyone who made Stu-widdu and this event possible.

She thanks her brother, Sam, and a huge cheer goes up from some random part of the crowd.

Tears run down Catelyn's cheeks. Mine too. She thanks Catelyn and me, she thanks the moderators, the people making contributions and the people making donation requests. She wraps up with a few words asking everyone to try and do the right thing, asking everyone to try not to be a cheater, even when cheating is easy and seems small, and they think no one will find out.

"Because we will find out," she says, using the same creepy voice that she used on Mr. Prescott in the principal's office a few weeks back, "and we can make the cheaters very, very sorry."

Then she dances on stage with Bruce Springsteen while he sings "Dancing in the Dark." Just like the Nineteen Eighties music video.

After the set, when we can actually hear each other enough to talk, when we've got a bead on Sam's position and are tracking Daisy as she moves through the Twitter feed groups, Catelyn asks me if I'm happy.

"I've honestly never been happier," I tell her and pull her waist tighter against my side.

"So, everything's moving in the right direction, right? We can kind of take a step back now, maybe more be part of the background noise for a while?" Catelyn asks.

"Sure," I reply. "That sounds like a great idea. I mean, if the wheels keep turning like they are now, there's not much left for us to do. I'm still just amazed that anything like this could ever happen. Between the kids and technology, I mean, what's left for us to do?"

"Nothing," Catelyn says.

"I mean, if we wanted to do something really good, I guess we could talk to Daisy about the amount of unchecked corruption that exists in the American political system…"

Catelyn punches me squarely in the sternum. Hard enough to double me over. She doesn't realize that I'm only kidding.

Maybe I'm not.

The End

Acknowledgments

The first draft of this book was truly awful.

I'd originally written the book to vent about a bunch of the stuff I'd witnessed when working in corporate America. The storyline was really just a placeholder for my rants. After several people had suffered through the first draft, I was gently advised to cut all of the soapbox stuff and just stick to the story. In other words, to cut out all of the parts that comprised why I wrote the book in the first place. Harsh. But, with the help of my editor, Rob Carr, I think it ended up a much less horrible book in the long run, and I want to thank Black Rose Writing for publishing it.

So, given the history, I think it's appropriate to thank everyone who read that miserable, soapbox rant of a first draft – especially Kate McGinty, Aimee Barrett, Joe and Maris Barrett, Cory Zimmerman, Amy Pelligra, Matt Kwan and the rest of my extended family at Sandbox Studio. I will always be sorry for the pain you endured while reading that first draft. You guys are awesome.

Most of all, I want to apologize to my wife Michelle, who had to read this book and deal with me throughout the editing process, so thank you, and I love you. Also, thanks to my son Joe, who rated this book a seven out of ten and thought that I should be really happy about that. And finally, thanks to my daughter Sophie who refuses to read any of my books but indirectly made it very easy for me to write about Daisy.

Note from the Author

Word-of-mouth is crucial for any author to succeed. If you enjoyed the book, please leave a review online—anywhere you are able. Even if it's just a sentence or two. It would make all the difference and would be very much appreciated.

Thanks!
Joe

About the Author

Joe Barrett has spent the past twenty-five years as a chief executive of entrepreneurial organizations ranging from private, venture-funded companies to large publicly-listed multinational corporations. He has been a frequent speaker at National Retail Federation conferences and has sat on the boards of several for-profit and non-profit companies. His short fiction has been published in *Iconoclast*, *The Storyteller* and *The Palo Alto Review*. He lives with his wife and two children in New Jersey.

Thank you so much for reading one of **Joe Barrett's** novels.
If you enjoyed the experience, please check out our recommended
title for your next great read!

Managed Care by Joe Barrett

"Witty, occasionally crass, and an unqualified delight." –*KIRKUS REVIEWS*

View other Black Rose Writing titles at
www.blackrosewriting.com/books and use promo code
PRINT to receive a **20% discount** when purchasing.